# THE FOURTH DIMENSION
## IS DEATH

# SAMUEL HOLT
# THE FOURTH DIMENSION IS DEATH

TOR

**A TOM DOHERTY ASSOCIATES BOOK**
**NEW YORK**

This is a work of fiction. All the characters and events portrayed in this book are fictitious, and any resemblance to real people or events is purely coincidental.

THE FOURTH DIMENSION IS DEATH

A TOR BOOK
Published by Tom Doherty Associates, Inc.
49 West 24 Street
New York, NY 10010

Library of Congress Cataloging-in-Publication Data
Holt, Samuel.
The fourth dimension is death / Samuel Holt.—1st ed.
p.        cm.
"A Tom Doherty Associates book."
ISBN 0-312-93140-9: $16.95.
I. Title
PS3558.042F68 1989
813' .54—dc19                                    88-29165

First edition: January 1989
0  9  8  7  6  5  4  3  2  1

# 1

I never did think Dale Wormley looked like me. We all have that experience, I suppose, the false twins out there in the world, people who are claimed by our relatives and friends to look astonishingly like us. A roommate or a brother comes home and says, "I just saw somebody on the bus and I could have *sworn* it was you, I almost *said* something, it was absolutely uncanny." And for a little while we find ourselves wondering about that doppelganger, what that other life might be, is it better or worse than our own, happier, sadder, easier, more exciting . . .

Well, I met my doppelganger, and I don't believe he looked that much like me. And I didn't envy his life, either. Nor his death.

If your face and voice become known to the public in a positive sense, because you're a famous politician, perhaps, or a major sports figure, or, like me, because you did time for five years as the lead in a successful television series, your doppelganger may turn out to be someone who will try to make a career out of that accident of similar appearance. There are now "talent" agencies specializing in celebrity look-alikes and celebrity sound-alikes (there's even a kind of ghostly living still to be made from looking like Charlie Chaplin or sounding like W. C. Fields, which is a joke on somebody), and the result is, from time to time it becomes necessary for a person in my position to guard the shores of his own existence, to beat back incursions made by the doppelganger into what is, after all, private turf.

And that's what happened between me and Dale Wormley. For five years I played the brilliant criminologist Jack Packard in the television series called PACK-ARD, and then three years after I was finished with the part (I hope) this Dale Wormley started playing a Jack Packard look-alike on television commercials for a supermarket chain throughout the northeast. The imitation of a living person and of a copyrighted fictional character was offensive to begin with, and the manner of the imitation made it even worse, since Jack Packard was portrayed in the commercials as a self-satisfied bully, so when we first became aware of the impersonation Morton Adler, my New York attorney, sent letters to the ad agency and the supermarket chain, requesting them to stop, and when that didn't convince them we sued.

Which was ironic enough to begin with. I had come to actively dislike Jack Packard, and here I was forced to defend him against unauthorized use. The five years I'd spent in the part had been fine, but once the series was finished—ended by the weariness of everyone connected with it, not by any lack of public enthusiasm—I had been ready to move on to other things, but it turned out Packard wasn't ready to let me go. My identification with that character and that series is still so strong that I'm essentially unemployable in any other role, though God knows my agent, Zack Novak, and I have both done our best to find me something. Not for the money, PACKARD reruns have solved my financial problems for the foreseeable future, but for the *work*. I don't want to hang around, I want a job.

So I certainly didn't feel like defending Jack Packard from imitation, but there it was. My co-owners of the syndication rights were also part of the suit, of course, and the actual process was being handled by Morton Adler, so it more or less progressed without me the first few weeks—except for a couple of long LA-NY phone calls with Morton—and didn't become an actual on-going thing in my life until October and my semi-annual migration to New York.

For a kid like me, who grew up on Long Island, New York City always was, is now, and ever will be the center of the known and unknown universe. As soon as I became rich enough to indulge my every whim, I bought a nice brick townhouse on West 10th Street in Greenwich Village, and filled it with dark comfortable furniture, and got on first-name terms with Tony, my neighborhood Italian greengrocer. Of course, since then Tony has retired to Florida, and his business has been taken over by a numerous and hardworking Korean family, with whom I am on merely smiling and nodding terms; I cannot attempt to find out the first names of people whose hand-lettered signs announce they are selling such items as reeks and arugura. ("Curryflower" is their finest and most complex creation so far, I think.)

However, despite being the center of the universe, New York City happens to have a climate which is at times inimical to man. Summer in the city duplicates the environment on the surface of the planet Mercury, and deep winter there is rather like downtown in the Asteroid Belt. Therefore, I keep my house in Bel Air as well, where I don't have to check the calendar before using the pool, and split my life between these two bases. I've heard my kind of bicoastal existence described as 'apples and oranges': spring and fall in New York, summer and winter in LA.

Fall. October 12th. The leaves were flying, and so was I. Normally, Robinson and I would have flown LAX-Kennedy on commercial air, but at a party recently in Malibu I'd met an executive of a multinational computer company called DSI, and had accepted his invitation to travel east on a company jet. In addition to the pilot and copilot and stewardess, there were six of us aboard, being Robinson and me, our host, and three other DSI executives, all on their way to DSI's world headquarters in New York. They'd be taking meetings there on some major drive DSI had planned for Great Britain, where the computer revolution is coming along briskly, just a few years behind ours. Their stock market had just recently undergone what they called the Big Bang, which in essence meant that British subsidiaries of American brokerages were permitted at last to do business in the City, and with American businesses would inevitably come American business

methods, which these days means one computer terminal per employee; a nice opportunity for DSI.

My own business has never reached Great Britain,
I'm not sure why. When PACKARD was still an active
show, it was sold in Italy and Sweden and parts of
South America, all dubbed into the foreign language,
and in Holland, where it was shown in English with
subtitles. Rerun money still comes sporadically from
all those places, but the British market was just never
interested in the affairs of Jack Packard. I've heard
theories ranging all the way from the idea that Packard
was too American, to the idea that he wasn't American
enough. Now, of course, with the show long gone and
only me left on my raft on the empty ocean, the
question is academic.

I thought the flight with the DSI people was pleasant
and fun, a superior way to get from one coast to the
other, but Robinson found it absolutely delightful, and
that's because he met a fan; a thing that doesn't happen
to Robinson very often. William Robinson, now 73,
was himself an actor for nearly forty years, coming into
his own in the movies of the thirties and forties, where
he played hoity-toity servants, far more upper class
than the people they worked for. He did disagreeable
butlers, disapproving valets, supercilious majordomos
and, in the war years, the occasional stiffbacked aide-
de-camp. He played a fifty-year-old for twenty years,
until he became a fifty-year-old, and then went on
playing the same age for another decade.

What happened to Robinson's career was neither age
nor ambition, but a simple profound change in American fiction. Gruff millionaires and their heedless head-
strong daughters faded from the scene, as did willowy
semi-male upper class amateur detectives, madcap

heirs and heiresses, luxury travelers on transAtlantic liners and lovable nouveau-riche midwesterners scaling the social walls of Boston and New York. With them, their trains of servants also disappeared, and there went Robinson's occupation.

Apparently—I didn't know him then—there was about a ten year transition period, when Robinson still found the occasional role (ultimately in television commercials) as the same old stuffy retainer, but in the increasingly long intervals of being, in actors' euphemism, "at liberty," he paid his rent by taking frequent work as an actual butler or valet for some of the stars he'd appeared with in movies. First he and William Powell, say (it wasn't William Powell, I don't think, but people like that), would appear in some film as master and man, and then for the next six months or year they'd recreate their roles in real life, which must have been strange for both of them.

By the end of this transitional decade, acting work had dried up entirely for Robinson, and he had become totally a servant, but with none of the subservience the word suggests. He brought his characterization along from the world of celluloid, and still plays the same old cantankerous pest as ever. Six years ago he was passed on to me by his then employer, a man I'd met as a guest star on PACKARD, and Robinson has been staring down his long nose at me ever since.

And here, on DSI's Lear, was a William Robinson fan. "I *know* you!" said the man, a portly sixtyish fellow named Kendall, who had the right look to have played those Robinson parts himself, though a bit more warmheartedly, less accerbically. "You were in the movies!"

"Several," Robinson murmured. A good servant—

that is, a good portrayer of servants—he always manages to simulate a subtle and long-suffering unease when required to sit with the gentry and be served by someone else; in this case, the very pretty stewardess.

"You were *great!*" Kendall told him. Our plush chairs swiveled, so we could turn toward each other for conversation, and now Kendall demanded one of the other execs switch seats so he could swivel closer to Robinson and tell him all about it. "You were with Joel McCrea," Kendall announced, tapping Robinson on the knee.

"Occasionally," Robinson admitted demurely.

Kendall mentioned a title. Robinson nodded, beginning to smile. Kendall quoted a Robinson line from that picture, and Robinson did his best, the old fraud, to look modest. Kendall mentioned other titles, other stars, quoted other lines, recounted bits of business with telephones and breakfast trays, and Robinson did everything but roll over on his back to have his belly scratched. While the rest of us conducted a grown-up discussion about worldwide computer sales, Kendall and Robinson ransacked every nook and cranny of Robinson's long and middling career. I sensed with foreboding—the kind of foreboding Robinson himself used to manifest when the various Bertie Woosters playing opposite him would describe their latest stratagem—that sooner or later Kendall would, in all innocence, ask Robinson why he wasn't acting any more, and I knew what then came next.

And he did, and it did, and Robinson raised his voice to be absolutely certain I heard his version of events; just in case I wanted to argue with him. Which I did not.

Here's the story. In LA I have a good friend named

Bly Quinn, who writes for television sitcoms, and last spring she had a pilot being shot for a new series called *Akers' Acres.* An irascible old servant named Leemy was to be a regular in the series, and Bly asked Robinson to play the part. After some hesitation, he said yes.

There are two versions of what happened next. Bly's is that Robinson tried to lord it over everybody in sight; that he rewrote all his own lines and most of everybody else's; that he argued with the director; that his time away from the profession had left him rigid and authoritarian and utterly incapable of following the simplest instructions. Robinson's version, delivered in the minutest detail to the enthralled Kendall, was that he was a professional with many years of experience to offer in this particular story milieu, and that his co-workers' refusal to be guided by his hardwon expertise had convinced him the show would be a disaster. In any event, he quit.

My only quibble, which I was much too cautious to mention, was with Robinson's assumption that, because Bly's my girlfriend, I was on her side. In fact, I've grown very used to having him around, prickly old fart though he may be, and if he'd stayed with the series he would have left my employ, so I'm just as happy things didn't work out, and I don't care who was right or wrong.

Anyway, the one-man William Robinson Fan Club took us most of the way through the second half of the journey, after our refueling stop at Grand Island, Nebraska, a dot on the map that isn't grand, is a thousand miles from a body of water large enough to have islands, but is certainly in Nebraska, possibly the flattest place on Earth. We had twenty minutes to stand there and look around and know exactly how an ant feels on a kitchen table, and then we were airborne again, and the Robinson retrospective took us all the way to New York.

Where Kendall insisted on driving us home. Usually I have a car pick me up, but since we were coming in non-scheduled and couldn't be sure of our arrival time I'd intended to call for the car from Butler Aviation, where we landed at Kennedy. But no; Kendall wouldn't hear of it. His own car and driver were there, Kendall had no pressing engagements, and this was probably his last opportunity to repay all the hours of pleasure Robinson had afforded him over the years. So we accepted the offer, and that's how it happened we had two outside witnesses—Kendall and his driver—when we got to 10th Street.

We'd landed at just after seven in the evening, having left LA at nine this morning West Coast time, so traffic to Manhattan wasn't too bad. We made good time, and pulled up in front of my place at quarter to eight. Thanks and appreciation were expressed on all sides, the driver and Robinson unloaded our luggage—not much of it; we keep duplicates of most things in our two houses—and Kendall and I shook hands, he belatedly and laughingly assuring me he'd always enjoyed *my* acting work as well; meaning Packard.

We were all four of us on the sidewalk in front of my house, then, when this big fellow came forward out of the semi-dark. I'm six foot six myself, a onetime basketball player, and this guy was at least the same height. I didn't notice much else about him, build or hair coloring or any of that, but I did see that his face was twisted and distorted by some strong emotion. He came striding forward out of nowhere, as though he'd been waiting years for this moment, and reached out to push his right hand against the upper left side of my chest, just below the shoulder, and *shove.* "You!" he said; he snarled, I mean. He shoved me again. "You!"

What was this? I pushed his hand away, while Robinson and Kendall and the driver stared in astonishment. "Watch it!" I said.

He glared at me. "You fucking think you're *something,* don't you?"

My doppelganger.

# 2

**A**t that moment, I had no idea who he was or why he thought he had a complaint. I only knew he was being physically violent, he was grimacing with rage or some other desperate emotion, he was large and strong and probably capable of doing some damage if that's what he had in mind, and I'd never seen him before in my life.

I used to be a cop a long time ago, for a year and a half on the force out in Mineola, Long Island, and an MP during my army tour in Germany before that. In both jobs, the unarmed neutralizing of the potentially violent is one of the things they teach you before they give you the gun and the shield. So when the hand I'd pushed away came reaching again, I reacted: My own left hand went out, closed around his right thumb, and held the thumb folded in on itself, cupped between my bent fingers and the heel of my hand. It's known as the come-along hold, because it doesn't take much of a squeeze to give that bent thumb excruciating pain and make the subject of the exercise more than willing to come along.

I didn't need this guy to come along, though; I just needed him to stop. Applying very slight pressure, but enough to let him know what had happened, that he was mine now, I said, "That's enough."

His eyes widened in hurt and surprise, his mouth opened in an exaggerated O, and he reached across himself toward the imprisoned thumb with his other hand. I gave him a quick short squeeze: "Hand at your side!"

That's like an electric shock, that pain. You don't think about it, you don't argue with it, you just do what it says. His hand snapped back to his side.

Kendall had found voice: "Good God!" he cried, with the astonished outrage of the proper burgher assaulted in a decent neighborhood. "Harry, help the man! Do something!"

Harry was the driver, who had the good sense to give me a questioning look, to be sure I wanted help before he offered any. I shook my head at him, and looked the stranger in his furious, frustrated eyes. "What's it about?" I asked him.

"You know what it's about!" His voice was artificially high-pitched and shrill, affected by emotion. "It all has to be yours, doesn't it?" he demanded, leaning his head and shoulders back away from me but making no effort to move that thumb. "Everything has to be the great *Packard's,* doesn't it?" Said with violent raging sarcasm bearing down on that name.

I said, "Buddy, I don't know you or what your problem is. If you—"

"You don't *know* me? You're *suing* me, aren't you?"

So I looked more closely at him, and then I began to see it, the way shapes change when a lamp is moved. The height was right, the hair coloring, and through the distortions that anger had brought to his face it was possible to make out something in the bone structure, the line of eyebrow, the shape of the nose . . .

Well, yes and no. That was not, absolutely not, the face I see when I look in a mirror, but it was him, all right; the doppelganger, the pseudo-Packard of Kwality FoodMarts. "For God's sake," I said. Startled, repelled, not wanting to know this other me, talk to him, look at him, certainly not *touch* him, I pushed his thumb away and stepped back. "Don't be stupid," I told him, feeling rattled and unclean.

Something in my manner broke the line of his attack, and he too became nervous and unsure. Instead of whatever forceful snarling statement he'd been rehearsing for hours—maybe for weeks—he stared at me almost as though confused, and said, "I've got a right to live too, you know."

I was vaguely aware of Kendall, somewhere behind my right shoulder, saying sharply, "Harry, the police!" I knew we didn't need police, but I wasn't sure what we did need. "Look," I said to the imitator, trying to remember his name, feeling somehow it would insult him not to remember, "look, *I'm* not suing you. A company's suing a company. PACKARD's owned by a corporation, they have to protect the asset."

"It doesn't matter to you," he insisted. He looked bruised and resentful, as though I were the one who'd forced the confrontation on a public sidewalk. "This is my chance," he explained, earnest now. "This is my chance." Then he looked at something past my shoulder, out in the street, and his face changed again, becoming desperate and harried. "Oh, *Christ!"* he said, and spun away, as though to run down the street.

"Hold it right there!"

I turned, and a police patrol car was now stopped just behind the limo. When I'd heard Kendall call to his driver about the police, it had been because this car was coming down the block. Harry had stopped it, Kendall had said a quick word of explanation, and my celebrity would do the rest. While the resentful and defeated imitator stood waiting, the two cops came to the sidewalk and asked, in that heavy intimidating manner that goes with the uniform, just what was going on.

"A misunderstanding, officers," I said. "It's all over now." The last thing I wanted was for this guy to be arrested, and it wasn't exclusively for humanitarian reasons. This thing, badly handled, could become a public relations nightmare, the big-wheel celeb dumping on the little guy.

Kendall, seeing the humanitarian motive and not the selfish one, would have nothing of it. "Misunderstanding, my eye!" he announced. "Sam, you don't have to bend over backwards with these people. Officer," he said to the nearest cop, "that fellow came charging out at us the instant we got out of the car. My name's Kendall, here's my card. I'm with DSI, my driver and I were bringing Mr. Holt and Mr. Robinson home, and this—"

"Yeah, right, right," the cop said, nodding seriously, holding Kendall's card like something he was glad to have been handed. "I got the picture," he assured

Kendall, and turned to me, saying, "You live here, don't you, Mr. Holt?"

It's part of their job, knowing the rich and/or famous on the beat. I said, "Yes, I do."

Turning to the imitator—what *was* his name?— asking as though it were merely a fact he was interested in for its own sake, the cop said, "You live around here, too?"

"Not *me*," he said; his resentment was in full flower again. "I don't have houses like that."

Tucking Kendall's card away in a pocket, the cop moved closer to the imitator, saying, "Could I see some ID, please?"

"Listen, officer," I said, then had to interrupt myself, saying, "Kendall, believe me, it's all right."

And now the other cop stepped in, effectively dividing us into two groups, his partner with the imitator, himself with us, as he said, "Mr. Holt, you were on your way home, is that right?"

"Yes," I said. "And nothing happened here except a couple words, it really doesn't matter, I'm not asking you to do a thing."

"Fine," he said, nodding. His partner was studying the imitator's driver's license, talking to him quietly, absorbing his attention, giving the imitator time to calm down and rethink his position. "Understood," our cop said to me, and turned to Kendall, saying, "Were you going in with Mr. Holt?"

"No, no, we were just dropping him off, when that fellow—"

"So everything's okay, then," the cop pointed out, and raised an eyebrow at me.

"We're just going in now," I told him, and picked up

one of our bags. To Kendall I said, "Thanks for the flight, I appreciated it. Not as much as Robinson, of course."

Which finally distracted Kendall from his desire to make a fuss. Grinning, he said, "I can't tell you what a treat it was, meeting the both of you."

We exchanged civilities, Robinson permitted his fan to shake his hand, and at last Kendall and his chauffeur got back into the limo and drove away. Both cops were now talking with the imitator, calmly, quietly, their backs to us. There was no point interrupting; they knew I wasn't going to press charges, so they were merely defusing the situation in a way calculated to keep it from happening again. Robinson and I went on into the house, and when I looked out my office window on the second floor a few minutes later the police car, the cops, and the imitator were all gone. It was over.

Dale Wormley. *Then* I remembered his name.

# 3

The next—and last—time our paths crossed was not Dale Wormley's fault. It was just an unfortunate accident, but no less unpleasant for that, and it was caused by the lunch arrangements I'd happened to make with my friend Brett Burgess.

Brett Burgess is an actor, I'm a star, and there's our story in a word. Two words. We met out on the Coast nearly a dozen years ago, before Packard entered my life. The same agent who changed my name to Sam Holt (because it sounded more manly than Holton Hickey, the name I'd been born with) changed his to Brett Burgess from whatever it had been. We got to know each other in that agent's office and in various waiting rooms where we'd been sent to try out for the same parts, and the friendship has luckily survived all the changes since.

There are two real differences between Brett and me. First, I got *the* part, the one that launched me and established me and made me rich, while he's still struggling along with small movie roles and brief uncertain stints off-Broadway. And second, while I just drifted into this profession, not even knowing it *was* a profession for quite a long time, Brett has been an actor, solid and talented and devoted, all his life. I know there are times when he wishes our positions were reversed, that he was the one with the fame and fortune, but mostly he realizes he's happier where he is, at work almost anonymously in the career he loves.

The silly thing is, I too have moments of feeling the grass must be greener on the other side. If I'd never been Packard, I could, like Brett, be working at *something* in the acting profession today. On the other hand, I wouldn't have the house in Bel Air, nor the house on West 10th Street. So Brett and I, in an odd way, embody each other's daydreams, and we like to stay in touch, see each other from time to time, get caught up on our fantasies of might-have-been.

I'd been back in the city four days when Brett and I had lunch. That morning he was auditioning in the Lucille Lortel theater on Christopher Street in the Village, so we arranged that I'd meet him there around twelve-thirty and then we'd stroll together up to Abingdon Square for lunch at Vitto Impero, the restaurant owned by my friend Anita Imperato. The weather was fine—New York in the fall can be absolutely beautiful—and I had time on my hands, so I walked across from home. Although I'm six foot six and have a rather well-known face, I've learned that if I wear a cap and keep my eyes front and walk as though I have a purpose in mind, I very rarely get bothered on the street. At least in New York.

I made my way without interruption over to the theater, arrived a few minutes early, and went in to find about twenty actors, all of the same outdoorsy leading man type, lounging in the rear seats, and one more of the same on stage with an earnest plain young woman, both holding red-bound scripts. The four people doing the casting were distributed in the front two rows. I saw Brett in the rear row on the other side and started toward him when a narrow balding young man with a goatee and a clipboard stopped me with a harshly whispered, "You're late! What's your name?"

"I'm not auditioning," I whispered back. Up on stage, the auditioning actor and the earnest girl were reading a scene together, full of artificial gaiety. I pointed toward Brett. "I'm here to meet my—"

"No one's permitted in *here,*" he whispered, fiercely self-important, "except—" Then he stopped, and squinted up at me, under the brim of my cap. I saw recognition change his face from disapproval to surprised delight. "Aren't you—?"

"Yes," I whispered, happy once again to accept this fringe benefit of celebrity; everybody thinks they already know you and already like you.

"Are you sure you *don't* want to audition?" He almost simpered when he said that, looking at me sidelong, virtually flirting with me.

And I considered it, by God, for one millisecond. All of the pros, all of the cons. I didn't even know if it was the lead; not that that mattered, since the idea was ridiculous anyway.

And what if I were to waltz in and take Brett's part away from him?

"Thanks, but no," I whispered, smiling back at my seducer with the clipboard. "All right if I sit over there?"

"Yes, of course." Rapping the backs of his fingers against the papers on his clipboard, he whispered, "Which one's your friend?"

"Brett Burgess."

"I'll call him next."

"Thank you," I said, pleased and surprised. "We both thank you."

I went on across the rear of the theater and slid into the seat next to Brett, nodding a silent greeting. He nodded back, then spread his hands to display helplessness. Leaning toward me, he whispered, "They're running late. As usual."

"You're next at bat."

That made his craggy face smile. (Not only does he look like the Marlboro Man, he's *been* the Marlboro Man, in a magazine ad.) "Used your influence, did you?"

"Yes. But from here on, you're on your own."

"I'm not sure I want this anyway," he whispered. "It's Alan Alda as a lumberjack."

"Isn't that a contradiction in terms?"

He grinned, but then looked toward the stage and gestured for me to wait. The actor who'd been reading was now coming down into the small auditorium, leaving the plain girl with both scripts. The goateed man with the clipboard gestured to him, then called, "Brett Burgess," and Brett squeezed my knee as he got to his feet and headed down the aisle, moving more heavily than usual; not a limp, exactly, but a stiffness in the knees as though he had arthritis there, or an old war wound. I suspected that meant he was already getting into the part.

While the previous contender and the goateed man murmured together briefly to one side, a stout man with a wheezy voice called questions up to Brett on stage from the second row; stage experience, parts played, theaters where he'd worked in different parts of the country, things like that. The information, I knew, wasn't so much wanted for its own sake as to give Brett a minute to get comfortable on stage and to give the people below a chance to see him separate from the part they wanted him to read. Then the previous man left, the goateed man faded into the darkness, the plain girl handed one of the scripts to Brett, and an angry voice near me yelled, "And what the fuck are *you* doing here?"

I looked over, astonished, and it was him again, one row down and over to the right. And of course he would be here; he was an actor. A part that Brett might be right for, that I might be right for, was naturally something he'd also take a run at. I shook my head at him, scrunching down as low as possible in my seat, hoping he'd understand there was no need to make a fuss, but one thing I already knew about Dale Wormley was that he was an emotional type. A fuss, unfortunately, was about to be made.

While everyone else in the theater craned around to see what was going on, and while poor Brett stood helpless and ignored on stage with the script in his hand, Dale Wormley came half-trotting sideways—a ludicrous comic crablike movement that could only make him madder—hurrying along the row toward me, yelling, "Come down to *sneer?* Come down to laugh at the *losers?"*

"Oh, for Christ's sake, don't be stupid," I muttered, but probably too low, still trying hopelessly not to attract unnecessary attention.

"I don't like your goddam *face,* you know that?" he demanded, almost parallel with me now; and that was another stupid thing to say, though I didn't point it out, since it was his presumed similarity to this face that was getting him whatever gainful employment he had these days. But then, his double-time sidle having brought him over directly in front of me, he backed up the stupid remark by taking a swing at the face he didn't like.

Sitting there, I parried that wild right, saying, "Cut it out." Meantime, people all over the theater were on their feet, moving this way, yelling at us to stop whatever we were doing, yelling that they wanted to know what was going on.

Wormley didn't cut it out. He swung again, the left now, and I blocked that one, too, saying, "Goddamit, grow *up."*

No. Teeth clenched, eyes glaring, he swung the right again.

Oh, enough. Still sitting there, I leaned forward and decked him.

# 4

**T**hanks a lot," Brett said.

"Think of it as an acting exercise," I suggested. "Practice in maintaining concentration on the part during a brawl."

We were in Vitto Impero, as planned, for our lunch, and Brett was pretty sure he hadn't gotten that part. The fact is, he had not managed to maintain his concentration during the brawl, which had been brief but dramatic. After I'd knocked Wormley down, a couple of the other auditioning actors carried him out and the wheezy stout man told Brett to go ahead, the distraction was over and everything was all right now. But it just hadn't been the same. Brett's reading with the girl was slow and wandering, as though his attention were elsewhere, and none of the intended lightness

in the lines came through. At the end, I could see the
disgusted expression on Brett's face when he went
through the final sidebar colloquy with the clipboard
man, a disgusted expression that remained intact all
the way up Hudson Street, as we walked along and I
explained who Dale Wormley was and why he felt he
had a gripe against me. "He's got a great sense of
timing, anyway," Brett said. "I'll give him that."

"I don't want him in my life any more," I said,
"that's all *I* know."

At the restaurant, Anita was too busy running the
place to sit with us, though she did come over and chat
from time to time. She and I were getting along very
well, having become reacquainted the first two nights at
her place upstairs from the restaurant and last night at
mine, and she went so far beyond her normal style in
the expression of her approval as to rest a hand on the
back of my neck while she stood at the table to talk.
From most people I wouldn't have cared for that
gesture, as being a little too cloyingly proprietary, but
Anita's so independent, so like a cat in her self-
sufficiency, that I could accept it from her as simply a
comradely statement.

A tall and sharply good-looking woman, slender to
the point of skinniness, Anita runs her life to her own
plan, and has done so for at least eight years, ever since
her husband, the man for whom the word "feckless"
was invented, skipped out and left her with a failing
restaurant and a sense of deep irritation. She rescued
the restaurant, got over the irritation, settled down to
an independent existence, and then met me.

Am I good for Anita? I know she's good for me, a
sharp-witted, sharp-tempered woman who keeps me in
line and makes me laugh. We're together as much as

possible when I'm in New York, but that means for half the year we don't see one another. I hang around instead with Bly Quinn out on the Coast; what Anita does then, I don't know. I've never asked, and she's never volunteered. She knows about Bly and mostly keeps her attitude to herself, only occasionally making an unfair—but usually funny—remark about my bubbleheaded Hollywood starlet. (Bly may look that part, but in fact she's a TV scriptwriter, with her own brains and wit.) Maybe the truth is, to have a fella like me for just a few months at a time is best for Anita, all the involvement her spirit can accept. I hope that's it.

Anyway, Vitto Impero does a good lunch trade, and not just of neighborhood people. Its reputation draws lunch customers ranging from midtown admen to lawyers from the courts way downtown. Anita prowls the place like a leopard, keeping it smooth and efficient, making a relaxed place by never relaxing herself; which meant Brett and I were left mostly on our own. There was a lot to get caught up on, we not having seen each other since spring, but Brett just couldn't leave this morning's experience alone. We'd talk briefly about a play he did in Canada in August, or about my recent near-miss in getting to perform Brick in a revival of *Cat On a Hot Tin Roof* in LA—the financing disappeared, and it would have been too uncomfortably like a vanity production if I'd financed it myself—but then Brett would veer off again, and be right back with this morning's disastrous audition. He knew he'd done badly, he knew what he'd intended to do instead, and he just couldn't seem to get it all behind him.

So we were there again, rehashing it yet once more, when Anita finally felt she could join us, a little after two. At that point, of course, the entire story had to be given a complete airing all over again for Anita's benefit, to bring her up to date. She knew about the PACKARD lawsuit against Kwality FoodMarts, but I hadn't seen any reason to mention the scene on the sidewalk, so she was hearing the whole story of the active and truculent Dale Wormley for the first time. Listening, managing to be both sympathetic toward Brett and amused toward me, she heard the whole saga out and then grinned and said, "You really slugged him?"

"He wouldn't stop swinging," I explained. "What would you have done?"

"I'm not saying you were wrong," she assured me. "I just wish I'd been there to see it."

Which was when Brett finally lightened up. With his own reluctant grin, he said, "It was pretty impressive, actually, Anita. I'll have to use it some time, in the right part. Sam didn't even stand up. He just leaned forward and *wham.*"

"Sitting *down?*" Gazing upon me in mock wonder, she said, "That's what I call insouciant."

"I've never called anything insouciant in my life," I said.

"Now, don't get bad-tempered," Anita told me, patting my arm.

"You've got to look out for him when he's seated," Brett warned her. Anita's presence at the table had done wonders for his mood.

"The question is," I said, "what am I going to do about Dale Wormley?"

"I thought you'd already done it," Anita said.

"I hope so. But what if I just made him madder? I don't want him hanging around, pestering me, lousing things up all the time."

Anita said, "Did you talk to Mort?"

Mort was Morton Adler, my New York attorney, who was taking part in the Kwality FoodMarts suit. "I mentioned the sidewalk thing," I said, "when I talked to him day before yesterday. You know, just in passing. I haven't called him today. Why? What do you want me to do, get a court order against the guy?"

"Why not?"

"It'd be kind of like running to the principal for protection," I said, feeling uncomfortable.

She shook her head at me, impatient with the tender sensibilities of the male. "Life is not a schoolyard, Sam," she said.

"May I quote you?"

"You may heed me," she said.

"Anita could be right," Brett told me. Even males don't worry a lot about the tender sensibilities of other males. "You can't just go around laying the guy out every time you see him. Sooner or later, *you'll* be the one in the wrong."

"All right," I said, reluctantly seeing the sense in it. "If he shows up again, I'll put Mort on the case."

But Dale Wormley never showed up again. He didn't get the chance.

# 5

**I** was in my lap pool when the police arrived. In Bel Air I have the normal swimming pool, but it's hard to find ways to exercise those long torso muscles back east, so when I bought the townhouse in the city I had a lap pool put in the basement, and a certain period down there every morning is a part of my routine. The in-house communication system includes a loud-speaker and microphone behind a grid high in the tile wall above the lap pool, and that combination of tile and water creates the only really good echo effect in Robinson's life these days. He loves opportunities to talk to me from upstairs when I'm down there, and enunciates even more unctuously than usual. Even with one ear in the water and both arms churning up spray, I had no trouble making out the reverberating tones of his, *"The police are here."*

I heard it. It threw me off, I floundered, I filled my mouth with chlorinated water, found my footing, stood up with wavelets at my chest, coughed, and called up at that grid, "What?" Even though I'd heard.

*"The police. Detectives, to be precise,"* he said precisely. *"They wish to speak to you."*

"Tell them to give me five minutes," I called, clambering out of the pool. I padded down to my robe flung over the back of the bench at one end of the pool, shrugged into it, and hurried upstairs.

It took more than five minutes. I had to shower off the chlorine, then dress. I moved as quickly as I could, but still it was probably a quarter of an hour before I reached the living room and found the two detectives seated there, chatting together, drinking coffee that Robinson must have offered. Robinson himself was not present.

Why had I expected them both to be men? I guess the ingrown assumptions don't change. Anyway, one was male, the other female, both probably in their late thirties. The man was short, chunky, with thinning brown hair and a blobby lumpy face, like something made of Play-Doh. The woman was an inch or so taller than he, big-boned rather than fat, with straight black Vampira hair and a long horsy face. The man wore a brown jacket, checked shirt, dark blue bow tie and gray slacks, while the woman was dressed in a severely cut dark blue suit, plain white blouse, dark hose and sensible shoes. All in all, he looked like a high school math teacher and she looked like the woman who interviews you when you plan to adopt a child. They both got to their feet when I came in, giving me expressionless looks. I said, "Sorry to hold you up."

"No problem," said the man, and the woman said, "We understand you were swimming."

"Exercise," I explained. Swimming indoors in one's own house in Manhattan in October would be the depth of decadence if it didn't have a morally correct purpose behind it.

"So your man said," the woman agreed, smiling faintly to let me know she accepted the morally correct purpose as an adequate excuse.

The man said, "I'm Detective Feeney and this is Detective LaMarca."

"How do you do? Sit down, sit down, drink your coffee."

They sat down, and so did I. They didn't say anything about how good the coffee was, so I could then tell them it was Robinson's pride and joy, and thus ease us forward through the civilities. In fact, they didn't go on with the chitchat at all. Detective Feeney said, "Do you know a man named Dale Wormley?"

This was four days after the incident in the Lucille Lortel theater, and my first reaction was surprise it had taken Wormley so long to try to make trouble out of it. Then my second reaction was surprise they'd send two detectives to my house over such a thing. And then my third reaction was disbelief; this was something else, some *further* annoyance from Wormley. Little I knew. I said, "I know who he is, yes."

Detective LaMarca laced her fingers in her lap, frowning at me slightly. "You know who he is? Does that mean you know him, or you don't know him?"

"We're not pals," I told her. "I've met him twice. He's on the other side of a lawsuit I'm party to."

"Kwality commercials," said Feeney.

"That's right."

"You met him twice," LaMarca said. "The first time was here?"

"Not in the house. Out on the sidewalk."

"Would you tell us about it?"

Maybe that was the point where I should have asked them to tell *me* about it, to ask what their interest was and why they were here, but I felt they'd prefer to run this interview in their own way at their own pace, so I simply told them the story of Dale Wormley accosting me on the street, Kendall bringing in the cops, and that being the end of it. "I don't know if the beat guys made a report," I finished.

"They did," Feeney told me.

LaMarca said, "Wormley complained you twisted his arm or something. Is that what happened?"

"Not exactly," I said. "He kept shoving me, putting his hand on my chest and shoving, so I put a come-along hold on his thumb to make him stop. As soon as he calmed down a little, I let him go."

"You bent his thumb, you mean," Feeney said.

"That's right."

LaMarca said, "Tell us about the other time you saw him."

"Is that why you're here?" I asked her, though I still didn't believe it.

"We'll get to that," she said. "Let's just take it in order, the way things happened."

"Okay," I said, and described round two. At the end, I said, "There were a lot of other people there. They can verify that he swung at me three times before I finally did something about it."

LaMarca said, "You knocked Wormley out?"

"I think he was groggy, or unconscious, something like that," I said. "He went down, and a couple of people there carried him out. He was gone when I left the theater."

Feeney said, grinning at me, "Just as well by you, huh?"

"I wasn't in any hurry to see him again," I agreed.

LaMarca leaned forward, hooking her laced fingers over her skirted knee. She said, "The first time, you saw Dale Wormley here and he shoved you and you bent his thumb. The second time, you saw him at the theater, and he swung at you and you knocked him out. And the next time you saw him?"

"There was no next time," I said.

She looked faintly surprised. "You just let it go at that?"

"Let what go? He was the one with the problem. As far as I'm concerned, the company that syndicates PACKARD is suing the company that hired Wormley to do a putdown parody of the Packard character. It's between them."

"'Putdown parody,'" LaMarca repeated. "You've seen these commercials?"

"Sure. I had to for the suit."

"And you don't like them."

"They're smarmy," I told her. "They make Packard out to be a bully and a blowhard. There's probably better ways to sell light bulbs and toilet paper."

"So you have to take it personally," LaMarca pointed out, being calm and reasonable. "It's *you* he's insulting, isn't it?"

"I could feel that way sometimes," I agreed, "but of course it isn't. I'm not *really* Packard, after all. I'm not a criminologist with a midwestern university."

"Solving crimes," Feeney said, grinning at me, man to man. "Being brilliant."

"Which is, of course, easy to make fun of," I told him. "When the show was on the air we were made fun of several times. *Mad Magazine* did a spoof, *Saturday Night Live* took off on us three or four times. Stuff like that."

"And it didn't bother you," LaMarca said. "That's the point you're trying to make, isn't it?"

"Look," I said. "If Wormley's made some sort of complaint against me—"

"He never did," Feeney told me. "From the way he acted with the beat cops here, that first incident here, he figured the law would just automatically be on your side because you're a celebrity."

"It doesn't work that way," I said.

"We know that, " LaMarca said, and then she said, "Does anyone live in this house besides you and the man who let us in?"

"No," I said, wondering what this abrupt change of subject was all about. "Why?"

Instead of LaMarca answering the question, Feeney asked one of his own: "Were you out last night, Mr. Holt?"

It was the first time either of them had called me by name; as though now they were getting down to it, whatever *it* was. I said, "Dinner with friends in Brooklyn."

"Excuse my asking this," Feeney said, with his friendly grin, "but you came home alone?"

"Yes." Anita had been working at her restaurant, of course, so I'd been alone at dinner at my friend Terry Young's house. Anita and I play our relationship casual, avoiding heavy plans, avoiding the requirements of habit. We wind up spending about half the nights together, at her place or mine; unfortunately, as I was now beginning to realize, last night had not been one of them.

"And at about what time did you get home, Mr. Holt?"

"I got home at about one o'clock in the morning, Detective Feeney," I said, feeling more comfortable about pressuring a male, "and I would really like to know why you want to know."

LaMarca said, "Did you see Dale Wormley on your way home?"

I felt unfriendly toward her, and allowed it to show. "I've already said," I pointed out, "that I haven't seen Wormley since the incident in the theater. That does include last night. So if he's decided to make trouble by claiming I—"

"Dale Wormley isn't claiming anything, Mr. Holt," Feeney told me. Then he grinned, almost boyishly, and sat back, shaking his head. "We probably should have mentioned this at the beginning," he said. "We aren't from the precinct."

"Oh, no?"

"No." Feeney's smile was utterly untrustworthy. "We're from Homicide," he said.

# 6

**S**hortly after six-thirty on that morning, three hours or so before Detectives Feeney and LaMarca came to talk to me, a neighbor of mine whom I don't know—I know none of my neighbors, in fact—a young woman named Crissy Ladbroke who is a stock analyst with a firm down in the financial district, left her floor-through second-story apartment in a converted brick brownstone essentially similar to mine and five doors away toward Sixth Avenue, and went downstairs for her usual pre-breakfast jog through the neighborhood. When she opened the inner door, however, she found a man crumpled on the floor in the tiny vestibule. Her initial impression that the man was a sleeping drunk lasted only a second or two, until she realized that the odd shape of his head was not a trick of early morning shadows but a result of it having been crushed by a blow with something very hard. Terrified, disgusted, she retreated back into the building and up to her apartment, where she dialed 911 and didn't emerge again until the first police arrived.

The man was Dale Wormley. According to the Medical Examiner's office's preliminary report, he had most likely died some time between midnight and three in the morning. The back of his head had been struck three times by a piece of wood, probably a two-by-four, minute shreds of which were now mixed with Wormley's flesh and blood and bone. For a number of reasons, it seemed unlikely that he had been killed where he had been found. There wasn't much room in that small vestibule, for instance, to swing a two-by-four, and no blood had been seen on the floor or walls. (Potential bloodstains, now being analyzed, had subsequently been found in the street in front of my house, near the curb, between two parked cars.)

Wormley's wallet, containing driver's license and credit cards and a moderate amount of money, was still in his pocket. There was no apparent violence to him other than the blows to the back of the head. His clothing had not been disarranged.

By seven-thirty, the police had reached Wormley's home, a studio apartment in a large building on West End Avenue in the eighties, where he had recently been living alone. Searching the apartment, they had found a letter he had written to me but never sent, dated the day after our encounter in the Lucille Lortel theater, in which he complained bitterly that I was depriving him of his "right to live," a phrase that appeared four times in the three page rambling hand-written letter. They had also found the name and current phone number of his former girlfriend, Julie Kaplan.

At first, Julie Kaplan was merely shocked and stunned by the news, but she then told the police that Wormley had had no enemies other than me. She told them that Dale had felt his life was totally bound up with mine, that he and I formed some sort of binary star in which I was the one with all the light and sustenance, and he was the "dark star," in his usual phrase for it, made dark by the fact of my existence. She said that his brooding about me, his obsessive belief that I was keeping him from his rightful destiny, was the principal reason she had left him, a few months ago.

Of course, now that I had murdered Dale Wormley, as Julie Kaplan explained to the police, she saw things in a different light and realized Dale must have been psychic to some degree, must have had a premonition of how it would all end. Of course Sam Holt must have been the one who'd killed Dale, she explained, because there was no one else with any reason. Wormley's crowding me, pestering me, pressuring me, imitating me, had inevitably led to this result. What other explanation could there be?

After they'd finished talking with Julie Kaplan, Detectives Feeney and LaMarca came to me, and after that period of preliminary nonsense they described to me this situation and what Julie Kaplan had said, and then they asked if they would have to go get a court order before I would let them search the house. "For a two-by-four?" I asked.

"Stranger things have happened," Feeney said, grinning cheerfully.

"I can't think of any," I told him. "Do you really and truly believe I went out last night and bludgeoned Dale Wormley to death, for being a pest?"

He looked as though he wanted to say *stranger things have happened* again, but he contented himself with an amiable smile while his partner LaMarca said, "Mr. Holt, up till now we don't believe anything. We're just taking this step by step, and you're the next step."

Feeney said, with his meaningless grin, "There's gonna be lots more to learn about Wormley before we're done. Other people with motives, maybe. An obsessive character like that, maybe you weren't the first one he leaned on. Or maybe Julie Kaplan did it herself, tried to shift suspicion over onto you."

"Or the Senator from Nebraska," LaMarca said.

I frowned at her. "The Senator from Nebraska?"

Feeney's grin turned into an actual laugh, and he said, "That's a little catch phrase of Marie's. Means you never know, when you start, work your way into your victim's life, where the road's gonna take you. First thing you know, the victim knew the Senator from Nebraska."

"Went to school with him," LaMarca explained, "or in the army with him. Sat beside him on a plane once."

"This time," I said, "I get the feeling *I'm* the Senator from Nebraska."

Laughing again, Feeney said, "See how much progress already."

LaMarca unlaced her fingers to gesture at the room, saying, "About having a little look through the house. Any problems?"

"Not at all," I told her, suddenly weary with it. Why

had Dale Wormley yoked himself to me like this? "Search to your hearts' content," I told them both.

And I wouldn't have been a bit surprised if they'd found a bloodstained two-by-four somewhere in the house; it felt like that all of a sudden. However, they didn't.

# 7

The suit was still alive. Dale Wormley's death really meant nothing at all in that regard, since the television commercials still existed and Kwality FoodMarts would have no particular reason to stop running them; except an order from a judge. But Wormley's death would delay things, confuse things, which is one of the reasons I spent most of the morning in Morton Adler's office high in the Graybar Building next to Grand Central.

A rumpled man with a neat round balding head, Mort's usual manner is one of shy amusement, as though he doesn't particularly see why everybody else wants to make such a fuss. His office, with its large windows overlooking the remaining air-rights in midtown Manhattan, is probably large enough, but is so cluttered and messy as to look small. Stacks of papers and books mound messily everywhere, most of them crowned by some recent copy of the New York *Times,* quarter-folded with the crossword puzzle on top, completed in neat black inked letters.

After we'd talked about the lawsuit a while, our conversation turned to the idea of me as a murder suspect, which made Mort lower his eyes and smile privately at the papers all over his desk. "The police are doing their job, Sam," he told the papers. "You know that. You've been in their shoes."

"Not really," I said.

"You've been a police officer," he insisted, shaking his head at the papers. "You know they're doing their work by the numbers, the way they should."

"It feels different," I said, "when I'm one of the numbers."

"Of course it does." Head still down, he glanced up through his eyebrows at me and smiled. *"You* know it's ridiculous to think you might have beaten this fellow with a stick," he said, "so you quite naturally resent the idea that anyone else might not see how ridiculous it is."

"In fact," I said, "I was violent with him twice before. The cops made a point of that."

"So your resentment," he said, nodding, looking at the messy desk again, raising his eyebrows as he followed the implications, "is combined with a little bit of nervousness. You *did* bend this fellow's thumb the first time you saw him. The second time, the physical violence increased."

"I knocked him out," I said. "It escalated."

"Escalated." He shook his head slowly and looked away out the window at the gray sky. "One of the more

minor bad effects of the Vietnam war," he said,
"though no less annoying for being minor, was the
emergence of that word out of the department stores
where it belonged and into uses in general speech where
it never really quite applies."

"Sorry," I said. "I didn't know that was one of your
pet peeves."

"Neither did I," he said, looking both surprised and
amused. "However, escalation or no, there is, I agree, a
progression in the level of violence between you and
Wormley. First he pushes you and you bend his thumb.
Second he tries to punch you and you knock him out.
Third . . ." And he grinned slyly at me.

"Sure," I said. "The police could see it that way.
Third, I come home tired and probably half drunk, late
at night—"

*"Were* you half drunk?"

"I had wine with dinner at the Youngs'. I don't
believe I was half drunk, no. But say I was, or just tired
and aggravated. And Wormley appears, and attacks me
again, and this time I lay him out with a two-by-four."

"But what then ensues . . ." he said, and shook his
head.

I hadn't so far thought about that part of it, the
events after the death of Wormley, but now I saw what
Mort meant. "That's right," I said. "Killing him I
might have done, but the rest no."

"It does seem unlikely," he agreed. "Have you, by
the way, ready access to heavy pieces of wood around
that place of yours? Any construction or repair work
going on, anything of that nature?"

"No," I said, "not in my house. But there's always
two or three dumpsters around that neighborhood."

He looked alert. "Dumpsters? Why don't I know that word?"

"Those are those large open-top metal boxes," I told him, "that look like a truck without cab or wheels. Construction crews use them for all the debris and trash. I think there's one on my block right now, down toward Fifth, on the other side of the street."

"The opposite way from where Wormley was found."

"Yes. Why?"

"I have no idea," he said. "But to return to the point, if Wormley *did* attack you a third time last night, and if you *did* go to this dumpster—thank you for that word, it makes up for escalate—and if you *did* take a piece of wood and hit him with it—"

"On the back of the head," I pointed out. "Three times."

"I agree," he said. "You would not, and you would not. Not with his back turned, and not more than once. But even so, you would not have then clumsily hidden the fellow just a few doors away from your own and gone to bed as though nothing had happened."

"That's right."

"What you *would* have done, Sam," he went on, smiling now reproachfully at me, "if you had just beaten Dale Wormley to death on your doorstep, you would have gone into your house and made two phone calls, the second one to the police."

I laughed, despite the grimness of the subject, seeing what he meant. "And the first one would have been to you," I said.

"Waking me, I assure you," he told me, "from an extremely pleasant sleep."

"None of this," I said, "does me much good when it

comes to convincing the police I didn't kill Dale Wormley."

He looked surprised. "But you don't have to," he said. "That isn't your job, it's theirs. They must find the evidence, sift it, come to a conclusion, convince their superiors. At the moment, I imagine you are a name on their suspect list, but not very earnestly, not enough to keep them from looking farther for more names to add."

"I suppose you're right." I felt a bit easier, but not much. *Do nothing* is always the hardest advice in the world to follow. "But there really is nothing for me to do, is there?"

"Of course not." He peered through his eyebrows at me again, with that sly amused smile. "Our old friend Packard isn't thinking of taking a hand, is he?"

"No no," I assured him, feeling embarrassed, and the intercom buzzer on his phone sounded. "I'll just wait and let the police work their way through it," I went on. "And if it ever looks as though there's something to worry about, the first thing I'll do is call you. That's a promise."

He nodded his approval, and rested his hand on the phone as he said, "But not, if you can possibly avoid it, in the wee hours."

"Do my best," I said.

Mort smiled and picked up the phone and said into it, "Yes, Myrtie?" Then he raised an eyebrow at me, and said, "Hmmm." He considered for a few seconds, then said, "I'll come out," and hung up. Then he looked at me. "We have a visitor," he said.

"We?"

"Julie Kaplan," Mort said.

# 8

"**T**he woman who told the police I was the only one who could possibly have murdered Dale Wormley?"

"Yes," Mort agreed, getting to his feet. "She is here, and wants to speak with me about you." Moving toward the closed door of his office, he said, "I'll leave the door slightly open, so you can hear. You needn't come out."

I also stood, and followed him to the door, and stood behind it as he went out, leaving it a few inches open behind himself. I heard Myrtie the secretary say, "Here's Mr. Adler," and then Mort's calm voice saying, "Miss Kaplan?"

"Yes. You're Sam Holt's lawyer, aren't you?" Her voice was young, breathy, the words pushed out in a rush. She sounded brisk, but unsure. As though she weren't used to being unsure.

"I am indeed," Mort told her. "How do you happen to know that, if I may ask?"

"Dale's papers," she said. "I wanted to find Sam Holt's address, but he didn't have it written down anywhere. But I found your name, with the lawsuit papers."

"Excuse me, Miss Kaplan," Mort said, "but let me understand something. You have Dale Wormley's papers? I'm afraid I don't quite follow that."

"At his apartment," she said. "I still have my key."

"Ah, I see."

"We used to live together."

"Yes, so I understand."

"Anyway," her quick breathy voice went on, "I have to talk to Sam Holt, but I couldn't find his address or anything at Dale's place, so that's why I'm here."

"Because you have to speak to Mr. Holt?"

"Yes. As soon as possible."

"May I ask why?"

"I owe him the most awful apology," the voice said, fast and urgent. "I want him to know I called the police back, I told them I was *crazy* before—"

"When you said that Mr. Holt was surely the murderer of your friend?"

"Oh, gosh," she said, and sounded younger than ever, and penitent, but in a hurried and careless way. "They told him, I guess," she said, "and he told you."

"Naturally."

"The thing is, I want to explain to him . . . Listen, Mr. Adler, I'll tell it all to you, okay? But I don't want to just leave a message or something like that, I want to tell Sam Holt face to face, I want him to know I'm really serious about this, I feel terrible if I made any trouble, and I just want him to understand why I said what I said. But I have to see him himself. I really do."

Well, I'm an actor, right? I know an entrance cue when I hear one. Besides, I didn't like eavesdropping from behind a door. So I stepped around it, pulled it open, stepped into the doorway, and said, "Okay, you can tell me then."

She was in profile to the doorway, facing Mort, her left side toward me. She turned at the sound of my voice, and her eyes widened, her mouth dropped open, she staggered as though she'd been punched. "Oh!" she said, and made a quick erasing kind of gesture with her free hand; then put that hand to her breast and looked faint, but no longer terrified. "Oh, my gosh," she said, more breathy and weak than ever. "Oh, you *do* look like him!"

Up till then, I'd always thought of the equation the other way; Dale Wormley looked like me. But this was the girlfriend, or former girlfriend, and when I made my unexpected appearance she reversed the order, and for just a second she'd seen her murdered lover in the doorway. "I'm sorry," I said, raising a hand, realizing what I'd done to her. Another reversal; she was here to apologize to me.

"Oh, wow," she said, panting for breath, shaking her head. She looked to be twenty-two or twenty-three, short, barely five feet, dressed in jogging sneakers and jeans and a bulky green jacket. A large floppy black leather shoulderbag hung at her left side, and in her left hand she carried a large maroon folder. She had a small pretty face with very large eyes, but then she also had a lot of heavy brown hair done in complex waves, like a shampoo model on television. The hair was a mistake, meant for a larger and older and more imposing woman, and making her face seem tinier than it was, almost pinched. When she shook her head, the hair moved like a large garment. "That's really amazing," she said, gazing at me. "To see you in person—"

Mort looked as though he wasn't entirely sure I'd done the right thing. His expression troubled, he extended a hand toward Julie Kaplan, saying, "Perhaps we should all go into my office, sit down, discuss—"

She was paying no attention to him. Still looking at me, she said, "It's even more than in the pictures. Here, let me show you—" And she opened the flap of the maroon folder.

I've never seen Mort move so fast. In fact, I didn't know fast movement was possible to him. But, before Julie Kaplan could reach into that maroon folder, he had lunged forward, knocked it out of her hand, pushed her back against the astonished Myrtie's desk, and planted one foot firmly on the folder on the floor.

"Ow!" the girl cried, more startled than hurt, and then continued to lean backward against Myrtie's desk, slightly off-balance, as she stared in disbelief at Mort, who looked more rumpled than usual, and very uncomfortable, but determined. "What—?" she started, and her voice broke, and she tried again: "What was *that* for?"

"Earlier today, young woman," Mort told her, his own voice trembling and out of breath, "you accused my client of having murdered your paramour. Now you insist on a face-to-face meeting with my client, which he has for some reason chosen to grant. Your immediate response is to reach inside this parcel you were carrying."

Staring now as though Mort were a dangerous lunatic, Julie Kaplan cried, "For Christ's sake, what did you think I was going to do, *shoot* him?" And as she said that, the most farfetched thing she could think of to say, I could see her realizing that, yes, that was exactly what Mort had thought. She gaped at him, and then at me. To me she said, in a hollow kind of voice, "I wanted to show you the *pictures.* The pictures on his resumé."

Mort, with a little grunt, bent and picked up the folder. Opening it, he looked inside, reached in, moved his hand this way and that, then closed the folder again and extended it toward Julie Kaplan. "My apologies for the melodramatic interpretation," he said, "but I thought it better to be safe than sorry. Stranger things have happened, you know."

That's what Feeney said, I thought.

What happened now was, the three of us went into Mort's office, leaving the connecting door open, and while Mort cleared stacks of documents and junk off another chair Julie Kaplan removed her green jacket, under which she wore a lightweight tan sweater. The three of us sat down, and Mort, smiling at the girl in what he clearly intended to be a reassuring fashion, said, "So you've changed your mind about Sam here. May I ask what made the change?"

"Well, I just saw it was crazy," she told him. "For weeks and weeks, all Dale could talk about was . . ." She moved her head, glanced at me, shrugged, said, "Well, you know."

"Me."

"That's all he could talk about," she repeated, "the pressure on him from you, how he couldn't breathe with you on top of him, how you didn't leave him room to live, and everything that went wrong in his whole life was somehow Sam Holt's fault. And I'd say, 'Dale, *he*

didn't make you fight with Matty Pierce in class, *he*
didn't make you punch that man from Paramount
Pictures, Sam *Holt* didn't make you get drunk and miss
performances and get fired from *Li'l Abner.'* So then
he'd get mad at *me* and say I was taking Sam Holt's
side, even his own girlfriend had to kowtow to the star
and all that, and finally I just said, 'Listen, Sam Holt
doesn't even know you're alive, he's got his own things
to think about—' "

I glanced over at Mort and saw him grinning faintly
in my direction. I grinned just as faintly back. We were
both, I knew, imagining the calmative effect she must
have had on Dale Wormley by pointing out to him that
his *bête noire,* Sam Holt, didn't even know he was alive.

She went on, not noticing our side glance: "That's
finally why I couldn't take it any more, why I just left,
three weeks ago. So *then*—"

"You and he," Mort interrupted gently, "have only
been apart three weeks?"

"It wasn't a *real* separation," she said, bright-eyed,
looking from him to me and back to Mort again. "It
was just I couldn't take his carrying on about, you
know, all the time. It was kooky. I think we both know
we're just, I mean we both knew—Oh, my gosh."

The eyes got brighter as she looked at us, overtaken
by her thoughts. She and Wormley had, after all, been
involved together emotionally and the fact of his death
was still very new to her. The way things like that work,
you don't learn the bad news all at once, you hear it and
absorb it just a little bit, and then later on you hear the
echo and absorb it some more, and so on, each time
getting the news fixed a little more deeply into your
brain; as much as you can stand, each time. Like waves
breaking over you one after another, until you're

thoroughly soaked. Julie Kaplan was right now feeling the effects of another wave.

Mort, frowning thoughtfully at the papers on his desk, seated well forward with one arm behind him, elbow up, hand clasped on chair-arm, said, "Let me see if I can guess what happened. Dale Wormley's attitude toward Sam Holt seemed to you obsessive and unreal—"

"That's right," she said, still very bright-eyed.

Mort nodded. He kept watching the desk. I knew he felt uncomfortable around high emotion, and this was his delicate way of keeping the temperature in the room bearable. "When the police came to you this morning," he said, "and told you what had happened, your immediate thought was, 'I was wrong, and Dale was right.' You thought he must have been telling you about a real danger, and you'd ignored him, and if you'd paid more attention and been—I think we say 'supportive' these days—if you'd been all that, nothing bad would have happened to him."

"That's the first thing I told the cops," she agreed, nodding, leaning toward Mort as though he were the physician with the diagnosis that would save her. "When they told me, right away I said, 'Dale was right! I should have listened to him!' "

"And so," Mort said, nodding slowly, seeming to read his words off the strewn papers on his desk, "having been converted to Dale's belief, you immediately passed it on to the police as your own."

"I did! That's exactly what I did!" She was bobbing up and down on her chair now, and she turned from Mort to me to say, "And I really believed it, I wasn't trying to just make trouble or anything like that. I believed it!"

"May I ask," Mort said, peering almost surreptitiously at her through his eyebrows, "what changed your mind?"

"Kim," she said.

He actually raised his head to look at her directly. "Kim?" he echoed.

"My roommate," she explained. "See, when I left Dale I just moved in with this friend of mine, Kim Peyser."

"A young woman," suggested Mort.

"Yes, sure," she said, and flashed a brief sunny smile, and said, "Dale and I aren't, weren't—You know, we weren't *through,* neither of us thought we were, well, you know. So Kim had room, and I moved in with her, cause it would just be for a while."

"Yes, of course."

"So when the police came and told me," she said, and shook her head at the memory, making that heavy garment of her hair lift and move in a slow wave around her face, "when they were going," she explained, "they said I shouldn't be alone for a while, so I called Kim at work and she—Kim works with one of those phone-survey places, you know? Call you up and ask you what toothpaste you use and all that. So it's kind of loose, you can come and go kind of when you want. So she came home, and I told her everything, and right away she said, 'Julie, you gotta be nuts. Sam Holt didn't kill Dale.' And right up till then I was believing it, believing the whole thing, I really was." Turning to me—as the injured party, I suppose—appealing directly to me, she said, "And the second Kim said that, it just fell apart. I mean, I *knew* you didn't do it."

"Thank you," I said.

"No, I *mean* it," she said, utterly serious and determined to make me understand. "It was like being with your friends and you get high," she said earnestly, "and you all talk about how the human race really came from another planet and all that, and everybody in the room really and truly *believes* it. And then you come down and you say, 'Oh, wow, that was weird.' You know what I mean?"

I had to grin and nod and say, "Yes, I do."

"Well," she said, "that's exactly what it was like. I told Kim the story, and she said, 'Julie, you gotta be nuts,' and that *second* I saw she was right, and it was crazy to think *you* were gonna go out and kill Dale. I mean, somebody who sues somebody is not somebody who goes out and kills somebody, it's like a whole other mindset, you know?"

Mort laughed. "Very cogent," he said. "Very well reasoned, Miss Kaplan."

"So I called the police," she told the both of us, "right away, and of course I couldn't get to the same people that talked to me before. It was a man and a woman and—"

"Feeney and LaMarca," I said.

She gave me a stricken look, reminded of her guilt. "They went right to you, didn't they? Right after me, they went to you."

"Of course," I said.

"Well, I left a message for them," she said, nodding to show her determination, her heavy hair nodding after her. "I told them I was crazy before, I explained the whole thing, but it was just a *message,* you know? Not like really talking to them or anything like that. I mean, who knows when they'll see it or what they'll think. So I just wandered around the apartment, and I said to myself, 'Julie, you've got to do more, you've got to fix this up somehow.' So that's when I decided the thing to do was find *you* and tell you what happened and explain how I was crazy, and tell you I'm ready to do anything I can to fix it up again. I'll talk to those cops, I'll do whatever you say."

"I appreciate that," I said, though I couldn't see much she could do to repair any damage she might have made.

"However," Mort said slowly, thoughtfully, and now his chin had sunk again, it was the desktop that absorbed his attention once more as he said, "At this point, Miss Kaplan, I'm afraid, by far the best thing you could do for Mr. Holt is nothing."

She leaned forward to stare at him, frowning, intense. "Nothing? But I want to—"

"You have made your statement to the police," Mort explained, not looking up. "They will now evaluate it, along with other statements from other concerned individuals, and along with whatever physical evidence they may obtain, and eventually they will decide the proper weight to give your statement. Now, however, if you approach them and say, 'I wish to retract my statement, I wish to make a quite different, in fact reversed, statement,' they will want to know what changed your mind. In the course of your interview with them, they will ask you if Mr. Holt has talked to you, and you will have to say yes, that you talked not only with Mr. Holt but also with his attorney."

Looking shocked, she said, "But that isn't—"

"You are going to say," he interrupted her, "that I am making the wrong inference. But I have made *no* inference, it's simply implicit in the statement of the facts. So the best thing you can do, Miss Kaplan, is not volunteer to state those facts."

She sat back, almost withdrawing within that cloak of hair as though into another room, to think about what he'd said. From the way her mouth moved, she was chewing the inside of her cheek. Then she shook her head—her hair heaved slowly after—and looked ruefully in my direction, saying, "I really loused up, didn't I?"

Why did I want to reassure her? After all, she was the one who'd wronged me. And yet I did; I said, "The police don't jump to conclusions, you know."

"I guess not." Then she brightened, saying, "I guess you'd know that for sure, wouldn't you? I mean, you used to be a cop and all."

"That's right," I agreed, surprised she knew that bit of my biography.

She must have seen the surprise in my face; she grinned back at it, saying, "I know a *lot* about you, Mr. Holt. Not through my own fault. Dale knew everything there was to know. He did scrapbooks. You were like his hobby."

The idea made me uncomfortable. I said, "I was?"

"He knew all kinds of things," she assured me, "stuff I bet you forgot yourself. He knew more than your biggest fan would know."

"But he wasn't a fan," I said.

The smile turned rueful again, and she said, "No, he wasn't." She'd put the maroon folder on the floor beside her chair, and now she stooped to pick it up, glancing at Mort half humorously and half apprehensively as she said, "Can I show the pictures now?"

Feeling uncomfortable, not wanting to *see* Dale Wormley try to be me, I said, "Why? What's the point?"

"I want you to see for yourself," she told me, "he

wasn't just—he was more than that. The part you
know." She drew a paper out of the folder, not quite
looking at it as she did so, and extended it toward me.

I recognized it; or, that is, I recognized the kind of
thing it was. I used to have such things of my own, in a
stack on the shelf in my closet, when I had the studio in
Santa Monica, before PACKARD was born. A
typewriter-size sheet of heavy paper. On one side is a
glossy black-and-white photo of the actor, posed to
look what he thinks of as his best. On the reverse,
usually on a separate sheet glued or taped in place but
sometimes more expensively printed on the back of the
photo itself, the actor's resumé, his list of credits.
Which parts in which shows at what theaters on what
dates; which movies; which television commercials;
maybe which industrial shows. Some resumés include
theatrical training history, and all include the name
and address and phone number of the agent or "contact" (a word meaning the actor doesn't yet have an
agent), plus an answering service number.

I took this photo reluctantly, and tried to keep my
expression blank as I looked at it. Or them, actually;
Wormley had chosen, as many actors do, a format
meant to show his versatility. Instead of one picture,
the glossy side of the resumé was divided into four
photos, showing Wormley in four different poses and
costumes and settings. In the upper left, he wore a
cowboy hat and an open-necked plaid shirt, and he
smiled openly and directly at the camera in a howdy-
ma'am style. In the upper right, he wore a tux and
leaned forward and down to his right a little, smiling
kind of suggestively and secretively up toward the
camera. In the bottom left, he wore boxing gloves and
trunks and stood in classic boxer-photo pose. And in

the bottom right, in trenchcoat, winking at the viewer, he was Packard.

Mm. A pretty good Packard, actually. If looking like that were all it took, the job was as much his as anybody's. Or was I being ridiculously defensive to even think that way?

Julie Kaplan said, with some strain in her voice, trying to convince me, "You see what I mean, that he wasn't *just* imitating you. I mean, he was a—"

"Yes, I see that."

"He was an *actor,*" she finished. "Before he ever got mixed up with you."

Mixed up with me? I turned the sheet over and saw that he'd spent some of his Kwality FoodMarts money having a first-class resumé prepared. The facts of his career were printed on the back of the photo itself. He had a pretty respectable history there, with a number of regional theaters, a few commercials before Kwality FoodMarts, and minor parts in a couple of drive-in type movies ("'State Trooper' in BIKERS FROM HELL"). There was probably no more than half here of what Brett Burgess's resumé could show, but to be honest it was a lot more than mine without PACK-ARD.

"He was an actor," Julie Kaplan said. It was important to her that I understand and accept that.

"I see he was."

"And things were going to get better for him, too," she told me, sitting up straighter, clenching her hands in her lap. "That's why I knew we'd get back together. Once he was in that show, he'd stop worrying about *you* all the time—" said, though unconsciously, as though I were the villain of the piece "—and things could be the way they used to be."

I looked at her. "Show?"

"*Four Square,*" she told me. "'The new play at Lincoln Center with Rita Colby. It's going into rehearsal in January."

Three months from now. I said, "He was cast in it?"

"Not officially, not yet. But he knows Rita Colby, he dated her a few times."

That surprised me, though on second thought it shouldn't have. In her early fifties, well-preserved in a gaunt but dramatically attractive way, Rita Colby would be about twenty years older than Dale Wormley; but why not? One of those rarities these days, a true *theater* star, Rita Colby was the closest thing America had to England's Maggie Smith. An extremely talented and dedicated performer, she was also maintaining the Broadway mythos of the overwrought grande dame, the Tallulah Bankhead tradition; a tall handsome blond fellow like Dale Wormley would be quite naturally one of the perks of that position. But in my eyes it lessened Wormley, and I wondered how he himself had taken it. I said, "Rita Colby promised him the part?"

"Oh, no," Julie Kaplan said. "Not like that. Kay did. Dale's agent. He's Rita's agent, too, and he absolutely promised Dale the second male lead in *Four Square.* Dale told me there was no question at all, he had the part."

I looked again at the back of the resumé, and saw that the agent listed was Kay Henry Associates, on Third Avenue here in New York. I didn't know the agency, but there was no particular reason why I should.

"May I see that?" Mort asked, reaching toward the resumé.

I handed it to him and, as he studied it, turning it over and over like an archaeologist with a particularly

with the house and whatever else might happen, I slipped out of the city just ahead of the rush hour.

After a pleasant evening with relatives, who've grown a lot calmer about me since PACKARD went off the air, and a restful night in the guestroom of Uncle Edgar's clifftop North Shore home, with its morning view of the Sound—a few hardy souls still sailed out there, ignoring the end of summer—I drove back to the city, arriving just at lunchtime, to find Detectives Feeney and LaMarca waiting for me. "I put them in the living room, as before," Robinson told me, taking my overnight bag.

"Call about having the car picked up, will you?" I asked him, and went into the living room to find the detectives dressed in different but similar clothing and seated in the same chairs as last time. Once again, Robinson had given them coffee. "My lawyer told me you'd be back," I greeted them.

Feeney raised his eyebrows and grinned at me, saying "He did?" LaMarca didn't react at all.

I said, "Because of the possibility that *I* was the one who was supposed to be killed."

Feeney smiled more broadly, and nodded, either in understanding or agreement. LaMarca, with frowning interest, said, "Do you think that's so?"

"No," I told her. "I've thought about it, and of course people in my position get crank letters and death threats every once in a while, but that hasn't happened since my show went off the air. The only person I can think of, in fact, who might want to kill me," I added, trying to return Feeney's smile but somehow unable to make contact with it, "is Dale Wormley."

LaMarca looked disapproving. Feeney laughed, and

said, "Killed himself by mistake, huh? Thought he was you."

"He *did* think he was me."

LaMarca was the no-nonsense partner. "We'd like to show you a picture," she said.

I waited, having not the slightest idea what was coming, as Feeney nodded at his partner and picked up a tan manila envelope from the floor beside his chair. He withdrew an 8 x 10 glossy color photograph—every day, someone was handing me an 8 x 10 photo—and extended it toward me.

It was a close-up, in excellent detail, well lit. The camera looked straight down at a linoleum or tile floor, probably a kitchen floor, of a light cream color. A hand and wrist and part of a forearm were visible on the floor, palm down, fingers partly curled. It was a slender hand and wrist, with pale rose polish on the nails and a small digital watch on the wrist. The clarity was such that I could read the time: 7:48. The sign for AM or PM was too small to make out. Above the hand, in some brownish impasto medium, capital letters were very shakily drawn: S A M, and then a space, and then ⊦. The index finger of the hand was at the right end of the crossbar on the last unfinished letter.

The photo, silent and clear and in beautifully realized color, was chilling. It was also enraging. I heard the tremor of anger in my voice as I said, trying to say it calmly, "Is that blood?"

"Her own blood," LaMarca said, unnecessarily.

It's Julie Kaplan, I thought, and visualized that heavy wool-like shawl of hair shrouding her head. I said, "Is that AM or PM?"

They both seemed surprised by the question. "PM," Feeney told me, then answered my next question before

I asked it. "We called here last night. Your man told us where you were and when you'd be back."

I said, holding up the photo toward them, "Is it Julie Kaplan?"

That also surprised them. Feeney said, "No," and LaMarca said, "It's Kim Peyser."

The name meant nothing to me. Frowning at them, I said, "Who's that?"

"Julie Kaplan's roommate," LaMarca told me, watching my face.

Of course; Julie Kaplan had mentioned the name yesterday. The girl she'd moved in with after leaving Wormley, the one who'd told her she was nuts to think I was Wormley's murderer. Handing the photo back to Feeney, I said, "Do you have any idea why they faked this?"

"Fake?" Feeney asked me, as though I was trying for a joke he didn't understand, and LaMarca looked almost outraged as she said, "You don't think she did it herself?"

"Of course not," I said. "Do you? The mortally wounded girl writes her killer's name in her own blood on the floor, managing to write just enough to make it identifiable before she dies? Do you *really* think that's what happened?"

"It can't be discounted," LaMarca told me.

"Sure it can. The thing's a fake. Can't you see that?"

"No," LaMarca said, and Feeney held the photo at arm's length, squinting at it, making a putdown routine out of it as he said, "Looks pretty good to me."

"Oh, for Christ's sake." I got to my feet, which startled them both. Realizing they both thought they might reach for their pistols—they *believed* that hokum—I stopped and faced them and carefully said,

"I am going to open that drawer over there and take out a pen and a piece of paper."

"Okay," Feeney said.

I did so, both of them watching me alertly, and brought both back to LaMarca. "Use the drum table here," I told her. "Print a capital H."

She looked at me, at Feeney, at the paper. She shrugged and printed a capital H.

"Good," I said. "Do it again."

"I don't see the point," she told me, "but all right."

She started to print another capital H. She drew two of the three lines of the letter, and I said, "Stop!" putting my hand on the paper to keep her from drawing the third. Then I took my hand away and said, "Take a look at it. *That's* how you print an H."

They looked at the two vertical lines. They looked at one another. Feeney looked at the photo.

I said, "Everybody who prints a capital H does the two vertical lines first and then connects them with the crossbar. But the name 'Sam' followed by two vertical lines wouldn't establish the accusation clearly enough. The killer wanted to be sure he'd made his point. Not an entire capital H, just enough to show that's what was intended. The last wonderful milligram of melodrama. So now you know something about the killer. He's an artiste."

"Just a minute," LaMarca said. "You had lunch with your lawyer yesterday in the Oyster Bar at Grand Central, and left him a little before two. You didn't get home until nearly three. Where were you in that hour?"

"That's when she was killed, huh? I walked home. I usually do in New York, in good weather."

Feeney said, "Aren't you kind of well-known to just *walk* around the—"

"No," I told him, and plucked the photo out of his hand and showed it to him. "Whatsername didn't write this," I told him. "The murdered girl. *She* didn't write it. If you come up with a reason why I would have written it, let me know." I dropped the photo back in his lap and he slapped at it to keep it from falling to the floor. "In the meantime," I told them both, "I'm busy." And I turned my back on them and walked to the door.

"We have more questions, Mr. Holt," LaMarca said.

I looked at her cold-schoolteacher face. "Screw you," I said, and went upstairs to unpack. When Robinson called me for lunch a little later, they were gone.

# 10

It isn't smart to say *screw you* to a pair of cops, no matter how much they irritate you, a fact I knew (from both sides of the equation) and of which Mort gloomily reminded me when I phoned him after lunch. I called because my irritation had departed, leaving nervousness, which Mort did little to ease. "I could have preferred, Sam," his voice said slowly and plaintively in my ear, "if you had chosen some other phraseology to express your discontent."

"So could I," I told him, "but they were being so deliberately obtuse, and—"

"Never," he interrupted, "accuse anyone of being stupid on purpose. Some people do it quite automatically and naturally."

"I'm not sure about those two," I said, thinking

about Feeney and LaMarca, unable to make up my mind about them. "But they were definitely just going through the routine they'd worked out ahead of time, regardless of what might happen."

"Twitting the celebrity, perhaps? Letting him know he gets no special treatment?"

"Maybe, I don't know. Anyway, I'd just had the long drive in from the Island, and I just didn't feel like putting up with them."

"Which you let them know."

"Which I let them know. And now, I guess, the question is, what can they do about it?"

"Well, they can't arrest you for the murder of Kim Peyser, we know that much," he said. (The murder itself, without the fakery about my name or my being connected with it in any way, had made this morning's papers, so Mort had already known about it when I phoned.) "But they *can* of course try to make life difficult in other ways," he went on. "What's your relationship generally with the officers in the precinct?"

"Slim but friendly," I told him. "I appeared at a PAL benefit for them six years ago when PACKARD was still on. Not much since. And these two are Homicide South, not precinct."

"I understand that. I was hoping you might have a champion somewhere in the force."

"Sorry," I said, meaning it.

He sighed. I hate it when Mort sighs. "Let me make some phone calls," he said, "see how bad the damage is, and what we can do to repair it."

"Thank you, Mort," I said humbly.

"I'll call you back," he promised, and I said, "I'll be here."

For the next half hour, I merely roamed the house,

waiting uselessly for the phone to ring. I sat at my desk, but there was nothing to do there but look out the window at West 10th Street and think about the death on that pavement of Dale Wormley. The dumpster from which the murder weapon had probably come was just visible down to the right, toward 5th Avenue.

I couldn't read. I looked at my cassettes, and there was nothing I wanted to watch. The idea of undressing and going down to the lap pool was no good; I wanted to be here, ready, when Mort phoned back.

Finally I found myself again at my desk, this time with the phone book open, looking for Julie Kaplan. There were no *Julie*s listed, but there were four *J*s; she would probably be one of them.

It was this not knowing anything that had eventually worn me down. Why was Kim Peyser killed? Was it connected to the murder of Dale Wormley? *Where* had it happened? Why did the killer make that rough and stupid attempt to put the blame on me?

Julie Kaplan was my only entree to that world, whatever world it was in which Dale Wormley and Kim Peyser had moved. She would know where her friend had been killed. She might even have an idea who had done it, who would think it a good plan to borrow her own suggestion that I was a murderer. That was what pushed me to act, plus the fact that the phone wasn't ringing, which meant I was stuck here with nothing to do but think. All of that is why I picked up the phone on my desk and started calling J. Kaplans.

The first was an answering machine, a nasal-voiced woman who was not the right one. The second was a suspicious older man. And the third was Dale Wormley:

"Hi," said the voice, in pleasanter tones than I'd ever

heard from him in life. "You've caught Dale Wormley's smart answering machine here." (Of course! Julie Kaplan had shared Wormley's apartment until three weeks ago, and would naturally have her own listing.) "I'm really sorry I can't be present to take your call, but you go ahead and tell this friendly machine whatever you want and I'll sure get back to you. In the meantime, have a nice day, y'hear?"

The studied folksiness of it grated, but under the circumstances I also found myself feeling sorry for the poor son of a bitch. He had simply been trying to make some sort of statement, trying to rise up out of the crowd, be noticed. That's what his life had been about, after all; that's what all actors' lives are about.

And that's where he and I were linked, however reluctant I was to admit it. I possessed something Dale Wormley had wanted, and this answering machine message of his made it clear: I was, through no fault of my own, someone. He had been, regardless of his efforts, no one. His message, by being neither sincere nor professional, had shown the hopelessness of his try.

I left no message.

Kim Peyser was in the phone book under her full name, with an address on West 74th Street. I called, and listened to another voice from beyond the grave: "Hi. Kim here. Or not here, you know what I mean. When you hear the beep, leave a message. See you later."

A cheerful, youthful, innocent voice. She shouldn't have been killed, I thought, while in those same few seconds I was also deciding whether or not this time to leave a message. Had Kim Peyser been killed right there, in the apartment she shared with Julie Kaplan? If she had, would Julie Kaplan continue to stay there? I think it was just the need I felt to do *something* that decided me: "Julie," I said, after the beep, "if you're still there, this is Sam, uh, Sam." At the last second, it had occurred to me I had no way to tell who'd be listening to this machine, and I didn't want to identify myself too closely. Julie Kaplan would recognize the voice and know who it was. I left one of my numbers—the general one, used in the less personal part of my life—and hung up. And then, once again, I had nothing to do.

Twenty minutes later, the phone did ring at last. I let Robinson answer as usual, while I sat at attention at the desk, and when he buzzed me it was to say the person calling was neither of the ones I'd expected, but was Terry Young. "I'll take it," I told him, and pressed the button.

Terry Young was the fellow I'd had dinner with in Brooklyn the night before last, when Dale Wormley was killed. We had first met nine years ago, he a reporter with the New York *Daily News* and I the hot new TV star he'd been sent to interview. We hated each other on sight, like cats, I seeing him as a professional fat slob, he seeing me as a posturing wimp, and it was only when our growing irritation with one another led to an honest—if loud-voiced—exchange of these views that we discovered it might be possible to get along after all. I now count Terry and his German-born wife, Gretchen, among my closest friends.

Picking up the phone, smiling already in anticipation, I said, "Hi. What's happening?"

"Well, you, to begin with," he said. He didn't sound cheerful.

Now what? I said it aloud: "Now what?"

"Have you annoyed a couple of cops recently?"

"Oh, Christ, yes. How do *you* know?"

"They're spreading the word," he told me sourly, "among their friends in the press."

Homicide detectives usually have a friend or two in the press, because the press quite naturally cultivates them. I said, "What word are they spreading?"

"This is third or fourth hand," he warned me, "but what I get is that you are *implicated* in two ongoing homicide investigations and—"

"Hell."

"—and are being uncooperative."

"Damn."

"Are you? And are you?"

"Not the way it sounds," I told him.

"In other words," he said, "yes."

"Damn it, Terry," I said, "does this mean I'm going to get a million reporters hanging around again?"

"Not a bit of it. In a situation like this, hearing from the other side could only spoil the story. You've already referred everybody to your PR people, haven't you?"

"Before this."

"So that's good enough for the troops. Mr. Holt declines comment through his spokesperson."

"Shit."

"May I quote you?"

"No."

"Well, how about for real, then?"

Was he serious? I said, "In your column, you mean?"

"It's up to you," he said. "If you want to get your side of the story out, I'm your man. If not, not."

"I hate to hear me saying this to you, Terry, but I'd better talk that over with Mort first."

"I don't hate to hear you saying it," he told me. "It shows a certain maturity at long last. These two homicides they're tying you to. The first one was the guy imitating you on the commercials, right?"

"That's right."

"What's the other?"

"A girl named Kim Peyser."

He had me spell it, and then said, "What's the link?"

"To me? There is none, that's the dumb part of it."

He let the silence on the phone line grow a certain amount of fur, and then he sighed and said, "Listen, Daddy. Do you want to tell me the facts yourself, or do you want me to hear them in the gutter?"

It was my turn to sigh. "They haven't released this yet," I said, "so far as I know."

"For my information only. Not for use without your consent, not for attribution without your consent."

So I told him about the name written in blood and why it was a fake, and he said, "Hold on," and there was a brief silence, and then he said, "By God, you're right. That's the way you make an H."

"I demonstrated that for Feeney and LaMarca," I told him, "and they just sailed over it and kept on asking questions about my whereabouts at the time of the murder and all that crap."

"Why, do you suppose?"

"I really don't know. Mort said it might have something to do with twitting a celebrity."

"Well," he said, "there are cops who like the idea of putting the arm on a celeb, because guess who else gets in the newstape at ten o'clock. Did you get the idea they were needling you?"

"No. To be honest, the only idea I had was that

they were ignoring me. And ignoring the facts of the case."

"I'll see what I can find out about them. Feeney and LaMarca?"

I agreed that was their names, and promised to check with Mort before the end of the day about granting him an interview, and we hung up, and then I had to decide if this was a legitimate excuse to call Mort before he got around to calling me. I knew it really wasn't, so it took me nearly ten minutes to convince myself it was and make the call. Mort came on the line saying, "No news yet, I'm afraid. I have some calls out and I'm waiting for a response."

"This is something else."

I told him about Terry's information, and the offer of a rebuttal in Terry's column. He brooded about that briefly, saying, "Mmmmmm," and, "Uh-huh, uh-huh, uh-huh," and finally deciding, "No. At least not yet."

"If you say so," I said, sorry that he had.

"If the rift is reparable," he pointed out, "it would be better to repair it. The only reason to make a public issue of this would be a desire to annoy the police officers involved."

"I do have that desire," I said, "but I can see you're right. All right, I'll tell Terry no."

"Try not to tell him anything else along the way," Mort suggested.

I laughed. "He already pumped me dry."

"I might have known." Mort sighed again, and said, "Well, I'll call you when there's anything to report."

"Thanks, Mort." I was about to hang up when another thought struck and I said, "Wait a second. Mort?"

"Yes, I'm still here."

"Do you have today's paper handy?" I knew he would, an infinitesimal part of the dumpster that was his office. "The one with Kim Peyser's death in it."

"Why?" he asked, suspicion deep in his voice.

"I want to know the address. Was she killed at home? She lived on West 74th Street."

"Sam," he said, "tell me something. Is our friend Packard taking an interest in this case after all?"

"No no no," I told him, hearing myself protest too much. "I just want to know where I was supposed to be while I was walking home from lunch with you."

"Hold on," he said, and I could hear shuffling and rattling in the background, and then he came back to say, "Here it is. An apartment at 497 West End Avenue."

West 74th Street crosses West End Avenue, so it could still be the same place. "Would that be in the seventies?"

"Well, let's see," he said. "I have my trusty Manhattan guide here, for the cross-streets. Let's see; West End Avenue. Drop the last number, divide by two, add fifty-nine or sixty. No, that would be just below 86th Street, a block or two."

So she wasn't killed at home. Whose kitchen floor was that? "Thanks, Mort," I said.

"Be good," he warned me.

"I'll do better than that," I assured him. "I'll be careful."

# 11

It was just a few minutes after I called Terry back, when we'd reluctantly agreed that Mort was undoubtedly right that I should keep my mouth shut in public for a while, when I noticed that I had written the same address twice today on the scratch pad on my desk. 497 West End Avenue. Once, it was the address Mort had given me of the place where Kim Peyser had been found murdered. The other time, it was the address in the phone book for the J Kaplan who had lived with Dale Wormley.

Kim was murdered in Dale Wormley's apartment? What on earth was she doing *there?*

I found out an hour later when Julie Kaplan phoned, sounding frightened and subdued, almost whispering.

She'd been reluctant to give Robinson her name, and
when I got on the line she sounded as though she might
hang up at any second. "You did call me, didn't you?"
asked the small voice.

"Yes. I wanted to know what happened to your
friend."

"The police . . ." Her voice faded away, then came
back, but fainter than before. "They think it was
supposed to be me."

"Supposed to be you? What was?"

"The— The victim. What did you *call* about?" she
demanded, sounding rattled and rebellious and on the
verge of hanging up.

I said, "Wait a minute. The police think the killer
was after *you?* Why?"

"She borrowed my coat," she said, sounding merely
harried and weary now. "And she was in my place,
and— You *didn't* do it, did you? I mean, no, never
mind, forget that, of course you didn't."

"The police showed you the picture, with the letters?"

"Yes."

I considered explaining the normal method of writing a letter H to this girl and realized she was beyond
that kind of comprehension. So I merely said, "They
showed me the picture, too. I don't know how much
they believe in it."

"Neither do I. I said it was crazy. I *told* them, the
same ones as before."

"Did they ask you if you'd met me?"

The long silence gave me the answer before she
finally half-whispered, "Yes. I had to tell them the
truth."

"Of course," I agreed, wondering if that had been

any part of the reason for Feeney and LaMarca's aggressive attitude toward me.

Almost plaintive now, she said, "I don't see why you want to call me."

"I want to know what's going on. Does this, this *thing*, make any kind of sense to you?"

"None!" she said, suddenly at full volume. "I never did anything to anybody in my life! And here I'm, I'm *hiding!*" As though reminded of that fact, she lowered her voice again, saying, "I can't go back to Kim's place, not now, and I'll *never* go to that, that other."

The apartment she'd shared with Dale Wormley, she meant, where her friend Kim had died, possibly in mistake for her. Which would make the killer an amazing blunderer, if all the guesses were right. According to those theories, first he killed Dale Wormley in front of my house, having mistaken him for me, and now he'd killed Kim Peyser in mistake for Julie Kaplan. Somehow, I didn't believe any of that. I believed the killer's moves were deliberate and careful, and that he'd done what he meant to do. Which didn't necessarily mean Julie Kaplan wasn't in danger. I said, "Where are you now?"

I could sense her hesitation, her reluctance to tell me where she was, and I felt a sudden shiver along my spine. By God, she thinks it's possible that I *am* a killer! But then, in a small voice, she said, "I'm at Kay Henry's, my agent. In the waiting room. I can hang out here."

So she was an actress, too, with the same agent as Dale Wormley. Possibly they'd met while hanging out in Kay Henry's waiting room; it wouldn't be the first time that had happened. But it was no solution now to

Julie Kaplan's problem. I said, "You can't stay there forever, you know."

"I know. I can't figure out where to go or what to do. The police want me in the city, but if I go to *anybody's* place, anybody I know, he could— Somebody could find me there. Wherever."

I said, "I have a suggestion."

The wariness in her voice gave me that cold feeling in the spine again, as she said, "What suggestion?"

I tried to speak calmly, normally, as though I had heard nothing wrong. "There's a woman I know," I said, "a friend of mine, she runs a restaurant in the Village. Her apartment is upstairs over the restaurant. She'd be happy to put you up for a couple of days, and since you don't know her, nobody else can know you're there."

"A restaurant?" She sounded bewildered. "What restaurant?"

"It's called Vitto Impero, in the West Village. You could—"

"Oh, I *know* that place!"

"You do? That's good."

"We ate there once after a show at the Cherry Lane. Dale and me. It was very good, we—" She stopped, and I heard a kind of shuddering sigh. Much more subdued, she said, "If you think it would be all right . . ."

"Her name is Anita Imperato," I said. "I'll call her now and tell her you'll be showing up some time this evening."

"You're *sure* it's all right."

"It's better than sleeping on a waiting room sofa," I pointed out.

That at least got a small laugh out of her. "It sure is," she said. "Thanks."

"I'll call her now. The name's Anita Imperato."

"Will you be there?"

The question had been neutrally phrased, and I wasn't exactly sure how to answer. "I could come over if you'd like," I said carefully. "If you're up to a restaurant meal. It's up to you."

"Maybe," she said slowly, "maybe we should talk. About all this."

"Fine. I'll come over late, around ten, so Anita can eat with us."

She agreed that that sounded good, so then I phoned Anita and told her what I'd just volunteered her for. "Sure," she said. "Is somebody really out to get her?"

"Beats me."

"Should be interesting," she decided.

# 12

I did it to Julie Kaplan again.

Maybe I should have remembered, and guarded against the situation somehow, but I'm not sure how. And in any event, I didn't remember. So I just walked into Vitto Impero a few minutes after ten that evening, saw most of the tables still full with people dawdling over their meals, saw Julie Kaplan and Anita at a table against the rear wall, both of them in profile to me, and simply moved toward them, threading my way through the diners. Anita glanced over, aware of every movement in her restaurant, smiled when she saw me, and Julie Kaplan's eyes followed. Abrupt shock turned her face into a black-and-white cartoon, all circles and ovals. The piece of roll she'd been holding fell from her hand, bouncing to table to floor, and she turned her head away, that heavy mantle of hair moving like a reproachful shroud as she leaned toward the wall.

Anita gaped at us both in astonishment as I reached the table. "I do look like him," I told her, feeling stupid, and said to the back of Julie's head, "I'm sorry. I forgot."

She took a long quavering breath, then turned to look almost fearfully at me, as though my hair might be made of snakes. "I'll get used to it," she said, in a low voice, and grimaced in self-irritation and embarrassment. "I'll have to, I guess."

I took the other chair, with my back to the room, and we got past the awkward moment with the help of menus and smalltalk about food. Angela the waitress took our orders and brought us bottles of Pinot Grigio and San Pellegrino water, and then Julie said, "I was just telling Anita, I'm only going to be a pest for two days. Nights, I mean."

"Oh? How come?"

"Kay got me a job," she said. "You know, Kay Henry, my agent?"

"You were hiding out in his waiting room."

"Well, not *hiding*. Taking sanctuary, I guess."

I laughed. "I never thought of an agent quite like that before."

"Well, he sure came through for me," she said. "He knew what had happened, of course, and I told him I couldn't go stay in *either* of those places, so he got on the phone, and just before I left there he came out and said I've got a job in Orlando starting the day after tomorrow."

"In Florida? Where, at Disney World?"

She laughed, though a little shakily, and said, "No, I'm not going to be Minnie Mouse or anything like that. It's dinner theater, some kind of musical of *Our Town.*"

Some kind of musical of *Our Town.* A chorus singing in its graves. Not all theater is wonderful. I said, "So you're a singer."

"No," she said, with a little ironic smile. "I'm an actress. I'll be *acting* a singer."

"I hope you don't have to pretend you can carry a tune."

"No, that I can do."

Angela brought the appetizers, then, and as she distributed them I said, "How long's the job?"

"Four weeks. It's just perfect. By then . . ." She shrugged, and looked down at her moules mariniere.

"Right," I said.

We were quiet a while, then, Julie eating her mussels, me ingesting calamari, and Anita picking at a radiccio salad. Being around food so much, Anita has a dismissive attitude toward the stuff, which is why I suppose she's so thin.

Finishing her mussels, Julie said, "If only it was tomorrow I was leaving."

"Hey, come on," Anita said. "The food's better than *that.*"

"The food's great," Julie told her, with honest enthusiasm. "It's Dale's mother I was thinking about."

"Dale's mother?"

"She's coming to town tomorrow. You know, take care of details, then bring Dale back to Iowa."

Iowa. Another proof of my belief that everyone in New York is from the midwest. (On the other hand, everyone in Los Angeles is from New York; I'm not sure how that works.) I said, "I get the feeling you and she don't get along that well."

Julie grimaced, then waited while the busboy cleared plates before she said, "She's a stage mother, you know?"

I said, "Wasn't Dale a little old to have a stage mother?"

"That was the problem, all right."

"Oh."

"Mom was going to be an opera singer," Julie explained, "but it didn't work out."

"It usually doesn't."

"Dale's father is dead," Julie went on, "and his mother's a secretary for an insurance agency in Iowa City. Dale sent her money when he could, and she kept all his clippings and theater programs and all that, and he was just terrified of when she'd be old enough to retire, because she already *told* him she was coming straight to New York to live with him and be his manager."

"Oh, goody," I said.

Anita said, "Living through her son. This has to be rough on her now."

"I wish she were a little more likable," Julie said, and paused while Angela put down our main courses, with another tiny salad for Anita. Angela made her runic passes with the peppermill and went away, and Julie said, "Actually, it's mostly that *she* never liked *me*. She's stuck in Iowa, and I was right there with Dale. He wasn't keeping *me* away."

Anita said, "Where will you be seeing Mom?"

"Well, that's a kind of a problem," Julie told her, looking uneasy. "She'll be staying at Dale's place, and I just don't want to go there again."

Anita said, "Do you want to give her lunch here?"

"Could I? I wouldn't get you involved at all, I promise."

"That's right," Anita assured her. "I'll be busy. Bring her around."

I said, "I'll keep my distance. I don't want to do to Mom what I keep doing to you."

Julie studied my face. "I'm getting used to it," she decided. "And the funny thing is, once you start talking, you don't really look that much like Dale at all."

"I never thought I did."

# 13

Since Julie's presence in Anita's apartment meant Anita and I would spend every night apart—Anita should be there with Julie, but I should not—I was very grateful that her agent had moved so quickly to get her a job out of town. Walking home across the dark and quiet Village after Vitto Impero closed—Anita had grinned and winked at me through the glass as she locked the front door—I considered that I'd brought it on myself; which didn't help.

The other trouble I'd brought on myself recently, being the bad blood between me and detectives Feeney and LaMarca, came to a head the next afternoon, in Mort's office up in the Graybar Building. Mort phoned in late morning to ask if I was available at three for a meeting with the detectives, and I said I'd be delighted; which we both knew meant I'd be delighted when it was over. "Some friends of ours have spoken with friends of theirs," Mort explained delicately, "and it's been agreed feathers were ruffled on both sides."

"No comment," I commented.

"Retain that attitude, please."

"Oh, I will, I will. Where's this meeting?"

"Here," he said, surprising me. "I spoke with Feeney just now, and it was his suggestion you might be more comfortable with me present."

"He wants to drag you into it," I said. "He wants to question you, too, about interfering with his witnesses."

"Well, we'll see," he said, unruffled. "And in any event, Sam, you will let me fight my own battles."

"Yes, sir," I said.

That afternoon, preparing to go uptown, I spent longer than usual deciding what to wear. I don't normally worry about such things, and I was disgusted with myself for thinking this way now, but I knew it would be best to appear like a regular guy and not like a star or a rich fella or anything else Feeney and LaMarca might be irritated by. I finally chose loafers and slacks and a button-down-collar striped shirt without a tie, plus my scruffiest windbreaker and cap. Shielded in my armor, I walked uptown, arrived five minutes early, and Feeney and LaMarca made us wait nearly half an hour.

Mort and I filled the time with other business, and in fact when the detectives finally arrived Myrtie let them into the office just in time to see me finish signing contracts in connection with a Japanese animated television show version of PACKARD (contractually forbidden from ever being shown in the United States, happily), which pretty well eliminated any advantage my costume might have bought me. "Well, here we all are," Feeney said, smiling falsely at me, offering neither apology nor excuse for their lateness.

"Nice to see you again," I lied, and gave him back his false smile doubled. Nobody offered to shake hands.

We all seated ourselves, me in a chair at right angles to Mort, in front of his desk and to his left, and the detectives side by side in a green naugahyde sofa facing the desk. We all watched Mort finish putting the contracts away in their manila folder and the folder on an already teetering pile of paperwork, and then he smiled at us all and said, "Yes. Here we all are. To clear the air, if that's needed, and for Sam to cooperate in your criminal investigation in any way he can."

"That's nice," Feeney said.

LaMarca gave me a cold look: "How did you come here today, Mr. Holt?"

I knew she was hoping I'd say I came here by cab or limo, so she could use that fact to try to demolish my earlier statement that I'd been walking home from this office at the time Kim Peyser had been killed. Deadpan, I said, "I walked. I almost always do."

LaMarca pursed her lips, but Feeney gave me a quizzical smile, saying, "Now, that's what I just can't get over. Do movie stars walk around the city? How come I never see any?"

"In the first place," I said, "I'm not a movie star. I'm a former television star. In the second place, New York is a walking city, in good weather, and most people here will leave famous faces alone when they see them.

Because they *do* see them. New York is full of them."
Looking at LaMarca, I said, "Your Senator from Nebraska is all over this town."

Mort said, "Beg pardon?"

I raised an eyebrow at the detectives. "Care to
explain?"

"Oh, I don't think so," Feeney said, with his sour
smile. "That's just one of Marie's little jokes."

The idea of Marie LaMarca being a person with a
battery of little jokes was impossible to think about.
These two had their own variant on good cop/bad cop:
they were nasty in completely different ways. While
Feeney was slyly comical and malicious, LaMarca was
cold and rigid and utterly without humor.

It was LaMarca who now said, "Have you had time
to think about who might have been trying to blame
you for Miss Peyser's murder?"

I said, "So you know she didn't write that name
herself, eh?"

Chuckling, Feeney said, "Oh, it was Kim Peyser's
finger that wrote it, all right. Blood under the nail,
fingerprint fragments at the ends of strokes. It was just
somebody else's penmanship, that's all."

"I thought you were going to cooperate," LaMarca
said.

I frowned at her. "I am cooper— Oh. I didn't answer
your question."

"No, you did not."

"Okay. Have I had time to think about who might
have been trying to pin that murder on me," I said,
echoing her question. "Yes, I've had time. Have I
thought of anyone? No, I haven't." I was aware of Mort
giving me a veiled disapproving look, and ignored it.

While LaMarca continued to look at me with

pinched lips, Feeney said, with his usual false offhandedness, "How long have you known Julie Kaplan?"

"I met her yesterday, in this office."

He raised an eyebrow, pretending surprise. "You arranged to meet her here, with your attorney? Why's that?"

"I didn't *arrange* to meet her."

"It was coincidence," he suggested. "She was passing through."

I looked over at Mort, who smiled amiably at me and said, "He asked *you* the question, Sam."

"Okay. I was here," I told Feeney, "discussing some matters, such as my earlier conversation with you two, when Julie Kaplan came here."

Feeney turned his magpie smile on Mort. "Is Miss Kaplan your client, too?"

"Not so far," Mort told him, smiling back. "And of course in this issue she can't be, as her interests may not always coincide with Mr. Holt's."

"Oh? Why's that?"

Mort's smile expanded, as though he were really enjoying Feeney. "Detective Feeney," he said, "I'm a bit older than you, and I can remember a time when most police officers already knew enough law so that they wouldn't have to ask a question of that sort. No two individuals in any action potentially before the court will have absolutely identical interests, and that is why an attorney cannot represent more than one of the principals involved. As I am already retained by a principal in this matter, being Mr. Holt, I could not represent Miss Kaplan as well, even were she to ask me, which she has not. Even if she were to offer me more money than Mr. Holt," he finished, with a little smile.

Feeney's smile had been looking very strained ever

since Mort's gentle crack about police officers of yester-
year. Now it twisted around his words as he said,
"Thank you for that *free* lesson in the law, Counselor,
but what I'm—"

Smoothly overriding Feeney, not even seeming rude
about it, Mort said, "There's an incident related to this
that might interest you, Detective Feeney. Several years
ago, a wealthy man in the Los Angeles area went to one
of the most prominent divorce attorneys in California
—Marvin Mitchelson, I think it was, to begin with—
and paid a considerable amount for an hour of legal
advice. He outlined his marital situation, his financial
situation, his reasons for wanting a divorce, and his
hopes for what he might realize from a divorce settlement. The attorney gave opinions and advice, and the
man left. This man then did the identical thing with
every other noted divorce attorney in the state, possibly
eight or ten people in the top rank. A considerable
expense, buying an hour of time from each. Finished,
he chose one of them to be his lawyer and sued for
divorce."

Feeney smirked. "Expensive kind of comparison
shopping," he said.

"Not really," Mort told him. "When the man's wife
went to look for an attorney, it turned out she couldn't
hire anyone she might want. They had all already been
consulted by her husband, who had exposed to each of
them his full financial condition. It would have been
unethical for any of those attorneys to represent any
other party in that matter. The best talent in that area
of law was closed off to the wife, and I would imagine
the husband saved quite a bit of money as a result."

Feeney's smile had been getting glassier and glassier,

while LaMarca's frown had grown deeper and deeper. Now, Feeney let a few seconds of silence go by, to be absolutely certain Mort was finished, and then he said, "Counselor, what does that have to do with anything?"

"Nothing," Mort told him blandly. "I thought you wouldn't mind an irrelevancy."

Feeney turned slowly to give LaMarca a theatrically wondering look, and LaMarca shrugged and turned toward me, saying, "You were telling us about Julie Kaplan."

So I told them about Julie Kaplan. They didn't interrupt, though Feeney kept looking as if he might, but was thinking better of it. When at last I finished, LaMarca said, "You're involving yourself in this thing a lot, aren't you?"

"How so? Miss Kaplan needed a place to stay and I knew of one. And it's only for two nights; her agent found her a job in Florida, so she'll be able to get away from here for a while."

Feeney looked dubious. "I'm not so sure about that," he said.

LaMarca said, "It sounds to me as though you're assisting a material witness to leave the state."

Before I could answer, Mort said, "If the witness's livelihood requires her to move temporarily to another jurisdiction, and if she so informs the police here, with her address in Florida, and reports to the police in Florida on arrival, and holds herself in readiness to return for any hearing or interrogation or other official need, she will surely be in substantial compliance with any order you may have given her."

Feeney said, "I thought she wasn't your client, Counselor."

"I was thinking of *you* as the client at that moment, Detective Feeney," Mort said. "Purely on a pro bono basis, of course."

Feeney was still swallowing that one when Myrtie came in, carrying the New York *Post*. She said, as she crossed to Mort's desk, "I'm sorry to interrupt, but I thought you might want to see this." She put the newspaper on all the other papers on Mort's desk, open to an inner page. She tapped a story with a fingertip, turned away, winked at me, and left the room.

We all watched Mort read, bent forward like a bombardier, looking straight down at the newspaper, his forehead braced on the splayed fingers of his left hand. The room was silent, except for one long drawn-out sigh from Mort. He kept reading, silent again, then raised his head, looked at Feeney and LaMarca, and said, "Dick Babcock is a friend of yours, I believe."

Feeney couldn't keep the smirk out of his face and voice. "He knows us. We know a lot of reporters."

Mort looked down at the paper again, and read aloud, "Mom charges celeb thumbs nose at cops."

Oh. 'Celeb' was me, of course; 'cops' were Feeney and LaMarca; and Julie had already told me about Mom, the stage mother from Iowa, in town to see to Dale Wormley's affairs.

"By Dick Babcock," Mort read, and glanced up.

Feeney spread his hands in a display of innocence, grinning, as LaMarca said, "He didn't get that from us."

Mort looked down and again read aloud: "Laura Wormley, mother of slain actor Dale Wormley, charged today that New York City police have, quote, knuckled under, end quote, to television celebrity Sam Holt. Holt, in front of whose Greenwich Village townhouse

Wormley was found brutally beaten to death late Monday night, is best known for the TV series PACK-ARD, in which he himself played a detective. Apparently feeling that TV detectives know best, Holt, according to police officials familiar with the case, has been uncooperative in the slayings of both Wormley and the related stabbing death of young actress Kim Peyser. Holt has been particularly unforthcoming, according to these sources, in connection with the details of his relationship with both Peyser and her roommate, Julie Kaplan, Wormley's former girlfriend."

I lifted my head at that, but neither Feeney nor LaMarca was meeting my eye, and Mort wasn't finished:

"According to Laura Wormley, police have told her their hands are tied in the investigation into her son's death because of Holt's unwillingness to talk. Quote, where I come from, end quote, paren, Mill Corner, Iowa, end paren, Mrs. Wormley said, quote, the law treats everybody alike. If my son hadn't been killed, he'd have been a big star himself some day, but he never would have thumbed his nose at the law the way Sam Holt does. And it looks like Holt can get away with it. End quote." Mort looked up, his expression mild. "It goes on," he said, "but I think the point is clear."

Feeney and LaMarca were both looking uncertain now. Feeney said, "I'm sure if Mr. Holt makes a public announcement, and we back him up on it—"

"No, I don't think so," Mort said. Tapping the newspaper, he said, "Babcock didn't get this slant originally from Mrs. Wormley, and we know he didn't get it from my client. I'm sure you didn't intend the story to be read this way, but Babcock let his enthusiasm carry him away, and the implication is crystal clear that my client has either bribed or intimidated you into keeping at arm's length."

Angrily, LaMarca said, "There isn't a word about bribes in there!"

"Nor is there anything about intimidation," Mort told her. "'Knuckled under' is the phrase used. And Mrs. Wormley is quoted as contrasting police behavior in New York with that at home in Iowa, where 'the law treats everybody alike.' Whereas here, a famous person like Sam Holt can 'get away with it,' presumably because you are either in awe of him or have been paid off by him." Rising, picking up the paper, Mort said, "Sam, I want you to go on cooperating with these two officers, answer anything they might ask that's even remotely connected to the matter at hand. I'll be in the other office, making phone calls."

LaMarca said, "What phone calls?"

"There are officials," Mort told her, "who I will want to reassure on this matter." He looked at her more directly than he usually does. Shaking the open paper out in the air beside himself, he said, "Are you sure this is what you wanted when you started all this?" Without waiting for an answer, he left the room.

I said, "Crap like that in the paper can't make either of us happy."

LaMarca, still icy, said, "Not everyone will interpret the story the same way your lawyer does."

"Not everyone," I agreed. "I've told you about Julie Kaplan. I've told you where I was while Kim Peyser was being killed. I've told you my relationship, such as it was, with Dale Wormley. Is there anything else?"

"Of course there is," LaMarca said, but beside her Feeney was getting to his feet. She looked up at him, surprised and irritated, and he said, "No, there isn't.

Thank you for your *cooperation,* Mr. Holt. If we need to talk to you again, we know where to find you."

"In this office," I said. "You've already searched my house, if you remember."

"Yes, that's right," Feeney said. Having discovered that his high horse was dead, he was doing his best to climb down from it. He didn't find that an easy job. "You were certainly cooperative in that," he assured me. "I'm sure we can work things out with Dick Babcock." Laughing uneasily—now *he* was the one trying and failing to make human contact—he said, "Nobody reads the *Post* anyway."

"Some will today," I suggested, "who don't usually."

By the time Mort came back, smiling grimly and looking triumphant, the law had fled.

# 14

From time to time, Zack Novak, my agent, sends me scripts to read, to see if I think I'm right for such-and-such a character; not that the producers have asked for me, but that Zack would volunteer me if I approved. I was in my office reading one of these, a pallid private eye story called *Murder For Four Hands,* in which Zack thought I might be right for Keller, the villain (bless his heart), but which was falling apart on the issue of credible motivation (there was no *reason* for the hero to go haring off in search of the killer, when the New York Police Department already has a staff of twenty-one thousand people), when Robinson buzzed to say the police were on the line.

This was about ten-thirty on the morning after my meeting with Feeney and LaMarca in Mort's office, and

I'd been wondering how long they'd take to regroup. There'd been no further nastiness in the newspapers— of course, today's *Post* wasn't out yet—and no developments in the murder investigation that I knew of. So it was with a combination of reluctance and curiosity that I said, "Okay, Robinson, I'll take it," and switched over to the outside line, to discover it wasn't my favorite detectives calling after all.

"Mr. Holt?" said a woman's voice that was not LaMarca. "This is Sergeant Shanley, we met back in February."

"Oh, yes, of course." My house had been broken into back then—I was away from it at the time, fortunately —and a man connected with an Arab terrorist group had been killed here. Sergeant Shanley, a blunt but smart woman, had been in charge of that case. But that was long finished. "What can I do for you today?"

"I've taken over the Wormley and Peyser homicides," she told me. "I wonder if I could come over now and talk with you for five or ten minutes."

Astonished, all I could think of to say was, "Sure. Come right ahead." And it wasn't till I'd hung up that I began to work out what this must mean.

Feeney and LaMarca had zapped themselves, that's what it meant. In trying to smear a little bad press onto me, they'd overshot and smeared the department instead. As a result, they were off the case.

And not only that, but clearly somebody in power had decided it would be a good idea to give me a signal that the war between Holt and the police was over, so they'd gone out of their way to find an officer I'd had satisfactory dealings with in the past, and turned the case over to her. So it was, I admit, with some satisfaction that I sat there waiting for Sergeant Shanley to arrive and thinking about the departed Feeney and LaMarca.

Not that she said a word about them, when she showed up twenty minutes later. A short, wide-hipped woman of about thirty, her pale blonde hair cut short and framing a round face with clear intelligent eyes and a snub nose, Sergeant Shanley arrived alone, her manner businesslike without rudeness, and she acted as though no one named Feeney or LaMarca had ever lived. She took me briskly and unemotionally through my meetings with Dale Wormley, my movements the night he was murdered and the day Kim Peyser was killed, and that was it. "I don't think we'll need to bother you again," she said, at the finish.

"No bother," I assured her, and it was the truth. Walking her back to the front door, I said, "Does this mean I won't be needed around here any more?"

She smiled, briefly, perhaps acknowledging the difference between her regime and the old one. "If you're asking," she said, "if you can leave town, of course you can. You could leave the country, if you wanted."

The publicity and problems all around me here would die away of their own accord if I weren't present to have my very existence fan the flames. "Leaving town is good enough for me," I assured her, and the next day—after an unsatisfactory evening at Vitto Impero with Anita and Julie Kaplan—Robinson and I flew back to LA. By commercial air. Without incident.

# 15

**M**onday, November 23rd; a month since the still-unsolved Dale Wormley murder had changed my normal procedures all around and dumped me back on the West Coast instead of the East at the wrong time of year, leaving me edgy and bored, with nothing to do but—for the first time since I'd bought this house—watch leaves fall into the pool. I'd always been away at this untidy season, and it was amazing to me just how many leaves there were on each and every tree on my property, and how unerringly they would spiral across driveway and lawn, catching the updrafts, spinning and tumbling, *stretching* like a runner sliding into third, to at last tap down as gently as a butterfly on the surface of the pool. And get wet. And sink.

My friend Bly Quinn had some time off from her TV

sitcom writing, so the two of us took a long weekend
away together, driving up the coast to look at some land
I own in Oregon, a tract partly wild and partly slated
for development that I'd bought when PACKARD first
provided me with a bunch of money and all my
advisers pointed out that Gene Autry might have
gotten rich by singing but he got *rich* rich by buying real
estate. So I bought real estate; in Oregon, for some
reason, I no longer remember why. It had seemed like a
good idea at the time. Various impact statements and
water tests and stuff like that are being done, year after
year, and the theory is that some day a bunch of
high-ticket houses will go up on large lots on the
developable part of the land, all of them backing onto
the permanently wild chunk, with its hills and rocks
and stream. From time to time, when at a loss for
anything better to do with myself, I hop into the open
Porsche and drive up to Oregon to look at my land. It's
always raining when I arrive.

We didn't talk about the Dale Wormley murder on
the trip, all of the conversation on that subject having
been used up the first couple of days I was back in LA.
Bly had put her scriptwriter's mind to work on the case,
coming up with plots and scenarios and murderers and
motivations that were all *much* better than any possible
reality, and once that phase wore itself out she grew as
tired of the subject as I was, and we got on with our
lives. So what we mostly talked about on the trip was
her recent desire to write a play for me.

Her idea was—and I suppose it's not that bad an
idea, really—that since I wanted a non-Packard role to
remind the world that I was still alive and still an actor
and still capable of performing other parts, and since so
far Zack Novak had failed to find any producer willing

to go along with that proposition, what I should do was
have a play tailor-made—or tailor-written—just for
me. Take it to backers, raise the money, put it on first in
Los Angeles and see what might happen next.

The initial flaw with the scheme was that neither of
us knew what this breakthrough play should be, and for
some stupid reason that seemed to create a great deal of
tension between us. It was a ridiculous reason to fight,
but neither of us seemed able to get out of its way. Bly's
point, apparently, was that if the play were to be
tailor-made for *me,* I was the one who should choose it.
But my point was, it's up to the playwright to write the
play; make a suggestion, see if I like it, that's how a
tailor-made play gets done.

This argument seemed, luckily, to be confined to the
car. It simmered between us all the way up the coast,
then disappeared for the weekend, then started up
again on the drive back, getting worse and worse,
reaching some sort of manic peak when I turned off the
San Diego Freeway at Sunset Boulevard and drove
eastward to the Bellagio Way entrance to Bel Air. We
squabbled up through the various Bellagios (Place,
Road, Terrace) and off onto San Miguel Way, at the
dead end of which I live.

Because of this bickering, I paid no particular attention to the dent-fendered orange Pinto parked to the
left of my drive, and didn't even notice—though I
should have—the young guy dressed like a tennis
player who climbed out of it, carrying a sheaf of papers,
as I stopped the Porsche and punched the button that
electronically opens my driveway gate. The broad
chainlink gate swung back in its inexorable but leisure-
ly fashion and I did at last become aware of the young
guy walking toward me, grinning amiably, the sheaf of

papers held like schoolbooks in his swinging left arm. "Mr. Holt?" he called.

I *knew* it wasn't a fan, looking for an autograph. I didn't know what it might be instead, or how seriously I should take it. I didn't know if I should crash my own gate, or back up, or just sit there; so I just sat there, head half-turned so I could watch both the young guy approach and the gate recede, and the guy swung his left arm out farther than usual, calling, "You've been served, sir!" as the sheaf of papers left his hand and rose fluttering like a pigeon coming apart, up over my raised side window and right into my lap.

A *bomb?* My hands were under it before it hit, lifting it, throwing it back over my shoulder, out of the car and onto the pavement behind me, as the young guy nonchalantly but smoothly got behind the wheel of his Pinto and drove quietly away, without any fuss.

"What—?" Bly's face was bloodless, her eyes huge. "What was *that?*"

"Jesus." I looked in the rearview mirror. The Pinto was disappearing around the curve of San Miguel toward Bellagio. The papers fluttered faintly on the ground, just visible beyond the trunk of the Porsche. *Served.* "By God," I said, finally recovering, "I think that was a process server."

"A what?" She twisted around, staring at the empty road where the Pinto had been, then at the forlorn papers on the ground. "Just a sec," she said, and jumped from the Porsche, and darted back to retrieve the papers. She returned slowly to the car, studying them, lifting the top sheet as she sat down beside me, shaking her head, murmuring, "Jarndyce and Jarndyce, by golly."

Bly does that. She makes references to things, things

in history or literature or wherever, and I rarely know
what they are, and I've learned not to be troubled by
them nor to ask what they mean nor to let them distract
me from the main point, which in this case was, "What
is it?"

"You've been served, all right," she told me. "Civil
suit, Federal court. Who's Laura Wormley?"

"Laura?" I frowned, trying to think, then vaguely
remembering a conversation with Julie Kaplan, back at
Vitto Impero a month ago. "I think it's— It may be
Dale Wormley's mother."

"Well, she's suing you," Bly said. "In Federal District
Court in New York County, New York State, which I
take to be Manhattan."

This made no sense. "Suing me for *what?*"

"For violating her son Dale's civil rights."

I just couldn't get it. "Violating his civil rights? How
in Christ's name am I supposed to have done that?"

Bly put the papers on her lap. She looked at me. "By
murdering him," she said.

# 16

The papers in her lap, Bly sat on the sofa and watched me pace my office, until the intercom buzzer sounded and I picked up the phone on my desk. "Yes?"

"I have Mr. Cooperman on the line."

"Thanks, Robinson," I said. Oscar Cooperman is my California attorney, and I'd never needed him so much in my life. I pushed the lit button and said, "Oscar?" and heard fuzzy air, full of static. "Goddamit, Oscar," I said, "are you in the goddam car again?"

Static. The words ". . . that impor . . ." drifted to the surface, and the static closed in again.

"You're goddam right it's that important, Oscar! Oscar? Where *are* you?"

Suddenly his voice was loud and clear, as though he were in the room with me: "You don't have to shout."

"Oh, yes, I do," I said. "I'm being sued."

"Of course you're being sued," he told me calmly. "Everybody in your income bracket is being sued. You're involved in three suits or countersuits that I know, and Mort may be handling one or two back in New York that I wot not of."

"Not like this, Oscar," I said.

"Oh, really?" He sounded skeptical. "And what makes this fright different from all other frights? And why should I—" Static. Furry static, with hairballs.

"God *damn* it, Oscar, come back! Where are you?" Static. "Coldwater Canyon." Static.

"Oscar? Can you hear me?"

"Perfectly," he said, imperfectly. *"You're* the one having trouble, not me. These cellular phones are—"

"Could we talk about the lawsuit, please? I'm not in the market for a car phone."

"Mistake on your part. I find it indispensable."

"So I've noticed. Oscar, do you remember somebody named Dale Wormley?"

Static: *thoughtful* static. "The lookalike, wasn't it? He died, Sam, he can't sue anybody any more."

"His mother is suing me," I said, enunciating carefully into that cellular telephone careening either up or down Coldwater Canyon, "for violating her son's civil rights by murdering him."

Silence. *Profound* silence, not even static. "I'll be right there," Oscar said.

# 17

"Well, that's very pretty," Oscar said, sitting in my living room, leafing yet again through the papers that had been served on me.

"You have a different sense of beauty than I do," I said.

"A poke of the sharp stick in the eye of the beholder," Bly said.

"I agree, I think," I told her.

"Hmmmmm," Oscar said, smiling indulgently on the papers like an uncle viewing his favorite nephew. Oscar is a stocky man in his mid-forties with a round baby-face, a gleaming bald dome, and a thick Brillo pad of gray hair around the sides, sticking out beyond his ears, making him look like an astonished and very old baby. Now, talking more to himself than to Bly and me, he said, "This wasn't, of course, the *intent* of the law, but it certainly comes within its range."

I said, "You mean, this can happen? She can do this thing to me?"

"Oh, absolutely," he assured me. "Sue you, that is. Not necessarily win. But she can certainly sue you under the cited statute."

"Even though I've never been found guilty of murdering her son, or even charged with it, or even very seriously considered for it?"

"Well," he said, "that's what the statute was all about, in the first place. When the civil rights struggle heated up, starting in the fifties, activists were murdered from time to time and very little was done about it, the crimes being against state laws and coming under the jurisdiction of state courts, most of whom were antithetical to the goals of the activists to begin with. This law was designed to find a way to bring those miscreants into Federal court, out of the state system, and at least find them guilty of *something*. Get the facts on record. Brand the killers in the public eye and cause them as much trouble and expense and inconvenience as possible."

"The law," Bly said perkily, in a singsong voice as though reciting a poem, "is the true embodiment/Of everything that's excellent."

Oscar considered her for a long moment, as though she were another set of tricky legal papers, and finally said, "Gilbert and Sullivan?"

"Just Gilbert, unless I sing it," she told him. *"Trial By Jury."*

"Well, that I *don't* recommend," Oscar said, returning his attention to me. "You don't want a jury in a case like this, full of people who can get even with you for being rich and famous."

I said, "Oscar, you mean this is going to *court?*"

"Well, I don't quite see how we could settle *out* of court," he told me. "Any settlement at all would imply some acceptance of their allegations, whether we publicly admitted to them or not."

"First thing we do," Bly said, "let's kill all the lawyers."

"Steady," Oscar told her.

I said, "Oscar, how can she do this?"

He hefted the papers. "Her new cause of action," he said, "is the transfer of the original investigating detectives off the case, which had the effect of ending all active efforts to solve the murder of Dale Wormley."

"That isn't why they were replaced," I objected, but even as I said that I could imagine how much Feeney and LaMarca would enjoy testifying against me in court. That was the instant when I stopped being merely astonished and started being scared.

Oscar was going blithely on, saying, "That's only her doorway into court. The suit itself is for violation of Dale Wormley's civil right to the uninterrupted enjoyment of his life, and the effect of that interruption on his mother. Her call for damages is based on her son's anticipated future support of her, projecting—quite optimistically, I think, though it hardly matters—her son's probable future earnings, now cut off. But those, of course, are not the details we wish to argue, or even pay much heed to. The main issue in this suit is the accusation of murder."

I said, "The fact is, this woman really and truly does think I killed her son. She told the papers in New York that I was getting away with it because I was rich and powerful and the police were afraid to come after me."

Oscar grinned. "That'll be the day."

"But she doesn't know that, does she?" I shook my head, answering my own question. "And now she's found some lawyer who sees publicity for himself in all this—"

"First thing we do," Bly said, and stopped, and grinned amiably at Oscar, who gave her a crooked grin and nod right back, his eyes on me.

I said, "So this way she gets to have me tried for the murder after all."

"That's true. And in a much worse venue," Oscar pointed out. "From your point of view, that is."

"Worse venue? Meaning what?"

"The rules of evidence," he told me, "are less rigorous in a civil court than in a criminal court. The standard of proof, for instance, in criminal cases, is that guilt must be established beyond a reasonable doubt. But in civil cases judgment can be derived merely from the preponderance of the evidence. *All* the rules are looser and simpler."

"Good God, Oscar," I said. Beside me, Bly looked as worried as I felt, and as though she wasn't even trying to find an appropriate quotation.

Oscar looked grim, as though he'd scared himself as much as us. "You're right," he said. "You're going to be tried for murder. And it's going to happen in a court that was never set up to fairly handle such a matter."

# 18

A conference call involving Oscar here in LA and Mort Adler in New York didn't add to my joy. Mort's assessment of the situation was at least as gloomy as Oscar's. And he had the additional bad news to convey that three civil rights legal organizations had joined the case as friends of the petitioner; for the publicity involved, of course, but so what? None of the three organizations were large or well-known or particularly respectable—nothing like the ACLU, for instance—but their names would still add a sheen of social responsibility to Mrs. Wormley's efforts.

Given the combination of a celebrity name and a novel legal situation, the publicity potential for the civil case was much broader than that for the original killing. Dale Wormley's murder, with my name attached, had made the wire services and the cable news programs, but only briefly, having then receded pretty much to the level of a local New York story, which I'd been able to defuse by moving back to California; this time, there would be no place to go. "Mort?" I asked, during the conference call. "Should I stay here, or go back there? Or does it make any difference?"

"You'll have to come back to be deposed," he told me. "Until then, do as you see fit."

"Deposed," I said. "Ah, yes." I'd been through that part of civil cases before, the part where the other guy's lawyer gets to ask you all kinds of irritating and irrelevant questions in his office while your attorney sits beside you being restrained and the whole thing is taken down by a court stenographer to haunt you later.

"I think Sam ought to stay here," Oscar's voice boomed from the phone and echoed from his person in the next room, and on the sofa near me Bly emphatically nodded. "If he starts moving around like a bug on a griddle," Oscar went on, an image I could only too unhappily identify with, "it'll look as though he's reacting to the suit."

"Which I will be," I pointed out, "no matter what I do."

"Still," Mort said, his manner such a measured contrast to Oscar's, "I do take Oscar's point. Unless you have some actual reason for returning to New York prior to the deposition, you might as well stay where you are."

Oscar said, "Mort? Anything to be gained by asking for a change of venue?"

"Out there? I don't see what. Delay and expense for both sides, an air of shiftiness on our part, and not much hope of success, since Sam is certainly a domiciliary of this state. And the alleged action took place here."

"I suppose you're right," Oscar said, sounding rueful. "I wish I could take part," he said, and then he added the absolute worst thing you can ever hear your own attorney say: "It's a fascinating case."

# 19

There's snow in the San Gabriel Mountains in late November; clean white drifts on the tan ground, with gray boulders elbowing through. The air is dry and crisp and cold, so that you can see with clarity for miles over the tumbled slopes, and the sky is so pale blue it's almost white. In fact, though you'd expect the sky to be closer when you drive up there, it seems farther away, higher and more remote and less comprehensible than usual, as though it were the sky of some other planet.

Thursday we drove up, Bly and I, fleeing the media's voracious interest in my murder trial and aiming for Zack Novak's ski lodge, which he was loaning me until further notice. I was driving the big Chrysler station wagon, for the weather and because we'd filled it with supplies. Robinson would stay at the house in Bel Air to feed the dogs and repel the press, and with luck we wouldn't be found until we wanted to be.

We took route 2, the Glendale Freeway, northeast out of LA. After it crosses the Foothill Freeway at La Canada it becomes Angeles Crest Highway, climbing and twisting steeply up into the mountains. A sign early on informed us that the road was closed well ahead, beyond the turnoff for San Gabrial Canyon Road but before Big Pines; there was that much snow up there already. But that was all right; Zack's place was not far past the turnoff, in one of the patches of private inholdings among Angeles National Forest and Devil's Punchbowl County Park and Crystal Lake Recreation Park and the Mount Wilson Observatory and all the rest.

We drove upward in silence a while, relaxing, looking at the spiky cactus plants in the snow like weird Christmas decorations, and then Bly turned and spoke in a tough gun-moll guttural, saying, "This is it, Earl. Our last job. Then we'll be happy."

"I get that one," I told her. *"High Sierra."* Glancing at her, beside me in the station wagon, I said, "You're even doing Ida Lupino's mouth."

"Have you ever considered getting a brush cut?" she asked, with a critical look at my hair.

"Never. And I think his *last* name was Earle. Roy Earle."

"You're right," she said, surprised, dropping the Ida Lupino bit. "Damn! I *hate* it when you know something better than I do."

"It won't happen again," I promised her.

Zack's ski lodge was very simple, really, not at all what the name implies. A small two-story clapboard house painted dark green, it was built against a steep slope, so that only the large living room and a half bath and the utilities were downstairs, everything else up: master bedroom and dining room above the living room, kitchen and two more bedrooms and two baths behind that, the structure built on and within the hillside, so that the two rear bedrooms and the kitchen all had ground-level outer doors. The furnishings throughout were studiedly simple and rustic, and the views at the front, out over scrambled gorges and thick descending stands of dark green pine, were fantastic. Both living and dining rooms had large stone fireplaces at the right side, out of the way of the view. Also out of the way of the view was the road in, a snowy slippery mix of gravel and mud, very narrow, angling in through thick second-growth pine, ending just to the left of the building.

The air was very cold and sweet, like thin apple cider, and our breath fogged as white as the snow mounds under the trees all around us as we made three trips to carry everything from the car into the house; luggage and groceries. We went in through the upper level to the kitchen, which was nearest to where we'd parked the station wagon, and then, while Bly opened a can of soup—she is *not* a cook, and on those rare occasions when she tries it's a horror—I went downstairs to turn the electricity on, the master switch being at the circuit breaker box in the half bath down there. Various hums started—heat pump, hot water heater, refrigerator— and I went out to bring split logs in from the pile beside the house. I laid two fires, one upstairs and one down, only lighting the one downstairs in the living room.

When I went back upstairs the soup was heating on the electric stove and Bly was in the master bedroom, unpacking. "Hello," I said.

She grinned over her shoulder at me, her arms full of jackets. "Hello."

She looked so good, and the setting was so snug, and my relief at being away from everything was so strong, that we then spent a considerable time longer in the bedroom than we'd planned, as a result of which we ruined that pot and had to open a second can of soup. Which was delicious.

All in all, it was a good day. Bly rummaged through Zack's cassettes and decided that thirties Duke Ellington was most appropriate to the circumstances, and so we spent the rest of the day surrounded by the dark, rich, urban, honey-aggressive sounds of that well-drilled big band, pulsing at us, prodding us, but gently, so we didn't become *too* vegetable in our relaxation.

After a while, we went out to check the woodpile and feel the air and get into a snowball fight, and then back in to play Scrabble—Bly always wins, or almost always —so that it was late afternoon before we sat down in front of the fire together in the living room and began at last to talk about what was going on.

Bly started it, by cutting—as she would say—to the car crash: "What are you going to do about it, Sam?"

"The lawsuit?"

"That's the dead baby on the table, yes."

"Lawsuits are for lawyers," I told her.

"This one?" She seemed really surprised, and really troubled. "Sam, hon, don't you realize how badly you could be smeared in this thing? You still have *some* hope for your career, don't you?"

"Well, don't say it like that," I said. "Of course I do. And in fact, the longer it is since PACKARD's off the air, the better chance I have to break out of this typecasting thing."

"Except for this lawsuit," she insisted. "They don't have to prove you murdered that fellow, all they have to do is *say* you did and then pretend to talk about something else, like civil rights and damages. You'll *never* live that down, you'll never work again or be asked to give your name to charities or present awards or talk to film classes in colleges or—"

"Some of that wouldn't be so bad," I said, trying for comedy, but hearing myself how hollow it sounded.

"Oh, yes, it would," she said. "For the rest of your life, you won't be Packard any more, you'll be the TV star who murdered the poor struggling actor, and got away with."

"Got *away* with it? How do you figure—"

"No electric chair," she said. "Not even prison. Just paid some *damages.* People will say you bought your way out of it, you'll be mentioned in editorials talking about justice being different for the rich and the poor. Sam," she said, "if you let the lawyers just do their normal gavotte through this one, there's no way you can win. Because the judge isn't even going to *rule* on whether or not you're a murderer, not really. He's going to rule on whether or not you owe damages to the dead man's mother. This is the worst example I've ever seen, Sam, of the old question, 'Do you still beat your wife, answer yes or no.' Do you owe Mrs. Wormley money for killing her son, answer yes or no."

"Jesus Christ," I said, "you make it sound even worse than I thought."

"It *is* even worse than you thought."

"But what am I supposed to do about it?"

"I don't *know,*" Bly said, staring at me. "Think about it, anyway, try to find some way . . ." She shook her head, waved her arms in frustration. "I don't know *what* to do, Sam, but we can't just sit here and wait for it to roll over you, and this is *not* just me making up stories again and doing sitcom plots."

"No, I know it isn't," I said. "You're right, I'm in trouble no matter what. Unless . . ."

"Unless what?"

"Unless the cops are going to break the case soon. Arrest the real murderer, and that makes the lawsuit moot."

"If that was going to happen," Bly said reasonably, "wouldn't it have happened by now?"

"Not necessarily."

"But probably," she said, and then she said, "What if you hired a private detective? Now, wait a minute," she said quickly, when I looked at her, "don't look at me like that. There *are* private detectives in the real world, and people hire them all the time—"

"Not to find murderers," I said. "In fact, Mort Adler probably will hire one or two, to do backgrounds on Mrs. Wormley and her son, see if we can prove she doesn't need the money, or her son never provided for her when he could, or something like that."

"Stuff that won't help you at all," she said.

"I agree completely," I told her. "But that's the kind of thing you hire a private detective for, in the real world." I raised a hand, saying, "Wait wait wait, let's find out a little more what's going on in the case, before we decide what we should or shouldn't do about it. It's almost nine o'clock at night in New York now, so I probably can't reach Sergeant Shanley any more today, but—"

"He's the one who took over the case?"

"She," I corrected, "and yes, she's the one. I'll try her in the morning, but I could at least call Terry Young tonight, and see what the press knows that it isn't saying, if anything."

"Then do it," she said.

I looked around at this pleasant rustic living room, with the fire crackling in the fireplace, and night spreading like blue smoke across the view out the big front windows, and soft illumination from the bedroom upstairs where we'd left the light on and the warmth of our lovemaking would still be in the air, and I said, "I guess I'm just not going to get away from it, am I?"

Bly looked at me sympathetically. "Apart from that, Mrs. Lincoln," she said, "how did you like the play?"

## 20

When I tried calling Terry Young that night I got a babysitter, who told me Terry and Gretchen were out to a screening in Manhattan and wouldn't be back till late. I didn't want to leave my number—that's right, I was feeling so harried and paranoid I didn't even want Terry to know where I was—so I just said I'd call back in the morning, and I did. "Well, well, it's the civil wrong," he said, when he heard my voice. "Betsy said you called last night. What's happening?"

"That's why I called," I said. "To ask you that same question."

"Well," he said, not getting it, "so far as I know, *you're* happening. On the international scene, of course, there's always the Middle East, but that's not the question, is it?"

"No. The question is, what's happening on the murder of Dale Wormley? Not this goddam lawsuit, the killing itself."

"Nothing that I know of," Terry told me. "When the lawsuit broke, an enterprising fella on *Newsday* asked the police if they expected to prove your guilt any time soon, and an official spokesman's answer was that the investigation was still proceeding."

"They opened it, in other words," I said.

"Exactly. They opened it."

In police parlance, to 'open' is to close, which is about as near as the American language has come so far to the Newspeak of *1984*. Since in theory the police can only actually close a case by solving it, all unsolved cases are open, but not all open cases are by any means active. Therefore, *active* really means 'open', and *open* really means 'closed', and that meant the Dale Wormley murder wasn't being worked on by anybody in this world.

Terry and I talked about this good news for a while, I promised him that when I had something public to say I'd say it to him, and then I went outside and stomped around by myself in the snow for a while, getting the stiffness out of my body and the negative feelings out of my brain, while Bly watched me from the living room window, like a sea captain's wife worried about storms. Then I went back inside and started calling Sergeant Shanley.

It took four tries, and when at last I reached her—again, I wouldn't leave a callback number with anybody—she said, "I was wondering if I'd hear from you. Where are you?"

"In California."

"And what can I do for you?"

"Find the murderer of Dale Wormley," I said.

She chuckled. "That would be a nice thing, wouldn't it? But at the moment, I'm afraid, it isn't looking very good."

"I understand you've opened the case," I said.

There was a little surprised silence, and then she said, "Oh, that's right, you used to be a cop."

"That's right."

"So I shouldn't blow smoke."

Myself surprised by that, I involuntarily laughed, and said, "I'd appreciate that, yes."

"Okay, then. If I'm called to testify in this civil trial of yours, I'll say there's no reason to suppose you killed Dale Wormley any more than anybody else did. Insufficient motive and no physical evidence."

"Thank you."

"But *then,*" she went on, "under questioning from the other side, and you know this is gonna happen, I'll say we don't have a prime suspect at all, that we don't know *anybody* with sufficient motive, that there isn't physical evidence pointing in any particular direction, and that yes, you did have opportunity, since the crime occurred in front of your house."

"Yeah," I said. "Yeah, I see that."

"I don't think I'll hurt your case much," she said, "but to be honest, Mr. Holt, I'm not gonna help it a whole hell of a lot either."

"I doped that out," I told her.

"Maybe we'll get a break between now and then," she said. "You're right, the case is open, but that means if anything new turns up, anything new at all, we'll notice it and we'll be ready to do something about it."

I said, "But up till now, there's no arrows pointing anywhere."

"Just at the files," she said. "Sorry."

What else was there to ask her? Nothing. I thanked her, said I expected I'd see her in court, and hung up.

Behind the house, a clear trail of packed earth and strategically placed stones led farther up the mountain to a huge flat boulder, windswept clear of drifting snow, with a view of what appeared to be the entire North American continent. I was feeling restless and edgy, naturally, so Bly and I climbed up there before lunch, not speaking, just concentrating on the movement of muscles and the crisp coolness of the air we pulled into our lungs. At the boulder, we stood hand in hand, looking out, the steeply slanted A-roof of Zack's lodge a short way below us down the slope, not another sign of humankind anywhere except for the insect-looking march of powerline poles across the shoulder of a hill far away.

"You know," I said, "how everybody, at one time or another, dreams about escaping from it all, going somewhere new, getting a new name, starting a new life? This is one of those moments for me."

Smiling in understanding, Bly said, "So here we are on Mount Cristo."

"I suppose."

"But you aren't Eddie Dantes," she said. "You know who you are, and you know what you're going to do."

"Oh, Christ," I said, feeling the weight of it landing like an Inverness cape on my shoulders. "It's so stupid."

"You don't have any choice," she told me. "This time, Sam, there's nobody else to do it."

She was right, dammit. I could feel the old stance

come back, the set of the head, position of the elbows, placement of the feet. I looked down at Bly, the old smile on my face, calm and superior but friendly, the assurance in the very lift of my eyebrows. "Packard's the name, Ma'am," I said. "Jack Packard."

# 21

After lunch, when we were both sure the list was complete, I phoned Robinson and read it to him; everything I wanted him to bring up here from the house. "The press has been *quite* intrusive," he said. "Despite the best efforts of your public relations person."

"Babs, you mean."

"That is what she would prefer me to call her, oddly enough," he agreed. "In any event, she has failed to satisfy them. They are not precisely *here*, but they are very much in the neighborhood."

"Take the Volvo," I told him, "and go out the back way." There's another driveway out from my place, down the slope of land behind the house and out between two houses on Thurston Avenue, closer to the

San Diego Freeway. "And bring an overnight bag for yourself," I said.

"And the dogs?"

"Leave out a bunch of food. You'll be back there tomorrow some time."

"But not you," he asked.

"That's right," I said, not satisfying his curiosity.

Having made the decision, having accepted the absurdity of my situation—"Hello; I'm not a crime solver, but I played one on TV"—I became more relaxed, able to think more clearly about my problems and plans, and to go over my ideas with Bly, whose worst regret was that she couldn't come along. "You know I want to," she said, "and I know why I can't. So that's that."

So we didn't discuss it, which was probably just as well. The fact is, although Bly and Anita are well aware of each other's existence, they've never met, and there's no desire on anybody's part that such a meeting should ever happen. I am part of two pairs, each complete, each in its own world. For Bly to come with me to New York and *not* meet Anita would be artificial and straining and awkward, but for her to come along and meet Anita would be chaos.

Which was more than usually unfair, given the situation. Bly would *love* a chance to play gumshoe, Robin the Girl Wonder to my Packard, the capeless crusader, whereas Anita—however concerned and interested she might be—would never even consider taking an active role in the case. If something like this had to happen to me, it should have been on the west coast, not the east. All of this we both knew and neither said; some knots can only get more tangled if you fuss with them.

I made some phone calls east, to set up a few meetings, but without quite explaining to anybody the mad scheme I had in mind, and then there was nothing to do but hang around and get beaten at Scrabble and wait for Robinson, who arrived in late afternoon, brimming with—sloshing over with—unasked questions. I volunteered nothing, and his portrayal of the crusty old servant prohibited him from admitting curiosity, so that was that. He took over the kitchen immediately upon arrival, to everybody's relief, while Bly and I carried all the new gear into the master bedroom and considered my disguise.

Which was going to be necessary, if I meant to accomplish anything. Unfortunately, when you're six foot six it's not that easy to adjust yourself to become less noticeable, and this problem is compounded if you've been the star of a recent popular television series for five years. But Packard wasn't going to get a chance to strut his stuff at all in a spotlight of avid attention, so some alternative would have to be found, even if only to get me east without heralding my arrival.

Fortunately, I'd kept a lot of stuff from the show, and Packard himself had not been above the occasional disguise; mostly moustaches and wigs and now and then a neat submarine-captain beard. These were good quality items, made specifically for me at the studio, so when I wore one of them it was impossible to tell it wasn't natural, no matter how close you got. Also, when thinking or otherwise displaying intelligence, Packard often used to wear clear-lensed dark-framed glasses; alone, those did for me about what they do for Christopher Reeve when he's being Clark Kent, but in conjunction with some facial hair and a graying-at-the-temples wig, a surprising difference could be obtained.

For the facial hair, I chose a slender Errol Flynn moustache that made me look somehow untrustworthy, as though I might try to get you into a card game or into bed or into a land deal; into trouble of some sort. "Why on earth do you want to look like *that?*" Bly asked me, and I said, "Because if somebody looks like a con man or a sleaze nobody studies him very closely. You don't want to catch his eye, because then *he* could catch *you.*"

"Holmes, you amaze me," Bly said, and shook her head.

For the same reason, I chose the most worn clothing in the batch; a baggy tan tweed jacket with shiny leather elbow patches, a patterned shirt with frayed collar, gray slacks in need of a pressing, and tasseled brown loafers I've always hated and can't remember why I ever bought in the first place. Without the seducer's moustache, and with Packard's old pipe, I could have been an associate professor in a small two-year college, but that wouldn't have given me the added protection of this slightly raffish appearance. "I'll buy a *Racing Form* at the airport tomorrow," I said, studying myself in the full-length bedroom mirror with no little satisfaction, "and carry it under my arm. That'll complete the picture."

Bly gave my reflection a rueful look. "Would you buy a used horse from this man," she commented.

"Exactly," I said.

When Robinson called us for dinner some time later, I walked into the dining room with all the gear on, and he looked at me appalled. "I hope the personality hasn't changed to match," he said.

"How do I look?" I asked him.

"Reprehensible," he told me. "Not like yourself at all, if that's any satisfaction."

"It is."

"If you were to come to the door unexpectedly," he said, peering at me closely, "I would assume you were some distant relative of Samuel Holt's, whose sudden presence in our lives would give no one pleasure."

"Terrific," I said. "Let's eat."

# 22

As it turned out, I wasn't going straight to New York after all, but to Miami, where Julie Kaplan had lengthened her employment after the dinner theater job her agent had found to get her out of town. I wanted a good long talk with Julie about the world she'd lived in with Dale Wormley, before trying to enter that world myself.

Starting my trip, I found it strange to be anonymous again, after several years of television celebrity. Maybe I should say it was a humbling experience, but it wasn't; just strange, and a little uncomfortable.

For instance. I didn't at all mind not being boarded onto the plane in the special ahead-of-time category reserved for celebrities and wheelchair-riders and infants in arms and unaccompanied minors, but by golly

I *did* mind traveling coach. There's no room back there, not for somebody six foot six. Also, the food in that part of the plane seems to have come directly from some northern European prison; to be presented with something that claims to be steak but is rectangular and curls *up* at the corners like old cardboard is never going to be pleasant. And finally, somehow the rear of the plane takes two or three hours longer to cross the country.

Robinson had bought my tickets, to Miami and on to New York, using his credit card, so I traveled as William Robinson, but other than that I was on my own in a very strange way; I had to live on cash. I haven't done that for years, but cash is the only anonymous way of paying for things like meals and hotel rooms. I also couldn't rent a car, of course, since I wasn't willing to show ID to anybody, so that meant all my ground travel would be by cab.

Beginning with the run from the airport over to Miami Beach, where I would be staying at one of the lesser hotels on Collins Avenue, that Art Deco area south of the acceptable zone. My being neither Jewish nor Hispanic was just as remarkable as my height in that neighborhood, but the moustache and *Racing Form* were just passport enough to support my claim to belonging there. (My paying for one night's residence in cash was not at all suspect, but merely served to bolster my bona fides in this place.) I signed the check-in card as 'Ed Dante', in honor of Bly's Monte Cristo conceit.

Alone in my small room with its view of Collins Avenue past the hotel sign—that wouldn't start flashing off and on tonight, would it, like an oldtime bad movie?—I immediately pulled off the wig, which had started to itch somewhere over St. Louis, and *scratched*.

This was going to be a problem. Miami was too hot and humid for most of my disguise, the moustache being about the only part that didn't eventually become uncomfortable. But the moustache was the wrong color to go with my natural hair, so that meant wearing the wig. And the glasses, too, though they pinched my nose after a few hours. In place of the raincoat and tweed jacket and trousers, a Hawaiian shirt worn outside lighter-weight slacks would just have to do, combined with a kind of hurried shuffling walk as though I were trying to cross a piece of open ground as rapidly as possible without being noticed. When I was a cop, I'd come to recognize that as a movement a lot of wrong guys had picked up in prison. And when I was on PACKARD I'd learned that observation and imitation are two of the most useful tools of the acting trade. So, when I left the Mar Vista Hotel a little after six, I wasn't Sam Holt at all, nor Jack Packard either. I looked like some sort of tough guy on one or the other side of the law. Whoever I was, your immediate instinct on seeing me would have been to look away, not wanting any kind of contact.

November sunset had come and gone, leaving Miami a plain of jagged black teeth against a darkening orange sky. Empty cabs did not drift this far south, so I headed on foot up Collins and had gone two blocks when I suddenly remembered that most of my money was still back in the room. I'd left the San Gabriel Mountains with a thousand dollars in cash, mostly in fifties and hundreds in a long zipper compartment in my belt, and I'd barely thought about that money since. And that belt was still on my other, heavier pants. (It's easy to forget cash, I was beginning to realize.)

Since the Mar Vista was partly a residence hotel, and

also since there wasn't necessarily always somebody on duty at the desk late at night, they didn't keep their keys attached to those large awkward artifacts meant to discourage guests from carrying their keys out of the building, so mine was still in my pocket and I merely climbed the stairs, to find my door open and two guys inside, going through my luggage.

They were both Hispanic, wiry guys with real moustaches much bushier than my false one. They were both more than a foot shorter than me, but that didn't bother them; when I walked in, they looked at me, looked at one another, shrugged in disgust, and came for me.

They were mean fellas, particularly after the first time I threw them across the room and they found knives in their pockets. They were mean, and they were two against one, but I had a few advantages they didn't know about, the first being that they didn't know I had any advantages at all. Such as police training, and such as MP unarmed combat training. On the other hand, they had a strong advantage over me in attitude. That is, I didn't particularly want to kill them, but they wouldn't have minded in the least killing me; an intensity of commitment that equalized the situation between us to some extent.

When the knives came out, I yanked an empty drawer from the dresser and used it as both a shield and a club, trying to keep them both in front of me. We were making a lot of noise, but I didn't expect that to draw much of a crowd in this place. Though I tried to keep my self-confidence intact—it's strategically better to think you're going to win than to think you're going to lose—I couldn't help feeling a certain angry disgust at the prospect of having it all come to an end like this:

Under an assumed name, in a stupid little false moustache, in a tiny room in a fleabag at the wrong end of Collins Avenue, dressed in a Hawaiian shirt featuring surfboards. This was *worse* than flying coach.

And it wasn't going to happen, dammit. I lunged and parried with the drawer, kicked a few near-misses at kneecaps, and seemed to be holding my own until all at once one of them jumped over the bed and got behind me and tried what should have been a guaranteed winning move: Grab my hair, yank my head back, run the knife across my Adam's apple. Except that when he grabbed my hair, of course, it came off in his hand and the force of his movement knocked him back ass over teakettle onto the floor and into the wall.

The other one stopped still, astonished, and stared at me. "Pah-*karr?*" he asked me, unbelieving, and I kicked him twice: First in the crotch and then, as he bent double, in the face.

The guy with my wig in his hand was coming off the floor, not caring who I was. I did a roundhouse swing with the drawer, which shattered into splinters against the side of his head, leaving me with a handle that did very well for brass knuckles. With his head bouncing between the handle and the wall, he decided to become as unconscious as his friend, and did.

They both wore jogging shoes. I took a shoelace from the guy who'd called me Packard and used it to tie his thumbs together, then repeated the operation with the other one; a quick and easy controlling method when you don't happen to have handcuffs available. Then, with my sleepers immobilized, I turned to the knives.

They were similar but not identical. Each was a three-inch blade, well-sharpened, that folded into a worn handle. I pocketed them both, then went into the bathroom to put myself back together again. First I adjusted the wig in place, then washed my face and hands, put the clear-lens glasses back on (they'd gone flying into a corner at the very beginning of the fight), switched to my money belt, and generally readjusted my clothing. Now I looked a little rougher around the edges than before, which was fine.

I came out to the main room to find my visitors both climbing shakily to their feet, looking sullen and bewildered and in pain. Both had bloody scrapes on their faces and surprise in their eyes. "Just hold it there a second, boys," I told them, and they blinked at me while I looked over the room's door, finding—as I'd expected—that it had not been forced.

"Well, well," I said, and knocked one of them to the floor again, to keep him out of my hair—or wig—while I searched the other. Then I reversed the process. I found a number of useful things, including about eighty dollars which, now that I was in a cash economy, I pocketed. I also found a key to my room. And in addition, I came up with a key to a Chrysler Corporation automobile. "Good," I said, and kept the car key, and pushed the boys ahead of me out the room and down to the lobby, where the desk clerk looked up with wary surprise as we three approached him. "What's this?" he said.

I said, "Do you know these fellas?"

"Me?" His innocence was wonderful to behold. "Why would I know these people?"

"One of them says he's married to your sister," I said.

The desk clerk's face flushed with rage. Glaring at my prisoners, he let loose a flood of Spanish that they responded to with their own versions of injured inno-

cence. While this was going on, I took the two knives
out of my pocket, opened them, and thumped them one
at a time point down into the counter, hard enough to
make it a little difficult for anybody to pull them out
again. This action ended the discussion; all three stared
at the knives. Then the desk clerk gaped wide-eyed at
me, wondering what next.

*You look the part, Sam,* I told myself. *Now play it.* "I
want you to hold onto these knives for me," I told the
desk clerk.

"Hold—? Why?"

"Because," I told him, putting on my face the kind of
mean smile that went with the moustache, "if anybody
else gets into my room, I'm going to use them on you.
Both of them."

"Me? What I got to do with it?"

"I just put you in charge," I told him. "Remember
that."

Then, while the desk clerk stood there and tried to
figure out what to say to get himself off the hook, I took
by the elbow the one who'd had the car keys. "Now you
show me your car," I said.

# 23

It was an eleven year old Plymouth Fury, orangy-tan in color and covered with the bumps and scars of a long hard life. It was parked a block and a half from the hotel, and in that distance no one at all had remarked on the oddness of a guy walking along with his thumbs tied together by a long dangling white shoelace.

This wasn't the guy who'd called me Packard. That one I'd left back at the hotel for the desk clerk to deal with. He couldn't have been sure he was right about my identity, he would have plenty of time to second-guess himself now that I was gone, and in any case he didn't strike me as somebody who made much of a habit of passing on information to the national media, so I doubted there'd be much trouble from that front. Things were looking up.

And I liked the idea that I was about to get a car.

It worked fine, the engine turning over the instant I tried it, while the guy stood in the street beside the open driver's door and expressionlessly watched me. I have no idea what he thought I was doing; maybe planning to drive him to the police station. In any event, he looked surprised when I shut the driver's door, opened the window, and said, "Take a walk."

"This my car," he said.

"Now it's mine," I told him.

"And you got my money."

"That's right," I agreed, and drove away from there.

# 24

Miami has no legitimate theater area as such, but merely has a few stages scattered here and there along the coast, ranging from Burt Reynolds' dinner theater up north of Fort Lauderdale down to the Coconut Grove Playhouse. New theatrical enterprises tend to nestle in somewhere near one of the established places, and that's where Julie Kaplan's employment had now taken her; to a small new theater in Coconut Grove, doing a revival of a Sam Shepard play. In a bare set supposed to be a motel room somewhere in the farthest boondocks of the empty American west, Julie Kaplan's small face and heavy helmet of hair seemed more appropriate than in ordinary life; as though she'd been outfitted for this part from birth.

It had taken three calls to reach her from Zack's ski

lodge before I'd flown east, the number she'd originally given me when we were both in New York having been superseded by a second which in its turn had been replaced by the third. When I'd finally tracked her down, she'd agreed to meet with me, and I'd said I would see the show, then talk to her afterward, and that's what happened. I got lost briefly on the way down, Coconut Grove somehow being half jungle and half city, with entire blocks where you can't see the sky for all the overhanging trees and vines. But I made it just before curtain time, and took a seat in the small half-empty theater as the lights went down.

Someone connected with the production, of course, would have called the place half full. Optimism is necessary in the theater, more so than in most places. Having been the most popular form of storytelling from Euripides to Gillette, it is now a minority sport, superseded by movies and television, which not only share the theater's basic attraction for the illiterate but also provide a fake reality the theater can't match. It's easier to pretend you're watching two people alone in a motel in the American southwest if they aren't actually *in the same room with you.* Every theatrical performance today, therefore, is an act of bravery; that's *really* relying on the kindness of strangers.

This production, in the shadow of the well-established Coconut Grove Playhouse, was a fairly standard example of mediocre regional theater today; technically competent, methodical and accurate, but rarely involving. Only once or twice did those people stop occupying space in the same room with us, the audience, and take up residence instead in that bleak motel room two thousand miles away.

I often wonder what the people who attend such

performances hope to get out of them. Culture? A change of pace from *Rocky XX* and Perry Mason number nine hundred and two? A chance to become involved in a story that hasn't been artificially pumped up with unmotivated and irrelevant scenes of violence? Whatever it is, such audiences tend to seem quietly satisfied no matter what they get, laughing too little along the way, applauding too much at the end, retreating to their cars afterward without much fuss.

This Saturday night audience was as normal as the show; I joined their shuffling departure from the small auditorium at the end and then hung around the pocket lobby waiting with a few other friends of the cast, my Hawaiian shirt and nasty moustache keeping the others from looking at me.

And keeping Julie from recognizing me, when she came out ten minutes later in jeans and a T-shirt. She frowned as she looked around the lobby, her gaze sliding rapidly past me twice before I went over to stand directly in front of her and say, quietly, "Hello, Julie."

She looked at me. Then she stared at me. "My God!" she said. "It *is* you!"

Which attracted exactly the kind of attention I didn't want, so I casually took Julie by the elbow and said, "Let's get out of here, okay?"

"Sure." As we headed from the poorly air-conditioned interior to the humid night outside, she said, "Did you see the show?"

"You were terrific," I told her. (I'm an actor, and I know this. We don't want to know about the play, we want to know about *us.)*

"Thanks!" she said, beaming all over. "It means more, coming from another pro, you know?"

"I know."

She hadn't eaten before the show, so I followed her directions to a Cuban-tinged hamburger and beer place, where we ordered hamburgers and beer and then Julie sat back and stared at me and said, "It's amazing, you know? It's a whole different personality. And where did you get that *car?"*

"Borrowed it from a fella."

"Well, it's perfect," she said. "It goes absolutely perfect with the image."

I grinned at her. "Props and costumes," I said. "That's what it's all about, isn't it?"

"I'm learning," she told me. "I'm sitting here learning all the time."

"Now it's my turn to learn." I took the play's program from my hip pocket—a simple typed-and-Xeroxed affair—and put it on the table with its blank back upward. I took my pen from my shirt pocket, poised it, and said, "Dale."

"Before we start," she said, "I want to try to explain about his mother."

"You don't have to."

"I know I don't have to, but I want to." She was very solemn and serious, and I could see there was nothing to do but let her have her say, so I sat back and listened, and she said, "Dale was her whole life, she lived his career almost as much as he did, he was the only thing that was—I don't know how to put it—that was *interesting* in her life. Now, it's as though she's the one that's dead, and nobody will let her just, just go away and get buried somewhere."

*"I'm* willing."

"She's mad at you," Julie said, "because you look so much like Dale—not now, but usually—and you're so much more successful than he ever was. And Dale's dead, and you're still alive."

"And she thinks I killed him."

"I'm not even sure about that," Julie said, surprising me. "That's the way she *talks,* I know, and I guess she believes it in some way or other. But I think the main thing is, you look like Dale, you rejected Dale, you're more successful than he was, and you're alive when Dale is dead."

"Not things you can sue me for," I said.

"I don't know whose idea that was," she said, shaking her head, her hair moving sorrowfully after. "Suing you. That wasn't Laura's idea."

"Mrs. Wormley?"

"She's not that sophisticated. I guess, when she was sounding off in the newspapers, some smart lawyer saw it and got the idea and suggested it to her."

Something else to thank Feeney and LaMarca for.

"But the other part of it is," Julie said, "now Laura's got something interesting in her life again."

"Ah," I said. "I hadn't thought of that. She used to live through Dale, and now she lives through suing me. Almost makes it seem worthwhile, as though I should be able to take her off as a charitable contribution."

"You know," she said, "you're sounding bitter. I didn't think you would."

"Neither did I," I admitted. "But, I got involved in a little trouble tonight, and I realized just how far I'm being pushed away from my normal quite comfortable life, and I guess yes, I'm feeling bitter about it."

"You're entitled," she told me, and grinned, and gestured at me, saying, "It goes with the new look."

Which made me laugh, as it was supposed to, and I said, "Okay. Now let's talk about Dale."

"Fine. What do you want to know?"

"Everything," I said. "Well, all right, more specific. You mentioned a couple of things one time. That he'd been fired from a production of *Li'l Abner,* for instance. And that he'd punched a man from some movie company."

"Paramount Pictures, when he was an extra." Julie gazed at me. "You want to know the troubles in his life, you mean."

"I want to know the people he rubbed the wrong way. I want to know who had reason to like him, or dislike him, or fear him."

"Fear him? Dale?" Julie offered a sad laugh, and shook her head again. "Nobody had any reason to be afraid of Dale," she said. "Not really afraid. He was bad-tempered and he got mad at things, but when I left him it wasn't because I was *afraid,* it was because when he was mad and frustrated all the time he just sounded petulant, like a little boy, and I didn't like to see him that way."

"That's about the only way I ever saw him."

"He cared about his career, that's all, and he thought he should have been farther along than he was. And then at the end, he thought he was finally just on the verge of his big break, and everything was going to be fine."

"That play you mentioned, you mean."

*"Four Square,* with Rita Colby."

"What I don't understand about that," I said, "is how he could have been so sure, so absolutely certain, that far ahead of time, that the part was definitely his. It wasn't the lead, and he wasn't a star, and that's usually the only two circumstances where casting is done that far ahead."

"It was Kay Henry who told him," Julie explained. "Who promised it to him."

"His agent."

"Right. Dale's agent. And mine. And Rita Colby's."

"Okay," I said. "If Henry had decided it was time to groom him, build him, then it makes sense."

"That's why Dale was so excited," Julie agreed, "because that's what he figured it had to mean. He was really really pleased."

"Then I wish he'd spent his time thinking about that," I said, "and not about being mad at me."

"Maybe," she said, "he thought you should treat him better from then on, because he wasn't going to be an also-ran any more."

"Maybe so. Tell me about this business of getting fired from *Li'l Abner.*"

So she did, and about the man from Paramount Pictures that Dale had punched, and a number of other incidents, most of them from periods of time when Wormley had been fueling his anger and frustration with booze. The hostility would apparently flare up for a while—as it had with me—and then either disappear when something good happened in his life and career, or be replaced by a fresher source of rage.

Soon I'd filled up the back of the play program, so I bummed a piece of notepaper from the Cuban waiter so we could go on to Wormley's circle of friends and acquaintances. Julie gave me the phone numbers of a couple of people who'd be able to tell me more—the agent, for instance, and someone who'd been in an acting class with Wormley—and promised to call them herself and let them know I'd be around. "Quietly," I said.

"Quietly," she agreed.

Mostly, in fact, I wouldn't be my normal self at all, but this new persona, Ed Dante; that's who Julie would announce me as.

So we ate our hamburgers and drank our beers; Julie gave me names and incidents and I wrote them down; I asked questions and she answered them; and through it all I could see that time had done its normal work. She could speak about Wormley much less emotionally now, less painfully. He was fixed in that receding moment in the past when his history had ended, and now he had *become* history, a story Julie told rather than an agony she was going through.

When we were finished, when I could think of nothing more to ask and she could think of nothing more to volunteer, when I'd given her Terry Young's phone number in Brooklyn and she'd promised to call if anything else useful occurred to her, she sat back and looked at me and said, "I don't know if it's because you don't look like Dale this way, or what it is, but it's easier to talk to you now."

"Time," I suggested.

"More than that," she said. "I'd like to take a look at you without all that stuff on, so I could see what difference it makes."

Grinning, I said, "Sorry. I can't unwig in here."

"Well," she said, slowly, as though she'd just now thought of the idea and were still considering whether or not it was a good one, "you could always come to my place. It isn't far. We could talk some more, and you could let me see you *au naturel.*"

Ah. I hadn't seen that coming. In the early days of my celebrity, these offers had been made rather often, and at first I'd accepted as many of them as I possibly could. Soon, though, I discovered two dismaying things: The women I most preferred to be around were the ones who didn't make any offers; and I wasn't really having that good a time getting myself listed on everybody's scorecard. Now that I'm no longer accepting offers, they aren't made so frequently—I guess we have unconscious ways to signal one another about such things —but when they do appear the problem has become how to turn them down without coming across as smug or a prig, and without embarrassing anybody or hurting anybody's feelings.

In this instance, though, there was a very simple reason to say no. "Julie," I said, "sometime in the middle of the night, you'd turn over and call me Dale, and neither one of us would get over it."

She studied me. "I don't think so," she said, slowly, thoughtfully, "but maybe you're right. Are you done here?"

"Oh, I think so," I said.

# 25

The reason the hotel's sign wouldn't be flashing all night in my window was that it was broken; which was all right with me. No one was on the desk when I arrived, and no one appeared to have been in my room while I was gone; which is to say, it was still the same mess my friends and I had left it. I reordered the place as much as necessary, wedged a chair under the doorknob to discourage visitors, took a long hot (though rusty) shower, and slept easily. In the morning, I drove the Plymouth over the causeway and through Miami out to the airport, where I left it at a meter and took my flight to New York, arriving in midafternoon.

Terry Young recognized me instantly as I came down the umbilical and into the terminal with the rest of the passengers. Approaching, grinning, hand out to be shaken, he said, "Who are you supposed to be? The teenage wolfman?"

"I'm supposed," I told him, "to be nobody you know."

"Or want to. Got any more luggage?"

"No, just what I'm carrying," I said. "And I've just learned the stews aren't as easygoing about carry-on luggage in coach."

"Oh, my God," he said, rearing back to gaze upon me in mock awe. "It isn't teenage wolfman, it's *The Prince And The Pauper.*"

Terry always makes me laugh. He's a burly Irishman with a fine brain distorted by years of observing the City of New York for the daily press. Rather than be embittered by his experiences, though, he's managed mostly to be amused by them, which has probably saved his sanity.

Now, in Terry's station wagon, salted with evidences of his children—everything from candy bar wrappers on the floor to a basketball rolling around the storage compartment—he drove me across Queens and Brooklyn toward his house and filled me in on the situation here in re the Dale Wormley murder investigation. Which didn't take long, because in effect there *wasn't* any Dale Wormley murder investigation. Nothing had changed since I'd talked with him from California, and nothing was likely to change. At least not on the official side.

"But it's all different now, right?" he asked me, taking his eyes from the Belt Parkway long enough to give me an ironic look. "Here comes Packard for real."

"I know, Terry, I know. I feel stupid about it, but what else is there? That lawsuit isn't going away."

"I realize that, Sam," he said, relenting. "I was just giving your leg a little tweak, that's all."

Terry and his wife Gretchen live in the Midwood section of Brooklyn, just east of Flatbush Avenue. A few blocks away are big chunky apartment buildings in beige brick, but the area around the Youngs is mostly, like their own place, sprawling one-family houses on large lots. When we arrived, Terry had to wait while I got out of the car to move a tricycle before he could park in the driveway, and then we went inside for a warm greeting from Gretchen, a gemütlich German girl Terry wooed and won when her job with Interpol brought her temporarily to New York several years ago. These days, she's the total hausfrau with her three kids, inexorably putting on a few pounds a year—though hardly anything to complain about as yet—and only rarely expressing a kind of wistfulness for the free soul she'd been before Terry Young came into her life.

She was at her most cheerful now, laughing uproariously over my disguise, insisting I let her try on my moustache—ever since Dietrich, German women have had this unhealthy interest in suggestive crossdressing —and then showing me the guest bedroom, where I'd stay. I'd seen that room before, and it was the attic to end all attics, crammed to the ceiling with last year's toys and last decade's clothes; now, it was clean, neat, spotless. "Gretchen," I said, "where'd you put all the *stuff?*"

"It was time some things were thrown out," she said, a glint in her eye hinting at a fierce family battle that had come out her way. With the moustache, it made her look sexy in a challenging fashion. I told her so, and she said, "Kiss me, my fool."

So I did. I'd never kissed a woman wearing a moustache before, and the tickle made me laugh. Which made Gretchen laugh, too. "You've spoiled all my illusions," she said, and put the moustache on my nose, and left me alone in the cleaned-up room to change back into my original self.

I was staying with the Youngs because at either of my normal places in New York—at home on 10th Street or with Anita in her apartment upstairs over Vitto Impero —there was too much likelihood that my presence would be noted. Gretchen had called Anita yesterday, at my request, to tell her what was going on, and since this was Sunday, a moderately slow night at the restaurant, Anita would be coming out to have dinner with us this evening, bringing along a suitcase of clothing for me from 10th Street.

It was a good evening, all in all, spent mostly on subjects other than Dale Wormley, though Terry did insist I put on my scoundrel drag for Anita's amusement. I did, Anita agreed she probably wouldn't serve me if I walked into the restaurant looking like that, I took it off, and that was the end of it. Anita decided to stay over, happily, and in the morning I put my gear back on and we drove into the city together with Terry, who at last raised the main subject, saying, as we neared the Manhattan Bridge, "Anita? What do you think of *Packard Rides Again?*"

"I think it's good," she said, surprising me.

I said, "You do? How come?"

"Do your own dirty work," she said, and shrugged. "Don't leave it to agents and lawyers and all those people all the time."

"But— They're *trained* in their jobs."

"So are you," she told me. "You're a trained cop, to begin with. And you're a trained observer. And you've been around all this mystery solution stuff for years."

"But that's make-believe."

"It's plausible, though, isn't it?" she asked me. "If it wasn't at least plausible, it wouldn't have been such a big hit."

This was the last reaction I'd expected. In fact, I'd been fully braced for Anita to share the same attitude of barely repressed scornful amusement as Terry. "Well, I'll be damned," I said.

Laughing, Terry said to me, "There you are, Sam. You should go ahead because otherwise you're nothing but a passive wimp. And because it is after all *your* life and reputation on the line. And because, even though your background for this sort of job may be halfassed, it's anyway plausible."

"Right," Anita said.

I nodded. "Thanks for the vote of confidence," I said.

## 26

**B**ecause I was trying to keep my presence in New York—and its reason—as quiet as possible, and also because I didn't want people to be on guard when talking with me, I'd asked Julie to use my false name, Ed Dante, when she phoned ahead to introduce me. I'd also asked her to give false reasons for my wanting to meet these people. With Kay Henry, for instance, Dale Wormley's agent, she had described me as an actor she'd met in Florida, who was without an agent and who she thought highly of; professionally, that is. At my request, she'd also suggested I might be right for the part in the Rita Colby play that Wormley had been cast for. This was a little dangerous, asking Henry to study me up close as a Dale Wormley substitute, but I couldn't think of a better way to get around to the subject I was actually interested in.

There wasn't much I could do about my raffish appearance, except dress a little more conservatively and comb my wig down more flat, but I thought I could get away with it if I acted like a conceited boob. Agents think of actors as conceited boobs anyway, so Henry shouldn't have any trouble believing I'd made the visual mistake of this moustache under the impression it made me look like a ladykiller. The hardest thing for any of us to do is deliberately place ourselves in a bad light, but that was my acting exercise for the day, so I'd give it my best shot.

My appointment with Henry was for ten. His address was a townhouse in the east forties off 3rd Avenue, converted to offices. He had the third floor of five, with the street floor shared by a travel agent and florist, the second occupied by a food brokerage (whatever that is), and the top two floors given over to InterArab Imports (whatever that is, and it doesn't sound good).

I arrived a few minutes early, on purpose, and took the slow small elevator up to three, stepping out to a receptionist's area doing its absolute damnedest—or Bloomingdale's damnedest, I guess—to look like a private person's living room, though what it actually looked like was a moderately important room in a small well-endowed museum. The receptionist, a cool anorexic English girl in black, sat at a Chippendale reproduction writing table, its legs as polished and curved and slender as her own, visible beneath. Chintz sofas and chairs, nice old floorlamps, and coffee tables and end tables echoing or complementing the writing table's design, all worked toward the same homey effect. It was an interior room without windows, its peach-colored walls furnished with 19th-century English family portraits: curly-haired little girls in white, with puppies; stern stout gentlemen with their hands on globes. It was a large room, with several seating areas, at two of which little clusters of people sat, talking together animatedly, gesturing broadly with hands and eyebrows, keeping one eye alert toward the elevator in case Liza Minelli should chance to drop by. It was easy to see how Julie Kaplan could have stayed here all day, after the killing of Kim Peyser, when she'd been afraid to go home.

The receptionist gave me a jaded look as I emerged from the elevator and sauntered toward her. "Hi, beautiful," I said, and smiled like an idiot under my moustache. "Would you tell Mr. Henry that Ed Dante's here?" Instead of trying to disguise my well-known voice, I used the flat nasal Long Island twang I'd grown up around.

"Of course," she said, cool and professional. "If you'll take a seat . . ."

I kept the stupid smile, and leaned forward, shifting some of my weight to my palm, pressed down on her table. "And what's *your* name?" I asked.

She was used to jerks. "Miss Colinville," she said, clipping the syllables off, her eyes astonishingly hostile.

"Brrrr," I said, still grinning as I turned up the collar of an imaginary overcoat. "I'll be over there fighting frostbite," I told her, pointing at an empty area of the room.

"You do that," she agreed, but she did release a faint and frosty smile as she reached for the phone to announce my presence.

That was sufficient. I wanted to be enough of a jerk to go with my appearance, but not so obnoxious that no one would talk to me. So I went over and sat on a flowery sofa and beamed at the groups of chatting people as though I'd just *love* to join in. As expected, they worked very hard not to be aware of me.

The fact is, within obvious limits we do decide what we look like. Our clothing, jewelry, eyeglasses, hairstyles, way of standing and walking, a hundred other things, all go together to create that person who is not exactly us but is the person the rest of the world sees. Every element of that involves a choice, and in our choices we make a lot of declarations, including which other human beings we're most comfortable having contact with.

So that's what I was using now. Ed Dante—that is, this Ed Dante, in Kay Henry's office—was an amiable but sleazy guy who tried to cover his inadequacies with a lover-boy image and failed. With very slight changes of appearance and manner, he had become much less dangerous and off-putting than the guy who'd been acting tough down in Miami. You probably still wouldn't want him for your best friend—unless you were a failed Errol Flynn yourself—but you wouldn't mind being in the same room with him for a while. At least, that was the idea.

It was twenty to eleven before the icy Miss Colinville ushered me into the inner office. In those forty-five minutes, a number of cast changes had taken place out here. A bright-eyed cheery girl who could have been Julie Kaplan's cousin came out from the inner sanctum and a couple of the people from one of the chatting groups went away in the elevator with her. Other people from this waiting area went inside, came out, left. A few times, the elevator opened to produce either a messenger delivering a package—scripts, mostly, from the look of them—or an actor to pick up a check; or at least a slim envelope. Most of these people (except the messengers) portrayed ebullience and hopefulness and happiness all the time, as though life itself were one endless audition.

As I sat there, the place got me more and more depressed—partly because it reminded me of my own early days in this trade, and partly because it emphasized how short and relatively painless my own apprenticeship had been—but I maintained the de rigueur ebullient brightness through it all, leafing through the *Billboard*s and *Variety*s on the coffee table near me, smiling at my fellow supplicants, occasionally winking at the oblivious Miss Colinville.

Who at last, after one more brief murmured conversation into her telephone, rose and nodded to me and turned toward that gleaming mahogany door. I dropped the month-old *Variety* I'd been leafing through, and followed, and found myself in a different world.

The corridor was white-walled, with sunken fluorescent ceiling lights. Theater and movie posters lined both sides, filling the left but broken by doorways on the right. Following Miss Colinville, I saw that these right-hand doorways led to two assistants' offices—both assistants deep in discussion with clients, at the moment—a supply room, a unisex restroom and an empty small conference room. At the far end, the corridor opened out, without doorway or door, into Kay Henry's office.

After all those interior spaces, the first thing you noticed about his office were the windows. Not that he had such a grand view, it being merely of the backs of several other buildings twenty feet or so away, but just that his room acknowledged the existence of the outside world. The office itself was very wide, walls and carpet and furniture all in varying soft shades of gray, with white or blond accents. The framed and autographed blowups of stars' photographs which were the only wall adornments were all in black-and-white. The lucite bowl of oranges on the glass and chrome Parson's table beside the entrance was clearly to be considered a color accent and not in any way a reference to food.

Kay Henry himself was much less self-conscious than his workspace. A bulky man of about forty, with badly thinning tan hair and a round optimistic face, he wore chinos and a polo shirt and a million dollar watch and very large-lensed tortoise-shell glasses. His casual clothing, near-baldness, roundness of both face and glasses, and an open cheeriness of manner all combined to give him a look of eager expectancy, a desire to be of help and use; not a bad facade for an agent.

As Miss Colinville departed, Henry came smiling forward, hand outstretched, saying, "Morning, Ed. Sorry we're running late around here today."

Clearly, this office "ran late" all the time, the way doctors do. "No problem," I said, grinning at him a little too boyishly, slumping my shoulders a bit as I shook his hand, letting his grasp be firmer than mine.

"Come sit down," he said, patting my arm and gesturing at the L of gray couches beside us. As we took seats, he said, "How's Julie doing?"

"Fine," I assured him. "I saw the show. She's really good in it."

"A very promising girl," he said, nodding and smiling. "Very promising."

"We're just pals, you know," I said, and grinned

sheepishly, and shrugged. "That's the way *she* wants it."

To his credit, Henry didn't wince at my crudeness. "Well, she's very high on you, Ed," he told me, "from a professional point of view. She tells me you don't have an agent at the moment."

I nodded, still sheepish, and laughed at myself, saying, "Right now, I don't even have a resumé. The airline lost my suitcase. They say I'll probably get it in a day or two. As soon as I do, I'll come right over with a few copies. I would have brought them now, but . . ." Another awkward shrug. (The fact was, any actor in my supposed position would automatically have brought his photo and resumé to this meeting, so I'd had to come up with a reason for not having done so, and the lost-suitcase gag was all I could think of.)

"No problem, Ed," Henry told me. A legal-size yellow pad and long well-sharpened pencil were on the glass coffee table before him. Leaning forward, picking up the pencil, poising it, he said, "Why not just give me a rundown?"

So I did, reeling off to him the history of a modest middling career over a stretch of eight years, combining elements I remembered from Brett Burgess's past with parallels to Dale Wormley's career, plus a few other times and places I happened to know about. It was a stuttering career, with hiatuses, no lead parts, bouncing around minor regional theaters, getting some regional TV ads, other minor work; and it all ended two years ago.

Kay Henry jotted all this down in some kind of personal shorthand, nodding, treating it as seriously as though it were Laurence Olivier's resumé, and at the end he brooded for a minute, lips pushed out, eraser end of the pencil tapping a slow drumbeat on the pad. "Nothing much recently, Ed," he finally commented.

"There's no point lying to you, Mr. Henry," I said, and he raised an eyebrow at that, giving me his full attention. I made awkward body movements, making it clear I was wishing there *was* some point in lying to him, and then I said, "It was drink."

"Drink?"

"I'm off it now," I told him, sitting up straighter, giving him my most honest and level look yet. "I'm AA. I'm one of those people, Mr. Henry, it's, I'm one of those people, it's poison."

Nodding sympathetically, his eyes friendly behind the large glasses, he said, "Actors, Ed, creative people like yourself, you've got to be so aware of that risk."

"I am," I said.

"You don't live a routine life," he told me. "Same thing, day after day. You live with variety, difference, always new places, new people, new things to think about. It's an exciting life. It's a great life, by golly." He looked at me with wide-eyed envy, as though he really and truly would have preferred my scruffy existence to this luxurious nest.

"It is a good life," I agreed solemnly, nodding at him.

"But it's unsettling, Ed," he went on. "Without that regularity of the average citizen's life, somebody in your position can be vulnerable."

Laughing bitterly, I said, "I sure was."

"It's happened to some of our finest actors," he said, nodding in sympathy with human frailty everywhere. "You're damn lucky you caught it in time."

"Oh, I know that."

He looked at the yellow pad again, smiled faintly, and said, "And that's why you need a new agent."

"Uh huh."

"Who *was* your agent, Ed?"

"Blair Knox," I told him, she being Brett Burgess's New York agent. She and Brett were good enough friends for me to be able to ask her through him the favor of backing up my story, should Henry phone her.

Again, Henry nodded, writing Blair Knox's name on the pad. "A good woman," he said. "If she took you on, that's a very strong recommendation all by itself."

"Well," I said, with that sheepish laugh again, "she did kind of have second thoughts there after a while."

"Sometimes we have to make hard decisions, Ed," he told me. "Don't blame Blair."

"I know who to blame, Mr. Henry," I said fervently.

"But that's the past," he said. "The thing to think about now is the future. Where can I reach you, Ed?"

"I just came back to the city," I told him, "don't really have a place of my own yet, or a service, or anything. I'm staying with friends in Brooklyn." And I gave him the Youngs' number.

Having written it down, Henry dropped the pencil and leaned back on the sofa, saying, "I'm not sure what I know about right now that you'd be good for. When I get your photo and resumé, my assistants can take a more extensive look, see what's coming up on the horizon, here in town. Or on the road." Lifting that eyebrow again, he said, "You don't mind going on the road, do you?"

"Well," I said, "if I have to, you know, to make a living. But it's easier, to, uh . . ."

"Stay on the wagon," he suggested gently. "If you're in one place."

"I wouldn't want that to keep me from a good part," I told him, looking worried.

"We'll keep that in mind," he assured me. "And there's a lot happening in this city right now, as a matter of fact. We'll have a look, see what we come up with."

This was supposed to be the end of the meeting, but instead of standing and thanking and departing I leaned forward, exhibiting many signs of embarrassment and hesitancy as I said, "Uh, Mr. Henry, there was one thing Julie told me about, a part she thought I might be right for."

Amused, Henry looked at me and said, "Oh? What was that, Ed?"

"It was something her boyfriend was going to do," I said, and gestured with head and hand as though directing our attention to the past. "You know, the guy who, uh . . . Dale Wormley."

Pain crossed Henry's features. "A terrible thing, that," he said. "Poor Dale. God damn it, poor Dale."

"I knew him," I said. "Not very much."

"A fine actor," he told me. "Great deal of promise. Cut down like that." He shook his head again. "We never know, Ed," he said. "We never know when it all stops."

"That's true, I guess," I said, and cleared my throat, and said, "Julie said there was this part, uh, with Rita Colby?"

Henry flipped at once from deep sadness to quiet pride. "A fine actress," he told me. "I'm honored to represent her." And he gestured at her photo, among those on the wall.

I looked at it, across the room. Rita Colby was one of those people who, by either nature or design, are very easy to caricature. Her short full auburn hair was worn in a helmet style, curling down around her earlobes. Her dark eyes were very large, always just a little surprised looking, and her mouth had a very individual quirky wrinkle to it, so that when she smiled just a little she looked as though she'd just heard a really terrific dirty joke, and when she frowned just a little she looked honestly and hopelessly heartbroken. It was a wonderful acting tool, that face, and she had the technique and talent to go with it.

Looking at that blown-up black-and-white picture, with its lavish inscription scrawled in white ink, I became aware for the first time that Rita Colby was just about the only famous face on these walls who was still alive. All the rest of those people had joined the late-greats. Was Rita Colby Henry's only living major client?

Had those other people ever been Kay Henry clients at all?

While I was looking at the pictures, thinking about them, Henry had been looking at me, thinking about me, and now he said, thoughtfully, "You know, Ed, Julie may have something there. You do look a bit like Dale, in fact. Different color hair, of course, and the moustache, but you're tall, and you have the same kind of well-defined bony face. As a matter of fact . . ." And he gazed past me, following some new thought.

I looked at him. Could he possibly be doing what I thought he was doing? "Mr. Henry?" I said.

He looked back at me, grinned, and shook his head. "Nothing," he said. "I'm pretty sure they'll be dropping that campaign anyway."

So it was true! He'd been thinking of offering me the job of parodying Packard, replacing Wormley in those commercials. This whole situation was getting too convoluted. I said, "But you think Julie may be right about me and that play?"

"It's a possibility," he told me. "Tell you what, Ed. Are you free about four this afternoon?"

"Oh, sure," I said, very eager.

"Rita Colby has cast approval," he explained. "She approved Dale, and she'll have to approve the replacement. She's dropping by this afternoon—"

"Here? She's coming here?"

He smiled at my eagerness. "Yes, she is," he said. "Why don't you come back then, about four o'clock, and I'll introduce you."

"That'd be great, Mr. Henry," I said, and now I did stand up, not as though in a hurry to leave but as though I'd become too excited to remain seated. "I'll be here at exactly four o'clock," I said.

Getting to his feet, Henry laughed lightly and said, "Just remember, we do sometimes run a little late."

"That's okay," I said. "I'll be here."

"That's good, Ed. I think you have the right attitude. Whatever problems you had in the past, I just have a hunch they're finished. Things are looking up."

"Yes, they are!"

"See you at four, then," he said, raising a graceful hand to usher me out.

Hesitating, I said, "Would it be a good idea for me to take a look at the script? To get some idea of the part, you know."

"Let's just let Rita have a look at you first," he told me, patting my arm gently, looking up at me with sympathetic friendliness. "Okay, Ed?"

"You know best," I told him, and he laughed and

said, "Well, I guess I'm supposed to, eh? That's my job."

I thanked him again, we shook hands, and I went back out to the receptionist's area. Having pressed the elevator button, I turned grinning to the cold Miss Colinville and said, "I'll tell you something, beautiful. I'm walking on air."

"That's nice," she said, without interest, and turned to answer the phone.

**27**

**B**rett and Blair Knox and I had lunch at one of the new trendy places in the west Twenties. Now that office rents in midtown have driven the book publishers south, restaurants have bloomed there as well, since apparently book publishing is a trade that can't exist without lunch. We'd wanted to eat somewhere respectable, but we didn't want to run into anyone we knew— particularly not Kay Henry. So the west Twenties it was.

Blair Knox began as an actress, sort of an Alexis Smith type, thirty-some years ago. She didn't have much success on stage, but she got interested in the agenting side of the business, went to work for one of the big outfits, and a few years later branched out on her own. Her client list has never included any major stars—no Rita Colbys—but she has a reputation for handling solid and reliable performers, and for being solid and reliable herself. Her clients find her a sympathetic and supportive force in their lives, her attitude probably coming from her early efforts to be an actress herself; she's been on their side of the street.

In photos from that time, she's a slender, straight-backed, regal-looking person, a little too aloof to be loved by an audience. Now, in her mid-fifties, a rigorous dieter and exerciser, she was more compact than slender, the regal appearance having hardened to a look of brisk efficiency. Slipping on tiny silver-framed reading glasses to study first the menu and second the list I'd given her, she looked somehow like the dean of a small private college. The list was the resumé I'd given Kay Henry; if he were to phone Blair, she should have some idea of Ed Dante's career. Scanning it, shaking her head, "Well," she said, "I don't seem to have done much for *you.*"

"I was a drinker," I explained. "Not always reliable. I've told you I'm on the wagon now, and you hope I mean it."

She grinned at me, removing the little specs. "But I wouldn't touch you with a barge pole, is that it?"

"Just about."

"Fine," she said, and put list and specs away in her purse.

We ordered, then talked generally for a while, ate our main courses, and over coffee it was Brett who returned us to the subject of the day, saying to Blair, "Tell us about Kay Henry."

Giving him an arch look, she said, "Thinking of making a change, are you, Brett?"

Now, Brett's a nice guy, and smart, but you can't joke

with him. Looking flustered, he said, "That isn't what I meant. It's Sam that—"

"Ed," I reminded him, and Blair smiled and patted his hand on the table, saying, "I know, dear, I was just teasing."

Then Brett felt stupid. "Of course you were," he said. "Sorry."

"About Kay Henry," Blair said, and looked at me. "What do you want to know?"

"Well, reputation, I guess," I told her. "But something more. In his office, there's all these signed photos of stars, but I noticed, Rita Colby's the only one of them who isn't dead."

Blair was delighted at this. "Is that true? Has he really done that? Sam—Ed, I mean—that's wonderful."

"It's all a phony, then? Those other people were never his clients?"

"Never," she agreed.

"But he's a legitimate agent, isn't he? He isn't a con man or anything."

"No, no," she said. "He's real, all right. He probably has somewhere between forty and sixty clients now, mostly kids starting out, a few older character actors and like that. There've been a few clients who hit big, but they always leave."

"The old story?" I asked. "Going with the major agency after the small agent works to get their career off the ground?"

"Not exactly," she said, and smiled at me, adding, "Though it's sweet of you to have such faith in that old story."

"It does happen a lot," I said.

Her smile turned crooked. "Tell me about it. It's

happened to *me* once or twice. But that isn't the Kay Henry story."

"What is?"

"Rita Colby," she said. "That's the whole story, beginning to end."

"Tell," I said, suddenly aware that at probably half the tables around us similar conversations were taking place; people putting their heads closer to dish professional acquaintances. But my purpose, of course, was more serious than simple gossip. On the other hand, gossip is fun, too.

"Well, of course," Blair said, "Henry isn't even his *first* name. God knows what it is."

"Blair," I said gently, "God knows what *my* name is. Or Brett's."

"All right," she said, nodding. "I was being catty. And thank you for not questioning *my* monicker."

"Mm? Blair Knox," I said, turning the syllables over, considering them. "Sounds perfectly ordinary," I decided.

She laughed and said, "Now, *you're* being catty. All right, Kay Henry. Years ago he worked for CRA, did you know them?"

"Sure. Career Representative Associates. They're the ones who merged with my old agent, to become CNA. Career-Novak-Allied."

Brett said, sounding grumpy, "All these damn initials. Everybody sounds like government agencies."

I said, "You mean, like the CIA and the FBI?"

"Any of them."

"Well," I told him, "CIA is the Culinary Institute of America, and FBI is the Food & Beverage Institute."

He stared at me. "You're putting me on."

"Nope. Those are absolutely real." Turning back to

Blair, I said, "Kay Henry worked for CRA. In the mailroom?"

"No," she said, "unfortunately not. He was a young agent here in their New York office, and he did some work for Rita Colby. She'd been pretty well known for a while, but she was just about breaking into the big time right then. What happens, the reason a lot of people change agents when they hit big, they get the feeling the agent still thinks of them as the old smalltimer. And maybe sometimes it's the truth. Or maybe the brand new star has trouble throwing her weight around as much as she'd like, when she's still surrounded by people who knew her when."

Brett said, "Before her head got too big for her hat."

"Pretty much so," Blair agreed.

I said, "But she's still with Henry."

"No, wait a minute," she said. "Rita Colby and Kay Henry were both with CRA, but he was just a lowly assistant. He was new and young, and he *didn't* act like he knew Rita Colby when, because he'd just got there himself. And what Colby wanted was a lap dog agent, somebody who knew how to do the job, but who would take orders and not give her a bad time."

"Ah," I said. I know of such agent/client relationships, and I've always thought they were mistakes. No matter how good you are, you're still better off to have an objective eye around, to keep you from going off the deep end. An agent whose job is to agree with the client can maybe make the deals right, but he can't necessarily make the right deals. I said, "So what you mean is, Rita Colby set Henry up in the agency business, with her as his first client."

"Sure," she said. "And he can have all the other

clients he wants, but as soon as one of them starts to become important—"

"A rival," Brett said.

"Out goes that client," Blair finished. "Male or female, it doesn't matter."

"But the rest can stay," I said, remembering that cosy clubhouse atmosphere in Kay Henry's waiting room. Some of those people hadn't been there to meet with Henry or his assistants at all, but merely to hang out together. For some of them, it would be a substitute for the acting career they'd originally planned. They'd earn their livings "temporarily", waiting tables or driving cabs, and instead of the career, they'd have that false tribe over at Henry's; comforting, accepting, encouraging, understanding. And since the agency did have Rita Colby, that one major star occasionally seen in their midst, it meant the lightning bolt could still strike.

Then there was the ambiguity of the relationship between Rita Colby and Dale Wormley; he'd escorted her to this or that function a few times, and she'd insisted on his being given the part in *Four Square*. Julie Kaplan was convinced there'd been nothing sexual between them, but was she necessarily right?

Was Kay Henry pimping for Rita Colby, out of the bullpen of that waiting room?

I said, "Blair, what do you know about Rita Colby's private life?"

"What private life? Sex life, you mean?"

"I guess so, yes."

"Nothing, thank God," she said, with a delicate shudder.

Brett said, "She isn't married. Not now, anyway."

"No?"

"Seems to me," he said, being a little awkward about it in front of Blair, "I've heard here and there she likes to have a handsome younger guy around sometimes."

"Kay Henry clients?" I asked.

Blair's eyes sparkled with the love of gossip. "Sam? Do you think so?"

"Well, as a matter of fact," I told her, "there's a possibility I'll be finding out for myself, some time later today."

# 28

The fellow who'd been in acting class with Dale Wormley, and who Julie had called on my behalf, was named Tom Lacroix, and we'd arranged to meet in his apartment in the East Village at three, so I walked down there after lunch with Brett and Blair. My background and persona—though not the Ed Dante name—were different for Tom Lacroix than for Kay Henry. This time, I was a freelance writer working on an article for *Vanity Fair* about success and failure in the arts, and the idea was that I wanted to use Dale Wormley's life and death—the fact that he had become best-known for imitating someone more successful than himself—to illustrate some of the themes of my article. I would also, of course, be mentioning Tom Lacroix himself in the piece, as someone still teetering between those extremes of victory and defeat; but the main subject would be Wormley.

Lacroix lived on East 10th Street off 3rd Avenue, an area that hasn't been gentrified exactly, but is moderately quiet and relatively safe, with rows of four and five story brick townhouses long ago converted to apartments and more recently converted to hot water and heat. His place was in one of these, on the fourth floor rear of a walkup. I identified myself on the intercom outside the front door, he buzzed me in, and I climbed to find him grinning down at me from the top of the stairs, saying, "I hope you're in good shape."

"Reasonably so," I told him. "But I'm just as glad you're not on six."

"Lordy, Lordy, me, too," he said, and I heard Texas—southwest, anyway—twanging in his voice. He was a rangy, athletic-looking fellow in his mid-twenties, with an amiable, unlined, not very memorable face. He wore jeans and a flannel shirt, and looked like the sort of actor they use to dress the bar set in beer commercials. When I reached the top of the stairs, he gave me a firm bony handshake and ushered me into an apartment approximately the size of a watch pocket. "If you sit there and I sit here," he said, "our knees won't bump."

"Thanks."

I sat where he suggested, and, true to his appearance, he asked if I'd like a beer. I said I would. "Lone Star," he offered, "or Dos Equis?"

I laughed and said, "By God, you are from Texas, aren't you?"

"Gave it away, did I?" He made a *drat* finger-snapping gesture. "Somehow, I always slip up."

"Dos Equis," I told him, and he crossed the room to a kind of bas-relief kitchen—all the necessary appliances in a wide shallow closet. Opening the refrigerator, he said, "I've noticed you Easterners tend to like glasses."

"Not necessarily."

"Good. Less work for mother."

He too had chosen Dos Equis. Handing me mine, he sat in the chair facing me—it was true, our knees did not quite touch—and raised his bottle in a toast: "Remember the Alamo."

I raised mine: "Remember the *Maine.*"

He thought about that, decided it was acceptable, and said, "Carthage must be destroyed."

"Fifty-four forty or fight," I suggested.

"Drink before it gets warm," he told me.

It was his house, so it was only right that he got to go last. We both drank from our bottles, and then he said, "So you write for *Vanity Fair.*"

"I'm not on staff," I told him, "just a freelance. In fact, this'll be my first piece for them."

"And it's about success in the arts?"

"Success and *failure* in the arts," I corrected. "Really, about the interface between the two." For this impersonation, this version of Ed Dante, I'd mussed up the wig a little and thought myself into a sub-Columbo guise; a careless cerebral guy, probably not first-rate at what he does, unaware of any negative impression he might be making with his moustache and his sloppiness. Success and failure, in other words; exemplifying my subject matter.

Lacroix said, "And you think Dale fits in there? The interface between success and failure?"

"Sure." I gestured with the bottle. "You couldn't call him a failure, he was making a living at his chosen profession. Not many do."

His mouth curved in a rueful smile. "You can say that again."

"But Wormley wasn't really a success either," I went on. "The highest he got was a parody of someone else's success."

"And that even got him killed," Lacroix said, "which is about as big a failure as you can get."

Bewildered, I said, "What do you mean?"

He seemed surprised by my surprise. "Well, Sam Holt killed him, didn't he?"

Whoops. I had to tread carefully here. Was this the common public view of the situation, or was Lacroix's opinion an odd one, a distortion caused by his having known Wormley? I said, "Did he? I didn't think that had been established."

"Oh, they'll never get him for it," Lacroix agreed, airily waving the Dos Equis bottle.

The old powerful-influence idea again. If only it were true. I said, "I'm not sure what the motive would be."

"Well," he said, the casual assurance of the uninvolved, "I don't suppose he *meant* to do it, do you? There was some sort of funny history of violence between them, you know, and I guess it just got out of hand. You know," he added, "you oughta talk to Holt, too, see what *he* thinks of success and failure."

"I wrote him, as a matter of fact," I said. "In California. Haven't heard anything yet."

"I bet you don't."

"Probably not," I agreed. "I suppose, guilty or innocent, he'll be keeping a low profile right now." I brooded, partly real and partly for effect. "You know,"

I said, "if Dale Wormley really was killed by Sam Holt, because he was mad at the imitation, that could screw up my whole article. I mean, the magazine might not want to touch it that way, I might have to start all over with a completely different approach."

"You mean, forget Dale."

"Yeah, I'm afraid so."

"And me," Lacroix said, with another crooked grin. "Story of my life, I'm afraid." He drank some beer.

I said, "Well, let's think about it. It's only the celebrity thing that's a real problem. You knew Wormley. If Sam Holt didn't kill him, who else might have?" And I was astonished at how easily it had been possible to come around to ask that question directly.

I was also disappointed by Lacroix's prompt answer: "Nobody. Or, that is, anybody who knew him might have, but that still comes out, really, to nobody. I mean, Dale was an irritation, a very irritating guy—don't tell Julie I said that; you know, she had a different attitude toward him—but he wasn't irritating enough to kill."

"In what way irritating?"

"Career," Lacroix said. "Anything at all about acting. He'd walk all over you without thinking twice. Even in class, in an exercise, he'd try to upstage you, steal the scene. People were always yelling at him to cut it out, lighten up, don't be such an asshole."

"Too competitive, you mean."

"Cutthroat," he said. "Myself, I like competition, I think it's a good thing, but you can overdo it."

"Sounds as though a lot of people would hold grudges against somebody like that," I said.

"Well, sure, anybody might have," Lacroix agreed, "if he was more successful at it. But he tried so *damn* hard, he screwed up most of the time. If you've got a guy trying to stick his thumb in your eye, but every time he makes a move he steps on his own dick instead, you can't get really mad at him."

I had no choice but to laugh at the image he'd conjured up, and he laughed along with me. "Still," I said, "in fact, there are people in this world without a terrific sense of humor."

"That's true," he conceded. "Down home, we say, '*Forget* the Alamo, it's *over,* man,' but some people just have to be mad all the time, it's the only way they can keep their heartbeat regular."

"Like Dale Wormley, for instance."

"A perfect example," he agreed, and then he looked surprised and said, "You know, though, there *is* another."

"Another what?"

"Another tough case, like Dale," he told me. "Now, *those* two made a pair. But I just can't see Matty taking it as far as all that."

"Matty?"

"Matty Pierce." Lacroix nodded, looking thoughtful. "He's been in our class, part of the group, longer than me. Longer than Dale, even."

Matty Pierce. The name rang a bell. It seemed to me Julie had said something about a Matty Pierce; not in Florida, but earlier than that, maybe in Mort's office. I said, "Tell me about this Matty Pierce."

"Well, one thing weird about him," Lacroix said, "oddball, I mean, is that he's a real New Yorker. The rest of us are all from to hell and gone, but Matty comes from Brooklyn."

"Oh?"

"He's kind of a tough guy," Lacroix said, "or at least he likes to play tough guy. He grew up in some tough neighborhood out there. In fact, he still lives out there, takes the subway in."

"I'm living in Brooklyn myself right now," I said. "In Midwood."

"Is there a section called Canarsie?"

"Yes. Way out by Jamaica Bay."

"Well, that's where Matty grew up," Lacroix told me. "And where he still lives. The story is, they made some TV movie out there a few years ago. You know, they shot some exteriors there, used some of the neighborhood kids."

I almost said, *That's how I got started,* which was the truth for Sam Holt but not for this journalist form of Ed Dante; so I stopped myself in time. But, in fact, I'd gotten into this career because a moive was being shot in Mineola, Long Island, where I worked as a cop on the town force. The movie people used a few of us cops as extras—to get on our good side, essentially, justify paying us some money that couldn't be called a bribe— and someone like the way I looked in the dailies; and the rest is pop history.

Lacroix was going on, saying, "Matty got the bug, he pestered the movie people, and somebody gave him an introduction to one of the casting agencies in Manhattan. And Matty *looks* good, he looks like your average run-of-the-mill rotten local boy, which is what he is, so he gets extra work a lot. But what he wants is to be a star. Charles Bronson, or at the very least Robert Blake."

"Stand in line," I suggested.

"Oh, you know it. In two words, Matty's getting no-where. And it makes him mad."

"Sounds like he and Dale Wormley were born for each other," I said.

"Sounded that way to Howard, too, for a while," Lacroix agreed.

"Howard?"

"Howard Moffitt, our teacher."

"Acting teacher."

"Yes, of course."

"Well," I said, "what changed his mind?"

"He assigned the two of them a scene together," Lacroix told me, grinning at the memory. "From *True West*. The brothers are supposed to be mad at each other, and Howard figured they could use their intensity, learn to get it under control that way. We had to peel them off each other."

"They fought?"

"It was grim," Lacroix said, but he chuckled when he said it, and shook his head. "Howard said we'd *all* learned something that day."

"Did Wormley and—What's his name?"

"Matty Pierce."

"Did they learn to get their intensity under control?"

"Not so's you'd notice," Lacroix said. "And they still hated each other afterward just as much. Maybe more."

"I wonder," I said, thinking about it, "if it'd be a good idea to talk to both of those people. Matty Pierce, and Howard."

"Well, Howard, anyway," Lacroix agreed. "If you want to talk about Dale in connection with success and failure, he's the guy to see."

"But also Matty Pierce," I said. "If I'm going to give a rounded picture of the guy, I should have a variety of people's viewpoints on him."

"Could be," he said, shrugging. "You know your business."

"Could you help me set it up?" I asked. "Call these

people, introduce me the way Julie did with you? I'd really appreciate it."

"Well, I'll see them both in class later today," he said. "I could tell them about you, what you're up to, see if they want to talk. Matty might not."

"Why not?"

"Oh, well," Lacroix said, grinning again, "he might feel he didn't want to say anything bad about the dead, you know, and I *know* he doesn't have anything good to say about Dale, so he might not want to say anything at all."

"I'd particularly like to talk with him," I said. "For the sake of balance. Tell him—Tell him I promise nothing he says will be for attribution."

Lacroix smiled at me. "He can speak ill of the dead anonymously."

"Not an offer you get all the time."

"Indeed not. Okay," he said. "I'll be seeing them both in class later on today, I'll ask them and see what they say."

"Thanks a lot."

"Give me a call late tomorrow morning," he said, "I'll tell you what happened."

"I appreciate it."

Pointing at my bottle with his bottle, he said, "You done with that beer? Want another?"

"I'd better not," I said. "I've still got more interviews to do this afternoon."

"More about Dale?"

"Yes." Then, to see what it might get me, I bounced the name off him. "Rita Colby, in fact."

"Ah," he said, with a knowing smile. "Now *there's* the interface between success and failure. It isn't who you know, it's who you fuck."

"Really? Julie didn't think—" I stopped at his little grin and headshake. "Oh," I said. "Wormley told you so, huh?"

"Well, no," he said. "I'll give the lad that much, he didn't kiss and tell. But figure it out for yourself. He meets Rita Colby through his agent. She's separated from her husband—this is before he died—so she needs somebody to be her escort at a couple of public occasions, and Dale looked good, knew how to dress, didn't spill things on himself when he ate, so he was it. And all of a sudden he's walking around with this little *grin,* you know."

"The cat that ate the canary."

"Yellow feathers in both corners of his mouth," Lacroix agreed. "And Rita Colby *insisting* he be in her next play."

"I see what you mean."

He grinned, shook his head, and looked at his empty bottle. "Well," he said, "*I* don't have to interview anybody today, I'm giving myself another beer. Sure you won't?"

"No, thanks."

Getting to his feet, crossing the tiny room, he said, "Of course, I'm just a rube from the sticks of downtown Dallas, could be I've just got a dirty mind. Could be, what Dale and Rita Colby had in common was Scrabble." He paused, a fresh Dos Equis in his hand, and grinned over at me. "What do *you* think?"

# 29

There were still cheerful cliquey conversational groups in the waiting room at Kay Henry's offices. And the icy Miss Colinville still manned the Chippendale. "Hi, there, beautiful," I said, with my stupidest grin, leaning again on her table. "Remember me?"

"Vividly," she said. "Do have a seat."

My former place was now in the middle of one of the campfires, so I sat on the other side, near the door to the offices, facing the opposite direction from before. I'd used up all the ancient *Variety*s and *Billboard*s in here, and in any event I now had Tom Lacroix's comments to brood on, so I did; particularly his assumption that Sam Holt was guilty of murder.

Just how prevalent was that assumption, in the great

world? If this was the common belief, would I *ever* live it down? To have trouble getting on with my career because I'd been typecast in a single role was one thing; to be unemployable because I was considered an unindicted murderer was something very different and far worse. I'd never seen myself as the Fatty Arbuckle of my generation.

In my new position in this room the offices were all behind me, and now I gradually became aware that the mutedly paneled wall ahead of me, beyond Miss Colinville and the chatterers, contained a modest and barely noticeable door. It wasn't hidden, exactly, but its lack of ornament and the placement of the pictures and furniture around it made it virtually disappear.

I had nothing much else to think about, beyond the unsolvable problem of Tom Lacroix's beliefs, so I spent a while looking at that door, wondering what was beyond it. All the offices were the other way, leading back to Kay Henry's room, with its view toward the rear of buildings on the next block. This waiting room was windowless, so beyond that door must be a front room of some sort, overlooking the street. Not more offices. Storage? A small screening room, maybe, except he'd be unlikely to pick one of the few rooms with windows for such a purpose.

I was rather fuzzily staring at that door, trying to guess what lay beyond it, when it opened, and Rita Colby came out, in dark wool skirt and linen blouse. Our eyes met, and she looked startled; probably because she hadn't expected to open the door into somebody's distracted stare. I was too surprised myself to politely and immediately break contact, so she looked away first, sketching a quick smile onto her face as she said a word to the gathered regulars. Her manner of noblesse oblige was perfectly matched by their gushed greetings, the peasants hallooing the lady of the manor. She accepted their obeisances, crossed the room, nodded briskly to Miss Colinville, and went through the other door toward the offices, without glancing my way again.

It was ten minutes more before I was called; then Miss Colinville turned to me with almost a hint of thaw in her expression as she said, "You can go on in now. You remember the way, don't you?"

"Sure do, beautiful," I said, getting to my feet. I winked at her. "I'll miss you."

Her lips curled with scorn, and she turned back to her duties. Still grinning, I went through the doorway and down the hall to Kay Henry's room, where Henry was pacing back and forth and Rita Colby was seated on one of the gray sofas, legs crossed, top leg fretfully moving.

At first, I was too interested in my own performance to really pay much attention to anybody else in the room. How would Ed Dante—*this* Ed Dante—react to the presence of Rita Colby? I decided he'd be awed, but that he'd try to cover it by clumsy joking mixed with overelaborate compliments. So, upon seeing the woman seated there, I immediately crossed to her, went down on one knee like a medieval knight, pressed both hands to my heart, and said, "Miss Colby, I'm your biggest fan. It's an honor to breathe the air in the same room with you."

She gave me a look of amused disbelief. "Well, *that's* baroque," she said.

"And I want you to know," I went on, twinkling Ed

Dante's personality at her like mad, "when I dream of you, I'm always respectful."

Laughing, but at the same time making a graceful brushing-away gesture in my direction, she looked up at Henry and said, "Make him stand up. I want a look at him."

Immediately, I popped to my feet, swept off an imaginary musketeer's cap, and performed a broad low bow, saying, "Ed Dante at your service, Madame."

"Yes, fine, just stand there," she said, sounding a bit impatient with me.

So I just stood there. I never wanted to take this character so far as to get him—and me with him— thrown out of anywhere. I stood, and Rita Colby looked me up and down, critically, studying me as though I were a piece of furniture she might add to the guest room. She made a waggly circling gesture with one down-pointing finger, so I turned in a slow circle, ploddingly, putting it on a little too broadly so she'd have to know this was another tiresome joke. When I faced her again, she said (to Henry, not to me), "Well, the moustache will have to go."

"Oh!" I said, in pain, and put one hand up to touch three protective fingertips to that narrow line of hair above my lip. (An impish desire came over me to yank the thing off and hand it to her, saying, "Well, if you don't like it, we'll get rid of it." Which would have been very foolish and very dangerous, so I didn't do it.)

Meanwhile, Kay Henry was saying, "I know what you mean. But let's not redesign the man until we know what we're doing."

"And whether or not," she commented, "we want to do it at all." Then, more irritably, she said, "You know, we don't *have* to cast that part this early. The circumstances aren't the same any more."

I listened intently, frozen there with my fingers against my moustache, feeling myself invisible inside this other personality, listening to them, waiting for them to say more, and thinking that Rita Colby didn't sound like a person referring to a part that had been given to a lover.

"I know, dear, I know," Henry said, soothing her, sounding well practiced at soothing her. "But Ed's here, and Julie Kaplan told him about the role, so why not look him over."

"Fine," she said, brisk and impatient. "We'll look him over." And she looked at me, making a business of it (more subtly than my bits), and said, "Well, he's tall enough. How tall are you?"

"Six foot six, Mum," I said, and released my moustache to tug a forelock. "Up a half."

She ignored that. "Have you ever played Nazis?" she aked me.

"I beg your pardon?"

"Nazi soldiers," she explained. "Gestapo men, that sort of thing. They usually cast big boys like you in that kind of part."

"As a matter of fact, yes," I said. And it was true; before PACKARD, the occasional one-shot small television roles I'd landed had included a couple of German soldiers in World War II stories.

"Good," she said, and pointed at Henry. "Go arrest him."

Very clever. It was a simple little exercise, a two-dimensional character I already knew, a scene I should have no trouble improvising. If awkward, jokey, pushy

Ed Dante showed through the character, that would be the end of it; she'd have no further use for me.

So now what? It seemed to me I'd better play the part as well as I knew how, that being the only way I could prolong this conversation. So I stepped back, lowered my head to think about it and to get all this other extraneous stuff out of the way, smoothed my jacket and tie to a better semblance of neatness, lifted my head, and looked over at Henry. I was aware of Rita Colby, of course, out of the corner of my eye, but I paid no attention to her. "Herr Henry," I said. I was doing just the faintest hint of an accent, no music hall stuff.

Henry played along fairly well, though with a distracting little grin: "Yes, officer?"

I stepped toward him, arms bent, hands out in front of me, turning palms up to indicate my helplessness as I said, with a touch of sympathy, "I am afraid, Herr Henry, they have sent me to bring you in."

His eyes widened. Overacting, he hunched up his shoulders—amateurs always do too much—saying, "But why? What have *I* done?"

"You know, Herr Henry," I said. "And they sent me, you see, because we know each other." Again I did the gesture of helplessness. "They know that, you see. They know everything."

He looked more honestly worried. He said, "But— What's going to happen?"

"Bad things," I told him. "It might be better for you to try to run away. Faster. Cleaner." More sympathy showed: "I promise I won't miss."

"By God," he said, breaking character, "you're scaring the shit out of me." Looking past me at Rita Colby, he said, "Well? Is that enough?"

"It is," said her voice, cool and thoughtful. I turned

toward her, grinning, and she said, "I'm very impressed, Ed."

"That's great, coming from you, Miss Colby," I said. Then I ducked my chin down, and grinned wide-eyed at her, and said, "But I'm better, you know, playing a lover."

# 30

**S**he didn't pick up that cue. In fact, she was all business, and not at all what Tom Lacroix, for instance, would have anticipated. Telling me I shouldn't think I definitely had the role, that others would have to be consulted—playwright, director, two producers—and that the casting wouldn't in any event be made until January, she nevertheless sat me down in Henry's office and described the play and my part in it; or, that is, the part I was being considered for.

*Four Square* was a suspense romantic comedy about a ménage à trois nearly becoming a ménage à quatre, and also nearly becoming a murder mystery. The principal characters were a United States senator, his wife and his longtime secretary, with whom he's been having a longtime affair. Rita Colby would be playing the secretary, who has now fallen in love with a younger man, a television news anchor; once Dale Wormley's part, now possibly Ed Dante's. The 'switch' in the story was that the wife didn't want her husband's affair with the secretary to end; it had provided a stability and safety in their lives, and without the secretary the husband might go off and become involved with women who would lead him into scandal and disgrace and loss of the next election.

Therefore—I suppose they could make this seem fairly reasonable—the senator and his wife proceed to scheme to murder the news anchor. But when the wife meets the news anchor—the character appears only in two brief scenes, of which that was the second—she *also* falls in love with him. When she tries to stop her husband's murder scheme, things go wrong, and at first it seems as though the senator has been killed by his own plot, at which point the secretary realizes it was the senator she truly loved all along. *So,* when the senator turns out to be alive, the couples switch, the senator and his wife amicably divorce, she goes off with the news anchor and the senator marries his secretary.

The plot construction of this trash was based on the known prejudices of the potential audience, which would mostly be middle-aged theater parties from Connecticut. These people liked stories of extramarital titillation, particularly among people of power or glamour—a United States senator, a television news anchor—but they didn't like stories that doubted the essential correctness of the social order. The situation at the beginning of the story could include adultery and a ménage à trois, but by the end the characters must have rearranged themselves into traditional couples. (Since most of the audience would themselves have gone through at least one divorce, the traditional couple no longer needed to be the *first-time* couple.)

Rita Colby didn't want me to have a copy of the script, since protocol required the other principals be consulted first, but she described it rather extensively, quoting—very well, in fact—some of her own better lines. Partway through this exercise, Kay Henry plaintively said, "Rita, darling, I really *do* have other things to do. *Must* you take over my office like this?"

"Oh, all right," she agreed, without fuss, and got to her feet, saying, "We'll go up front, then." To me, she said, "Do you have time for this?"

"I sure do," I told her, grinning and grinning. "I wouldn't miss it for the world." And here was a point where Ed Dante and I converged and became one.

After thanking Kay Henry for all his help, shaking his hand a little too fervently and grinning all over him, I followed Rita Colby back down the hall and through the door into the waiting area, where her presence caused a little flurry among the campers and Miss Colinville briefly lifted an ironic eyebrow before deciding to ignore me. It was nearly five by now, so fewer people were hanging around, but the cozy clubby atmosphere remained the same.

We crossed the waiting room, Rita Colby opened the door that had so interested me before, and I followed her into a neat but impersonal studio apartment; with, as I'd guessed, windows overlooking the street. The place looked like an upscale hotel room, with a kitchenette in one corner. A kingsize bed dominated the right side of the room, a seating area with couch and two armchairs grouped around a glass coffee table filled the left. Traffic noise was suddenly audible.

Closing the door after us, Rita Colby said, "Do you want a Coke? Perrier?"

"Perrier would be good," I said, dropping out of character—though not badly—while I looked around the room. "What is this place?"

On her way to the kitchenette, opening the low refrigerator—well-stocked with snack foods and non-alcoholic beverages—she said, "A kind of crash pad, really. Kay lives upstate. If he stays in town, for a show or anything, he'll sleep over here. And the same thing if one of his clients needs a place."

I said, "Do *all* of his clients get that privilege?"

She gave me a knowing smile, neither of us looking toward the door and the chattering fellas and gals outside. "Not all," she said. "Here's your Perrier."

"Thanks." I took the bottle and glass from her hands.

She stood looking at me, a can of Diet Coke now in her hand. "You're not quite what you seem, are you?" she asked.

Whoops. Time to get back in character: grinning my awful grin, I said, "I'm a man of parts, I am. And a man of mystery. And here's looking at *you,* kid." I clinked my glass against the Diet Coke can and slugged back some of the Perrier, managing to make a little noise while I did it.

When next I looked at Rita Colby, that little moment of interest had come to an end; she was turning away, toward the sofa and chairs. "Come sit down," she said. "Where was I in the story?"

"The wife has decided to kill me."

"Oh, yes. Come sit down."

So then she told me the rest of the story, and explained my part in it: "The thing is, he's this younger guy that both women fall in love with, so he should be a hunk, and when the audience first sees him they should think that's all there is to him. But *then,* for the wife to credibly go off with him at the end, we have to see there's more to the guy than that. Dale Wormley would have done it very well, he would have brought that *edge* of his to the part. You didn't know him, did you?"

"No, I didn't." I offered my dopey grin again. "Julie Kaplan thinks he was a terrific guy."

"Not exactly," she said. "He was pretty sour, in fact, but he could *use* that anger in his work, it could make him seem as though there were depths there." With a small smile and a dismissive shrug, she said, "For all I know, there *were* depths there." Then, studying me critically, she said, "You know, you really should get rid of that moustache."

"Really?" I made myself sound sad at the prospect. "Some women tell me they like it," I said, and sparkled a bit.

"Some women like beehive hairdos, Ed." She shook her head, continuing to study me. "You know, without the moustache, and if you did something about your hair—"

"I'm not gonna shave my *head!"* I exclaimed, doing a big show of mock-fear.

"We'll get a makeup man on you, don't you worry," she told me. "You know, you look like Dale a bit. You don't have that anger he had, but the features are rather similar. In fact, with just a few changes, you could look like . . . I'll tell you who you could look like," she decided. "Like that television actor Dale did the takeoff on."

Feeling very nervous, I said, "Sam Holt, you mean?"

"That's the one."

"Somebody told me he's the guy that killed Dale Wormley."

She reared back, frowning at me in astonishment. "For what earthly reason?"

"I guess, because of those supermarket commercials."

"Because of a *parody?*" Rita Colby emphatically shook her head. "That's ridiculous," she assured me. "Somebody mugged poor Dale because he was out on the street in the middle of the night, when he had no reason to be out there except that anger of his."

"So it isn't a murder mystery."

She thought about that. "Well, it isn't *solved,*" she said. "But murders in the street *don't* get solved, do they?"

In this case, I thought, that would be very bad news; for me at least. Aloud, I said, "I guess they don't. It was just something that somebody told me."

"Rumor," she said, with contempt. "There was probably something in the *National Enquirer.*" Then she became brisk, saying, "Well, that's the whole story of *Four Square,* anyway. Kay knows how to get in touch with you?"

"Sure." This was dismissal, but rather than accept it I slouched lower in the chair, my legs stretched out, one arm flung over the chairback. Grinning lazily at Rita Colby, I said, "You know, I think you and I could be really great together, if you get what I mean."

She was amused by me, but distantly. "I think probably I do," she said. "Forgive me, I have another appointment."

"That's too bad." I beamed my rays of sunshine into her skeptical eyes. "I thought, we're nice and cozy here, we might get a little better acquainted."

She nodded slowly, thinking that over, and then she gave me a level look and said, "I don't want to hurt your feelings, Ed, but if you're going to be offered the part of Clint, and if you're going to take it, we really should understand one another."

"Well, you're right about that," I told her, cheerful as a puppy.

"I'm glad you agree."

I played dumb, spreading my hands, saying, "So what's the point?"

"The point is, dear," she said, her voice very soft, almost sympathetic, "I don't sleep with the help."

# 31

It was after five o'clock when I dragged my slaughtered carcass out of Kay Henry's crash pad, leaving Rita Colby in sole command of the place and finding the social clusters all gone from the waiting room. Miss Colinville was gone, too, which was a relief. I didn't think I was up to playing Ed Dante with that girl yet again today, particularly after the disemboweling I'd just received from Rita Colby. What a surgeon that woman would have made!

And if that's the way she viewed life, what the *hell* was the link between her and Dale Wormley?

I brooded on that question as I rode down in the elevator and walked across town to the subway entrance for the BMT, reaching the platform just in time to squeeze into a Brooklyn-bound Q train. This was the height of rush hour, so I stood crammed in with a million other people on the whole long ride down into Brooklyn. I got off at Avenue J, and walked the few blocks into Midwood and over to the Youngs' house, reflecting as I did so that Rita Colby's attitude toward me didn't necessarily mean she'd had the same attitude toward Dale Wormley. She'd spoken of him dispassionately enough, but had drawn complete contrasts between him and me, emphasizing his anger. Maybe she'd responded to that anger in some way. Or maybe it was merely that I'd presented her with a character who simply had to be slapped down.

That was Gretchen's theory, when I recapped my day over dinner. Anita hadn't felt she could take two evenings in a row away from the restaurant, so it was just Gretchen and Terry and me. And the three kids, of course, but they existed in a parallel universe of their own, next to ours. While the kids pursued their own concerns, I made my report and Gretchen said, "Well, the way you were carrying on, she had to do that."

"I wasn't exactly carrying on," I said.

"Oh, yes, you were." She shook her head at me, saying, "You don't know what you look like in that disguise. When you look at yourself in the mirror, you're just standing there, you're still yourself. But then when you come out and move around, in character, you have this awful toothy *smile* all the time, and kind of puppy eyes, and you slouch around like Groucho Marx. Any woman in the world would take one look at you and know the best thing to do is just immediately slap you across the face."

I laughed, and said, "In that case, I'm glad the women I'm meeting show such restraint."

Terry said, "What were you going to do if she *didn't*

slap you down? What if she'd said, 'Sure, honey, let's party'? Were you going to go to bed with her?"

"I was counting on Ed to be oafish enough to louse up the opportunity," I told him, and grinned open-mouthed at him like Ed, and said, with my twang, "Hey, great, baby. Just lemme call my girlfriend first, tell her I'll be a little late."

Terry laughed, and choked on his food. "Okay, okay," he said. "You were safe."

"Now, *then*," I said, "she would have been justified to bring up the nuclear warheads. But she came on like Darth Vader right *away.*"

"Well," Gretchen suggested, "what I think happened is, Rita Colby saw how good an actor you are, when you did the Nazi soldier, so she knew she'd want you in the play. But she didn't want to put up with you being a pest all the time, so she slapped you down hard at the beginning, to get all that out of the way."

"And very effective she was, too," I said.

Terry said, "But, the question is, are you getting anywhere? Somebody killed Dale Wormley and the girl, whatsername—"

"Kim Peyser."

"Right. And tried to pin the blame on you. What makes you think it has something to do with that play?"

"Nothing," I admitted. "Terry, I'm not necessarily going to go now and scrape up introductions to the playwright and the director and the producers and all these people, and try to find out if somebody had artistic reasons not to want Wormley in the part, and they killed him for the good of the theater."

"Not necessarily," Terry echoed.

I said, "I'm just following wherever the circumstances lead me. I talked with Julie Kaplan down in

Miami, and really the only two things that were hot and current in Wormley's life at the end were the lawsuit with me and the part in *Four Square*. Now, he was a bad-tempered guy, who made enemies pretty easily, and I'm following through on a guy named Matty Pierce he had trouble with in his acting class, but that kind of thing doesn't very often lead to murder, you know."

"What about the commercials?" Terry asked me. "The ones you were suing him for. What about the supermarket company, the ad agency, all the people involved with that stuff?"

"No conflicts and nothing current," I said. "He shot those commercials almost a year ago, and had just about nothing to do with any of those people since, except minor things connected with the lawsuit."

Terry said, "Well, you know, it doesn't have to be something current in his life. People have been known to hold grudges."

"So far," I said, "I haven't found anything like that. Julie gave me the keys to Wormley's apartment; it's still hers, too, I guess. I'll go there tomorrow and see what I can find. The thing is, Terry," I said, "I've been asking myself the same kind of question. What am I accomplishing? Am I just spinning my wheels? Is Packard going through the motions, playing the part only because it's better to do that than just sit at home and do nothing? I don't know. Maybe that's the truth. For now, all I can do is follow a very cold trail, and see where it leads me."

# 32

My cash was running low—when all you can spend is cash, it does tend to run low pretty rapidly—so I'd arranged for Robinson to transfer a couple thousand to Terry Young's checking account. Next morning, we started the day with Terry taking out five hundred for me from his bank. "By God, it's nice to have a healthy-looking balance for a change," he commented, when he came back out to the car. (I'd waited in it, parked by a fire hydrant on Flatbush Avenue, down the block from the bank.) "Even when it's not real." And he handed me my cash.

"Thanks, Terry," I said, stuffing the money away. Twenty-five twenties make a thick wad, but I'd discovered that anything over a twenty dollar bill attracts attention and suspicion. No matter how much inflation pushes the cost of things up, people still notice a fifty.

Again we drove into Manhattan together, Terry dropping me off downtown and me then taking a cab up to 497 West End; just below 86th Street. The name slot beside the bell for apartment 4-E read *Wormley Kaplan* in careful black-ink lettering on a bit of white cardboard; Julie's work, I guessed. I rang the bell next to the card, just in case the police still had someone there—though that was extremely unlikely, six weeks after the event on a very dead case—and when there was no answer I used one of Julie's keys to let myself into the building. After a slow ride up to the fourth floor in the elevator, I used her other key to enter the apartment.

It was two long narrow rooms next to one another, with a small kitchen carved out at the front of the first, next to the entry door, and a bathroom in the equivalent position of the second. At the far end of both rooms were large double-hung windows overlooking a featureless central court; just the stone building walls around a rectangle the size of a large car, with concrete four stories down and a glimpse of sky seven stories up.

The living room had been furnished with a look to utility and expense rather than style. The sofa, long and low and old and covered with a Mexican-influenced cotton spread, was the largest piece of furniture, with a couple of mismatched easy chairs and tables and lamps grouped in traditional manner around it. The television set and VCR and tape deck and trays of cassettes —mostly original cast show albums, male singers, some easy jazz—were stacked on a wooden bench facing the sofa, with the stereo system's speakers under the bench.

And here was the cream-colored linoleum kitchen floor I had once seen in a photograph. Nothing showed now; the letters in blood had been cleaned away.

Terry Young had looked up the details of that murder, and so now I knew at least what had been done here, if not yet why nor by whom. Kim Peyser, wearing Julie Kaplan's coat, had been stabbed, in this room, with a large kitchen knife. She had been stabbed twice, first in the back and then in the chest—the first cut not having killed her, she'd turned around to confront her murderer, who presumably had been startled not to see Julie Kaplan's face above that coat, but who could no longer pull back from his actions—and the knife had been left in the second wound; it had snagged on a rib. The knife had come from this kitchen, had been the only large useful knife in here.

The immediate result of the stabbings was a trauma, in which Kim Peyser fell to the floor, but didn't immediately die. So long as she was alive, her heart kept beating, and blood kept pumping from the rips in her body; that would have been for five to ten minutes. It was unlikely but dimly within the range of the possible that she could have been conscious part of that time, and used her own freshly-drawn blood to start writing my name on the linoleum floor. What had in fact happened was that the killer had turned her awkwardly—the awkwardness because of the knife hilt sticking out of the middle of her chest—and arranged the scene, with the letters and the positioning of her hand. And then he'd left.

Who was he? Why had he been here? If Julie Kaplan had been his intended victim, why hadn't he pursued her to Florida and tried again? If Kim Peyser was the intended victim, did her death link with Dale

Wormley's at all? If she were the intended victim, why did the killing take place *here?* Had the killer actually come here with Kim? Had he followed, and rung the bell? Had he been here already when she arrived? Did they know each other? Did he have a key to this place? Was he the same person who killed Wormley, or not? *Why* had he come to this apartment?

There were so many answers I didn't know. Packard, it seemed to me, was proving not to be such hot stuff without a scriptwriter.

I opened the refrigerator, and was surprised to find it half filled with food. Current food, that is, not spoiled old food from six weeks ago. There was a quart of low-calorie milk, half a grapefruit face down on a saucer, leafy vegetables in the crisper, a jar of diet strawberry jelly, a number of other things.

Somebody was living here. But who? Julie hadn't loaned the place to anybody, or she would have told me so. If she'd known someone was in residence, whether through her doing or not, she would have warned me about it when she gave me these keys.

I went back out to the living room, where the signs of occupancy were subtler but finally just as clear. The *TV Guide* atop the television set was this week's. A plate on an end table beside the sofa contained crumbs—cookie crumbs, I thought—that were not entirely hard; last night's midnight snack.

Who was living in here? Was it somebody who knew the situation—one tenant dead, the other away for an extended stay in Florida—and just decided to take advantage of the empty apartment and move in? Was it a friend of Dale Wormley's, or Julie's, or was it a stranger?

Was it the killer?

Since none of this made the slightest sense, that last idea was no more nonsensical than any other. And while I was standing there in the living room, rolling cookie crumbs between my fingertips, thinking about the lack of sense in this affair, I heard the key grate in the lock and knew the interloper—the other interloper, actually, since I was an interloper, too—was home.

I had no desire to begin with a confrontation; I preferred first to find out who this person was and what was going on. At the entranceway, at that door about to be opened, there were three choices of movement: One could come straight ahead into the living room. One could turn left into the kitchen. Or one could turn right through a doorway and then left through another doorway into the bedroom. Striding, trying to be silent, I went into the bedroom.

And when I saw the black leather purse on the bed, large, rather shiny, with a short black strap and a big clunky chrome clasp on the top in the shape of a rose, I knew exactly who'd moved in here. Even before she got the door open—still unused to the complexity of city locks—I knew Dale Wormley's mother had taken up residence in his abandoned nest.

She must not see me. She must not find me here. I looked around the room, knowing she would come in here first to hang her coat in the closet—if she then went into the bathroom, I'd have an opportunity to make my escape—which meant I couldn't hide in the closet. Nor in the bathroom. Which meant, God damn it to hell, there was only one choice.

I went under the bed.

Fortunately, it was a king-size bed, so there was room to get all of me underneath it, but it was very low to the floor, so that every time I lifted my head from the carpet I hit the bottom of the box spring. I felt absurd, as though I'd wandered into a very old farce indeed, but this situation was serious and very dangerous. This woman was suing me. She had publicly accused me of killing her son. I could *not* be found in this apartment, wearing a disguise, hiding under the bed. It was impossible even to think about the consequences, and therefore it could not be permitted to happen.

The bed had a skirt, almost to the floor, but under its hem I could look out and see her feet as she came into the bedroom. She crossed first to the closet, as expected, to hang up her coat, but then, instead of going to the bathroom, she went back out the way she'd come in, and a minute later I heard water in the kitchen being run into a kettle.

I didn't dare move. I could only wait, and hope, and feel like the world's prime idiot. What if I'd stood my ground when she'd come in? What if I'd claimed to be an old friend of Julie's, showed the keys Julie had given me? It was too late for that now, but what if I'd done it at the very beginning?

No. In the first place, I hadn't yet realized who was living here when I made my decision to duck into the bedroom. And in the second place, with the lawsuit coming up, it was just too dangerous to actually meet the woman, in disguise, pretending to be somebody else. Whatever credibility I might have in court would vanish, if she ever recognized me.

The kettle boiled. When I heard a voice a minute later, in the living room, I thought at first she'd turned on the television set, but then I realized it must be her own voice, and that she was on the phone.

I squirmed out from under the bed. Tiptoeing, I

crossed to the doorway, and leaned against the wall to listen:

"... another two or three weeks. Julie's still in Florida, avoiding me, you know the way she is—Helen, she was never what you would call warm to me when Dale was alive, and nothing has—Well, that's very forgiving of you. Yes, she probably does feel that way, I don't doubt it. But I am not going to call her, because then it would look as though I was asking *permission* to stay in my own son's apartment, which I am not. Those newspaper people haven't thought to look for me here, so it's been very restful."

Could it be she was embarrassed to be going behind Julie's back this way? Could that be why she sounded so aggressive? In any event, she abruptly changed the subject, apparently at the instigation of Helen, because she suddenly said, "Him! Well, he's disappeared!"

That was me she must be talking about. I leaned closer to the doorway, listening.

"Yes, the detectives are watching his house. Both his houses, you know he has one here, too. But he's just gone, and nobody knows where he is. McCormack says I shouldn't worry, but *I* think he's up to something."

McCormack was her attorney, or one of her attorneys. I remembered the name from those legal papers that had been dumped on me.

I didn't much like Mrs. Wormley's voice. (I couldn't remember her first name; probably blocking it.) It was a hoarse voice, as though it had been used too much, and there were arrogant, impatient, imperial tones in it. Some spoiled brats remain spoiled brats all their lives, and from the sound of her voice I would guess Mrs. Wormley was one of those.

Now she was saying, "McCormack thinks it's possible he'll never even show up in court, just do it all through his lawyers, not even really contest anything."

Don't count on that, I thought.

"No, Helen, it would not. I'd *hate* it. Why, because I want to confront the man, that's why. He thinks he's above it all, doesn't he, wouldn't deign to even *notice* the likes of us. Well, I'm going to rub that man's nose in it, you see if I don't."

I remembered Julie Kaplan's suggestion that suing me had become this woman's vicarious life, to take the place of her previous vicarious life through her son's acting career. It seemed to me, now, listening to her, that Julie had been right but incomplete. Another part of Mrs. Wormley's motivation was just good old-fashioned envy. Spite can make a wonderful fuel.

"Yes," she was saying, "no more than two weeks. Then I'll have to come back for the trial, of course, but God *knows* when that will be. Yes, I will. Be sure to water the plants, now. Yes, I will. Yes, I will. I have to go now, Helen, I'm supposed to call McCormack this morning, I was just out to get the paper. I have no idea, I haven't really looked at it yet, but there hasn't been anything for days now, because there isn't any *news,* you know. When we find Sam Holt, though, and serve the rest of the papers on him, *then* there'll be some news. I bet we make the TV again."

Nasty old bitch, I thought, while Mrs. Wormley slowly wound down her conversation with Helen, repeating things, agreeing to things, adding one more reminder about watering the plants. Why does the nasty old bitch, I thought, have to live her life through *me?* Why doesn't she devote herself to good works?

Become a Gray Lady, join the Peace Corps, go down among the lepers. Maybe she'd catch something.

At last she ended that phone call, and I heard her immediately dial another one. "Mr. McCormack, please. It's Laura Wormley."

Laura; somehow the name seemed inappropriate. She should be a Hannah, or a Bertha. Of course, I still hadn't seen her, but I visualized the kind of battleaxe who used to give W. C. Fields so much trouble. I was so happy with this image that I didn't even want to know the truth.

"Mr. McCormack? Laura Wormley. Did they find him yet?"

Me again.

"Really?" Sounding *very* interested. "Right here in New York? Are they sure?"

I leaned almost through the doorway, listening.

But then, sounding disappointed, she said, "Oh, *them.* I know that kind of paper, they don't know anything, they just make it all up." And I leaned back again.

Then she said, "Do I have to? Well, yes, of course I want to flush him out. Well, it just seems all I do is go to your office and *sign* things, and nothing ever happens." A long put-upon sigh; poor lady. "Well, if I have to, I will. But it takes *forever* to get way over there from here, I'll be lucky to be back in time for lunch." Another sigh; but then, in a steelier voice, she said, "You *know* I'm not losing interest, Mr. McCormack. I told you at the beginning, I'll do whatever it takes. All right. I'll be there as soon as I can."

She cradled the phone, with an exasperated sniff, and I went back under the bed.

# 33

At last the door slammed shut behind her. Then she rattled the knob from outside, to be certain it was locked. And then there was silence.

I waited three or four minutes, lying there, to be sure she hadn't forgotten something that would make her come abruptly back, and then finally, feeling stiff by now—I hadn't been exercising or swimming my laps lately, and it was beginning to tell—I crawled out from under the bed for what I hoped was the last time.

And while I'd been under there, waiting, I'd had another thought, another way of looking at the Kim Peyser murder, induced by my own current experience. One of the questions I'd been asking myself about her murderer was: Why here? Why did he kill Kim Peyser in Dale Wormley's apartment (and Julie Kaplan's)?

And the idea that had now come to me was: What if he were here first, as I had been here first when Mrs. Wormley arrived? What if she had surprised him, as Mrs. Wormley had almost surprised me? And what if, like me, he'd been here because he was searching for something? (Unlike me, he would probably have known what he was searching for.)

Let's look at it from that angle. Let's say the murderer killed Wormley in the first place because Wormley was some sort of threat to him. But with Wormley dead the threat still continued in some way, and the killer had to come here to look for *it,* whatever it was; the thing that continued the threat after Wormley was dead. And while he was here, Kim Peyser came in, and Kim Peyser *knew him.*

The story hung together this way, better than all the theories about Kim Peyser having been killed in error. In the first place, the error theory required him always to be behind her, not seeing her face; and that couldn't be for very long. Now, looking at the layout of this apartment, the only scenario I could come up with that made that idea workable at all would be if the killer had been in the bedroom when Kim Peyser entered the apartment, that he *already had the knife* for some reason, and that when she came into the apartment the first thing she did was turn away from both bedroom and living room and enter the kitchen. That version seemed to me improbable, for a number of reasons.

So let's say he's here to search the place, not to kill anybody, and Kim Peyser walks in, surprising him. There was no sign of struggle before the killing, so she knew the guy. He gave her some reason or excuse for his being here, something that would seem plausible for the moment but would break down later; so she wasn't suspicious right then, but he didn't dare let her leave. One of them, let's say, suggested a cup of coffee. So they went into the kitchen together. He opened drawers, making a show of being unfamiliar with the kitchen, and when he found the knife he simply turned and used it.

The next question, the big question after that, is: Did he then go back to searching the apartment, with Kim Peyser dead in the kitchen, or did he leave, spooked by what had happened? And, in either case, did he find whatever it was he was looking for?

I was making a lot of assumptions here, but it seemed to me these assumptions had a feeling of coherence I hadn't found up till now in all the various ways that had been tried of looking at these two murders. And they seemed to me to be coherent enough to make just one more assumption worth making: That it would probably pay me to search this apartment.

I knew I had time. From the way Mrs. Wormley had talked on the phone, she'd be gone at least an hour, possibly more. So I started in the kitchen, and I gave the place as complete a toss as I could without actual carpentry; that is, without removing molding strips and window frames and such. I did unscrew switchplates and disassemble lamps, but mostly it was a matter of simply moving everything in the apartment, from the largest to the smallest. That's the essence of a search right there; you touch everything, lift everything, move everything, study everything, and at the end you put it all back the way you found it. The work was hot and dusty, and before I was half-finished I was down to socks and shorts; if Mrs. Wormley had come back then, we both would have gotten a hell of a surprise.

And I did find something. Or, that is, I found an anomaly that suggested there had been something to find. The kitchen had contained nothing of interest, and the only oddity in the living room was that one of the audio cassette boxes was empty. It was supposed to contain the original cast recording of the musical *Grease*. I looked in the cassette player, but it wasn't there, so I went on, and in the bedroom I found the *Grease* tape in the top dresser drawer, under Dale Wormley's socks and underwear.

Why? I put the tape back where I'd found it—leave everything where you found it—and thought about that anomaly while finishing my search, coming across nothing else of interest and ending in the bathroom, where I washed and cleaned myself up, and where the medicine chest seemed to have been taken over mostly by Mrs. Wormley's nostrums. (All of the bottles and boxes contained, as best as I could tell, only what they were supposed to.)

When I was finished with everything, and back into my clothes, the tape of *Grease* was the only oddity I'd found. And it seemed to me that putting the tape of *Grease* in that drawer had not been an innocent act. It wasn't a mistake or carelessness, there being no natural reason to have moved the tape from one room to the next in the first place, since it could only be played on the machine in the living room. Which meant it had been hidden there. And the only reason I could think of for hiding that tape was because the box it had come in was being used for something else, and Dale Wormley hadn't wanted to draw attention to the box by leaving its tape lying around.

What had Wormley concealed in that box? Another

tape? Probably so. And if that's what the killer had been looking for, he'd found it.

Which made my new set of assumptions look better than ever.

# 34

**B**efore I left the Wormley apartment I phoned Tom Lacroix, this being the time he'd suggested I do so, and he said both the acting teacher, Howard Moffitt, and Matty Pierce, the guy Dale had fought with in class, had agreed to meet with me at five this afternoon, following the class. Lacroix sounded surprised that Pierce had agreed without having to be urged; he said, "I didn't even have to tell him your speak-ill-of-the-dead-anonymously offer."

"Then I'm really looking forward to what he has to say. Thanks for setting it up."

"No problem."

"Will you be there?"

"Just to introduce you," he said. "Then I have to go to work. I'm a waiter, at the moment."

"Waiting for a show," I said.

"Oh, you know it."

He gave me the address, I promised to see him there at five, and then I left the Wormley apartment at last, and walked across and downtown toward the Graybar Building, since I had a twelve-thirty lunch appointment with Mort Adler.

Myrtie, Mort's receptionist/secretary, didn't recognize me at first and gave me an extremely dubious look when I walked into the office; this wasn't the sort of client she wanted for the firm. "It's okay, Myrtie," I told her, grinning (like myself, not like Ed Dante), "down inside here I'm Sam Holt."

"Oh, my God," she said. "Whatever you've done, undo it."

I promised her the transformation was merely temporary, and she buzzed Mort to tell him I was here, adding, "And you will *not* believe it."

Whether he believed it or not, Mort was certainly amused by it. "Come in, come in," he said, chuckling to himself, looking down at various pieces of baseboard as he reached up to pat me on the shoulder like a basketball coach with a star center who just booted the ball into the stands.

We sat together in his office, and I explained what I was doing and why, feeling only moderately foolish in the telling. He sighed a long sigh when I mentioned hiding under the bed while Mrs. Wormley walked around the Kaplan/Wormley apartment, but he said nothing one way or the other until I was finished, and then he glanced at me briefly from under his eyebrows and said, "Would you care for advice?"

"I think I can imagine the advice," I told him. "It would consist mostly of the word *don't.*"

"Not entirely." Leaning back in his chair, frowning at his desk as though he'd just noticed how sloppy it was, he said, "You do have some background in this sort of thing, of course. And I understand your frustration at the moment. But you see the danger."

"With Mrs. Wormley, you mean."

"Well, that primarily," he agreed, "though not exclusively. But let's take that situation in the apartment, yes. Technically, you had more right to be there than she did, since you had the tenant's keys and the tenant's permission to enter, but the instant you slid under that bed—an instant I would pay a considerable amount to have seen, by the way—you placed yourself irrevocably in the wrong."

"I know I did. The alternative . . ." I shrugged. "The alternative was to introduce myself, as somebody or other, to Mrs. Wormley."

"The alternative," he agreed, "was equally unhappy, *once you were there.* And you can't be certain you won't find yourself in other difficult situations, while this goes on. So now let me get to my advice."

"Sure."

He leaned even farther back, twisting around to look out his window at the air rights over Grand Central, enclosed by gray dull slabs of plate glass and stone. "You have a good working relationship with the police officer who took over the Wormley case," he suggested.

"Sergeant Shanley," I said. "Yes, I do. A lot better than Feeney and LaMarca."

Turning back to me, smiling at his desk drawers, he said, "Of whom we hope to hear no more."

"Amen."

"I strongly urge you, Sam," he said, "to telephone to Sergeant Shanley, meet with her at the earliest opportunity, and tell her precisely what you're doing and what you've already done."

I said, "Ask her okay, you mean?"

"Not at all," he said. "If she's any good, she won't give you an okay. Partly because she shouldn't, and partly because she can't."

"What if she tells me to stop?"

Smiling faintly, Mort shook his head. "Nor can she do that," he told me. "She can tell you not to break the law, of course, but she can't tell you not to go around asking people questions. She can't even tell you not to wear a ridiculous moustache or call yourself by made-up names. What she *can* do is tell you to stay within the law; which of course you will agree to do."

"Of course."

"And then," he said, "if another delicate situation arises, you won't have to crawl under any beds. You can merely stand your ground and announce that the police officer in charge of the Wormley homicide investigation is aware of your activities."

"I see," I said. "It could take the heat off, you mean, in a situation with someone like Mrs. Wormley."

"Not," Mort told me, "if she were to find you lying about under her bed. But certainly it would be a help if she were to find you standing in an ordinary fashion in the living room, Julie Kaplan's keys in your hand."

"All right," I said. "I'll call Sergeant Shanley right after lunch."

"Speaking of which," he said, bracing both hands on the edge of the desk preparatory to rising, then pausing to look up at me with a slightly pained expression and to say, "Is it your intention to wear all that excess hair at lunch?"

"Absolutely," I told him. "From what I heard of Mrs. Wormley's conversation with her lawyer—"

"And *that* went over the line," he pointed out. "Eavesdropping on a conversation between your court adversary and her attorney is absolutely and totally improper."

"I won't do it again," I promised. "But from what I heard the last time, they have private detectives looking for me, here in the city. I really don't want to go anywhere in public as Sam Holt."

"I accept that, unfortunately," he said, and got to his feet, adding, "Not the face I would prefer across the lunch table, but we will survive. After you."

# 35

After lunch, we went back up to Mort's office, where Myrtie told me Gretchen Young had called and wanted me to get back to her at home. So I did, and Gretchen said Blair Knox, Brett's agent, was trying to get in touch with me. Delaying Sergeant Shanley, I called Blair and she came on the line to say, "Well, Kay Henry is definitely interested in you."

"Talent will out," I said.

"Do you think that's true? Anyway, he called this morning to discuss you. He went through that resumé you gave him item by item, wanting to know how you'd handled each part and what sort of reviews you'd got, and how you'd related with the rest of the cast and the director and all that."

"Wow."

Laughing a bit shakily, she said, "I had no idea, Sam, what you were going to put me through."

"Neither did I," I told her. "I'm really sorry, Blair. I thought at the most he'd just call to see what your opinion of Ed Dante was."

"Oh, he wanted that, too," she said. "But he was very interested in the career. I think I held my end up."

"I'm sure you did."

"In any case," she said, "he seemed satisfied when he hung up. But I thought you should know, he's out there, tracking you down."

This investigation better not take much longer, I thought, my little construction is an extremely temporary affair. Living inside a house of cards. "Thanks for the warning," I told Blair, and tried calling Sergeant Shanley, to be told she was out of the office but was expected back within half an hour. I left my name and Mort's number, and then Mort and I retired to his office to discuss the lawsuit against Kwality Food-Marts that had gotten me into all this mess in the first place.

What it came down to at this point was that the lawsuit was going to die of inertia—or perhaps had already died of inertia—and all that was left to discuss was how to bury it. *Court costs* was the name of the game by now; Kwality FoodMarts had no intention of finding another Packard lookalike to do more commercials, the earlier commercials with Dale Wormley had finished their run and would never be seen again in this world, so Kwality had no interest now but to defend their right to have arrogated my appearance and the Packard persona in the first place. If we would accept a consent from them not to offend any more in the future (which they didn't intend to do anyway), with no acknowledgment of wrongdoing on their part in the past, we could all go home and forget about it.

And right here was where the alliance on my side of the issue fell apart. So far as Mort was concerned, it made no economic sense for me to go on paying for a lawsuit on an issue that had become moot. So far as the syndicators who were my co-copyright owners and co-suers were concerned, however, the point here was to make Kwality FoodMarts hurt sufficiently badly that other potential infringers—both of PACKARD and of other shows these syndicators controlled—wouldn't dare take the field against them.

So Mort's principal dealings now were not with Kwality's attorneys but with our own partners' attorneys, with Mort trying to get them to agree to pick up one hundred per cent of continuing costs of the litigation from this stage forward. "If they win," Mort pointed out, "they'll be reimbursed out of the settlement. If they lose, you didn't want to be a party to it anyway, so it's improper for you to share in the burden of expense."

"Whatever you say, Mort," I said.

"That's probably best," Mort said, judiciously, and Myrtie buzzed to say that Sergeant Shanley was on the line.

The sergeant expressed surprise without pleasure at my presence in New York, and when I asked for an appointment she said, "You know, we really don't have anything new. I'm sorry, but that's the way it is."

"That's all right," I said. "I do."

Startled, she said, "New information?"

"No," I said. "New activity. *My* activity. Do you have time to see me this afternoon?"

"I think I'd better make time," she said.

# 36

I walked over to Midtown Precinct South on West 35th Street, and announced myself to the officer at the desk. He gave me a skeptical look, but phoned Sergeant Shanley and she came right out. When she saw me in my Ed Dante fig she sighed and nodded and said, "Uh huh. You've got things to tell me, all right."

She led me back to a small impersonal office with plain bare walls and a gray metal desk holding nothing but a telephone. There were a couple of slat-backed wooden chairs as well, as uncomfortable as they looked, and there we sat, Sergeant Shanley leaning her elbows on the desk while I described my reaction to Mrs. Wormley's civil suit and the lack of progress on the murder investigation. Nodding, she said, "You know how it is yourself, Mr. Holt. When there's no one else to interview, no more physical evidence to study, no informants to come forward, you can only wait for something to happen."

"A civil case," I said, "doesn't have to find me guilty beyond a reasonable doubt."

"I know that, too," she said. "I think it's very rough, and very unfair, what's happening to you, but there really isn't anything we can do about it. And to tell the truth, I see Mrs. Wormley's side, too. She's just as frustrated about this thing as you are. And she's more personally involved."

"Not any more. Not if I'm going to go into civil court and not only be branded a murderer but a murderer who *got away with it.*"

She thought about that. "Yeah, I guess so," she decided. "Celebrity can make it a little rougher, can't it?"

"It can. Sergeant Shanley," I said, leaning toward her, "I'm not some jerk coming in here trying to do your job better than you. I'm *involved,* and I can't just sit on the sidelines and wait for the steamroller to drive on over me."

"So you've come to town to try to see what you can learn," she said. Then she grinned faintly and gestured at my head, saying, "And you're wearing the caterpillar and the rug so you won't be recognized."

"I feel pretty foolish about it," I admitted. "But if I go around as Sam Holt I *really* won't get anywhere, except to make things worse."

She nodded. "Have you actually made any contacts yet? Got up like this?"

"Yes," I said. "In fact, the reason I wanted to talk to

you is to tell you what I've done so far, and what I plan to do. Because, frankly, it does get kind of tricky sometimes."

"I guess it might," she agreed. "Okay, Mr. Holt, tell me what you've done."

So I told her what I'd done, and she nodded, listening, not interrupting; though her eyes did widen a bit when I went under the bed in the Kaplan/Wormley apartment. When I finished, she said, "Well, you're a lucky man."

"So far."

"I'm glad you realize that," she said. "Mr. Holt, from what you've told me, it seems to me you've pretty well established that you can't do yourself any good at all, but you *can* make a lot of trouble for yourself. You're very lucky you haven't fallen into that trouble already."

"I know I am."

"But what are you gonna *gain?*" she wanted to know.

"Well, I'll tell you what I've gained so far," I answered. "The physical layout of the Kaplan/Wormley apartment tells me the Kim Peyser murder wasn't mistaken identity. The killer had to know who he was stabbing."

She nodded. "We'd about come to the same conclusion ourselves."

"And," I said, "that means the killer and Kim Peyser knew each other, or there would have been some sign of struggle prior to the stabbing."

"Which lets you out, of course."

But there I had to shake my head and tell her, "Well, no, it doesn't. Part of the up side of being a celebrity is that people think they *do* know you. If I'd been the person in there when Kim Peyser walked in, she would have known who I was even though we'd never met, and I could have rattled off some song and dance to keep her calm while I reached for the knife."

Shanley sat back in her chair, folded her arms, and grinned at me. "I should have thought of that myself," she acknowledged. "Here I went and took you off the list, and now look."

"Well, you needn't put me back on the list."

"I wasn't going to," she assured me. "What else have you learned? Anything?"

"The missing tape."

She frowned, unfolding her arms and resting her hands on her knees. "Now, that," she said, "is a leap, if you don't mind my saying so. You find an empty tape box in with the rest of the cassette tapes. Then you find the tape that belongs in it, only it's in the other room."

"Hidden," I pointed out, "or at least buried, under clothing in a dresser drawer."

"And you jump to the conclusion," she said, "that some sort of tape—a *different* tape—had been kept in that tape box, that the killer was in the apartment looking for that different tape when Kim Peyser came in, and that after he killed her he found the tape and took it away." She shook her head. "That's a whole *bunch* of conclusions to jump to."

"And that isn't even all of them," I told her. "I'm jumping to more conclusions than that. But first, what other explanation is there? You don't just accidentally put a tape in the back of a drawer *under* all the clothing, and in fact you don't even carry that tape without its box into the bedroom in the first place, because there's nothing you can do with it in there *except* hide it."

"That isn't absolutely necessarily true," she told me,

"but all right, I'll go along with you this far: It *looks* as though the tape was carried into the bedroom and hidden on purpose."

"And the box, in its place in the living room, was empty," I added.

She nodded. "So, *if* the box was being used to hide something else, and *if* the killer was looking for that something else, then *probably* he found it and took it away with him. A lot of ifs."

"But they make sense," I insisted. "And what would that something else be? The something else that was hidden in the tape box." I spread my hands, suggesting the answer was obvious. "Those tape boxes are small, and they have two little plastic projections in them that the tape fits over. You might be able to put two or three cigarettes in one of those boxes, or maybe a folded note, but it seems to me if you're going to hide something in a tape box, what you're probably going to hide in there is another tape."

"And here comes the big final jump to a conclusion," she said. "Am I right?"

"You can see where I'm going."

"Sure," she said. "But tell me anyway."

"The motive for killing Dale Wormley was blackmail," I said. "And the hidden tape was the evidence."

She nodded, but dubiously, and then she said, "Mr. Holt, you make a very neat package there, and that's what I don't like about it."

"The neatness?"

"That's right. I've seen this kind of thing happen a lot," she told me. "I've seen it happen in this building. A fella gets a theory about a case, all the evidence he has so far dovetails in nice and neat, and the fella decides that *is* what happened. Then, when some other evidence comes along that doesn't fit into that package so neatly, the fella refuses to see it, refuses to admit that evidence even exists. Your kind of package there, it isn't a way to close a case so much as it's a way to close a mind."

"I'll remember that," I said, impressed by her. "You may be right, and I thank you for saying it."

She grinned: "But you still like your theory."

"Oh, I *like* it, but not enough to make a fool out of myself," I assured her. "Not if I can help it. I really do appreciate the warning, Sergeant. I still think the hidden tape is meaningful, but I'll remember that I can't be *sure* about it, not yet."

"That'll do," she said, and got to her feet. The interview was over. "I can't tell you to stop what you're doing," she admitted, as I also stood up, "but I *can* tell you, if anybody makes a complaint against you, don't hope for any help from over here. The department doesn't like free-lancers. If they get a chance, they'll land on you with both feet."

"I'll be careful," I promised.

"More careful than you've been," she suggested.

# 37

**M**atty Pierce, the acting student who'd had the fistfight with Dale Wormley, had that indefinable look of the actor who plays tough guys. It's all layers of pose and posture, veneer over veneer, with no apparent reality beneath at all. These guys, with thick gleaming black hair, chunky bodies, overly bright eyes as though they'd had a plastic surgery eye-tuck at the age of ten, cocky smile, slightly lumpy "rugged" good looks, are palpably different from actual street toughs. There's no anger in them, for one thing (though there is arrogance), and none of the defensiveness of the real punk. These are guys who've never had their bluff called. They get a lot of work in teen movies, riding motorcycles.

Tom Lacroix introduced me to Pierce and to Howard

Moffitt, their acting teacher, at five that afternoon in
the narrow old building on Bethune Street in the West
Village—not far from Anita and Vitto Impero—where
Moffitt's class and theater were located. Moffitt, a
stooped and craggy tall man of about sixty, reminded
me of three or four other acting teachers I've met in my
career, people who are theoretically fine actors, who
not only know how it's done but—much rarer—know
how to communicate their knowledge, but nevertheless
their credits in actual performances and productions
are amazingly skimpy. Whenever one of these people
takes a small part in a movie or a play, talked into it by
some old student who's made good, you see what the
problem is: There they are, in the corner of the screen
or the stage, *acting*. You can see them do it. Their
strength as teachers is their weakness as performers:
they don't know how to not show you how it's done.

Moffitt's building was very narrow, probably twenty
feet, and three stories high, wedged in among other
quaint nineteenth-century brick townhouses, most of
them now broken up into tiny apartments, a few
converted to nursery schools or doctors' and dentists'
offices. The ground floor of Moffitt's place, behind a
broad wooden garage door painted brown and apparently non-functional, had been turned into a small
theater, with sixty or seventy seats—whatever maxi-
mum number would permit non-union productions in
here—and the most basic lighting and backstage area.
Minimalist experimental theater was the only kind
possible here.

One entered the building through a small ornate door
next to the garage door. A tiny box office and doorway
on the right led to the theater, and a warped steep
staircase straight ahead led up to the acting studio and

theater's storage rooms and male and female restrooms on the second floor. Moffitt's living quarters were one more flight up, at the top.

We met on the second floor, in the studio classroom at the rear of the building. The room was nearly square, the width of the building, with two tall broad windows facing back yards filled with starkly leafless plane trees. The floor was well-oiled old broad planks, one side wall was brick and the other mirrored with black curtains drawn in front of the mirrors, and the furniture consisted of about fifteen metal folding chairs or wooden kitchen chairs, plus three battered wooden tables of various sizes. The front wall, opposite the view, contained a closed door and a large green blackboard on which the word MOTIVATION had been incompletely erased.

Tom Lacroix, anxiously looking at his watch, made the introductions and then went ka-drumming down the stairs, on the way to his waiter job. He'd already given both Pierce and Moffitt a rundown on my alleged background and interest here—the article for *Vanity Fair* about the interface between success and failure, with the peg of Dale Wormley as having been somehow midway between the two—so I could go straight into it, saying to Pierce, "I understand you and Wormley had a disagreement a while ago."

He did the aggressive grin of his style of actor and said, "We had a disagreement every time we looked at each other. You're not gonna put that in *Vanity Fair*."

"No, I'm not," I agreed. "I just want to get the background here, so I can be sure what *does* go into the piece is accurate. This is the part of the iceberg that stays underwater."

Moffitt nodded judiciously, as though thinking of

giving me a good mark, and said, "We work the same way in the theater. I tell my students, if all you know about the character is what you're going to show the audience, you aren't ready to take that part out on stage."

Pierce, concentrating on me rather than acting lessons at the moment, said, "But I'll be *in* the piece, right?"

"I'm not even sure," I told him, not wanting to go so far as to promise an actor publicity in a non-existent article. "I'm just trying to get a handle on the subject matter at this point," I explained.

He was wearing, naturally, a black leather jacket with many zippers, and now, from inside it, he drew a manila envelope and handed it to me, saying, "Just in case, here's my resumé."

"Fine." Feeling awkward, but having to go through with the pretense, I put the folder away in my raincoat pocket and said, "Just what was it about Dale Wormley that rubbed you the wrong way?"

He shook his head, with a twisted grin; then, to emphasize the negative, he lifted a hand and shook his upraised thumb back and forth, as though telling me the bridge was out. "The other way around," he said. "Dale was pissed off *all* the time. The way you got along with that guy was to back down. I'm not into backing down."

"Why was he so angry?" I asked. "Because of his career?"

"I never cared enough to ask," Pierce said, and hooked his thumbs into his jeans pockets, and sat there looking tough.

Moffitt interjected, "Matty's right about that. Dale *was* angry all the time. I think it was a true personality

trait, not anything specific that happened or that anyone did to him."

"He was a big guy," Pierce said. "Like you. So he
figured he could get away with stuff."

"Be a bully, you mean," I suggested, and Pierce
shrugged. He probably was thinking it would sound
sissy of him to accuse someone else of being a bully.

Moffitt said, "I've often wondered if that kind of
aggressive hostile drive isn't somehow an asset for
somebody trying to succeed in a competitive field like
acting. I suppose, Mr. Dante, you'll be getting into that
in your piece."

"Yes, I will," I agreed. "But what I'm interested in at
this point is the background on Wormley himself, his
relationships with the people around him." Turning
back to Pierce, I said, "Tom Lacroix kind of led me to
believe there was a particular feud between you and
Wormley, but you say he acted toward you the way he
acted toward everybody, and it was just your refusal to
be a doormat that made for any special problem
between you."

"Damn right," Pierce said. "I know a couple people
—you know them, too, Howard—that would just roll
over and play dead if Wormley gave them a look. So
*there* there's no problem, right?"

"Resentment, though, I should think," I said.

"Well, yeah," Pierce said, "a couple people were
always talking big, they're gonna do this, gonna do that,
but they *weren't,* you know?"

"Anyone I ought to talk to?" I asked. "I mean,
anybody in par—"

Moffitt, smoothly interrupting, said, "Matty, get the
playbook, will you? Let's take a look at the casts Dale
worked with. You know where it is?"

Rising, looking a bit confused, Pierce said, "Sure. I don't know what you need it for. It's in one of those drawers under the lightboard, right?"

"That's right," Moffitt agreed. "I think Mr. Dante should get a sense of the ambience here, the kind of group Dale was interacting with."

"Okay," Pierce said, shrugging. He went away downstairs, his feet thumping more deliberately and heavily than Lacroix's had, and Moffitt turned to me, smiling amiably as he said, "I'd say you have about one minute, Mr. Holt, to tell me why I shouldn't tell Matty who you really are."

# 38

**W**hich meant I had about one second to decide on a response. When time is tight, there's always the truth: "Wormley's mother," I said, "is suing me in civil court for violation of her son's civil rights by killing him. I'll get less of a fair shake in civil court than in criminal court. The official murder investigation is absolutely inactive. I just met this afternoon with the detective on the case, and there's nothing doing there."

Moffitt frowned at me. "So you're trying to put the blame on Matty?"

"I'm trying to find out where the blame *goes,"* I told him. "Somebody killed Wormley, and I know it wasn't me. So who was it?"

Pierce was coming back up the stairs. Moffitt glanced

in that direction, then said to me, "Matty didn't do it, I can tell you that much."

"And the others in the class? The resentful ones?"

"Follow my lead," he said, and Pierce arrived, carrying a large black looseleaf notebook.

The next ten minutes were very strange. Moffitt and I were running a scene together, an acting exercise, for an audience of one: Pierce. Our prop was the notebook, a record of all productions and extended scenes done by Moffitt's classes in the last two and a half years. The scene we were playing was *Interview,* with Moffitt both performing and directing, and Pierce both audience and unwitting cast member. Because all I had to do now was follow Moffitt's lead and play my part, because I didn't have to warp my questions to suit a secret agenda, I actually gave a better performance than before, and was almost sorry to see it end.

Almost. On the other hand, when Moffitt moved us into end game I went along with a real sense of relief; if Matty Pierce had seen through what was happening here, there would have been another fistfight in Moffitt's acting studio, no question.

But finally Moffitt said, "Matty, I know you have to get to work, and I'd like to discuss this theme of Mr. Dante's from my point of view. For a teacher in this profession, his ideas might be very interesting." With an innocent gaze in my direction, he added, "If you have time?"

"Sure," I said. "The more I learn, the better."

"That's undoubtedly true," Moffitt agreed.

Pierce had been growing increasingly restless, in fact, as the conversation had moved farther away from himself, and was very happy to leave. "Don't lose the picture and resumé, now," he told me, shaking my hand, squeezing harder than necessary. "You'll be able to say you knew me when."

"I'm looking forward to it," I told him.

Pierce went hammering back down the stairs, and Moffitt and I waited till we heard the front door slam behind him. Then Moffitt smiled at me and said, "Please excuse my stretching that. I admit it was an elitist impulse."

"It was?"

"I don't expect a television actor to have much by way of technique," he explained.

Was he trying to get a rise out of me, push me off-balance a bit and see what happened? I said, "Acting is acting, isn't it?"

"Oh, absolutely not," he said, eyes widening; I'd touched on some bugbear of his, obviously. But then he waved the matter away, saying, "In any event, it was pleasant to have my prejudices confounded. What are you working at these days?"

"I'm between jobs," I said, that being the standard face-saving answer from an actor who isn't working at anything at the moment.

I expected Moffitt to recognize that and respect it, and he did, with a faint smile, saying, "You should work. Exercises can only go so far."

"If that civil court endorses the idea I'm an unconvicted murderer," I said, "I'll never work again."

He raised a surprised eyebrow: "Not even as the notorious Sam Holt? Wouldn't there be some publicity value in that?"

I shuddered. "That would be worse."

"All of my prejudices are in ruins," he said.

Looking at his ascetic and satisfied face, I decided I didn't have to like him. "Not all, I think," I said.

Surprised, he laughed and said, "My God, I'm still responding to your Mr. Dante, who wasn't that intelligent. All right, Mr. Holt, forgive me. Let's get down to cases. The fact is, whatever it was in Dale's life that led someone to kill him, it would not have derived from this class, or the people he dealt with here."

I said, "Are you sure you aren't just defending your turf?"

"Oh, yes," he said. "You see, the *raison d'être* of this class is its artificiality, its separation from real life. I have had my successes, Mr. Holt; there are former students of mine who have gone on to some fame and accomplishment in this profession."

"I'm aware of that."

"But they, I must admit, are the exceptions," he went on, and shrugged, saying, "Which must be true, in any of the arts. The students come, they learn what they can about the art and about themselves, and then they go on, into the world, toward the narrow end of the funnel. Very few will make it, which most of them know. But it's impossible ahead of time to be sure which ones will succeed. So they all, when they come here, have the *potential,* but that's all. In their real lives, they work as waiters or carpenters or cabdrivers or receptionists or sales clerks. *Here,* they are stars in embryo. A great deal of passion is released in our classes, passion being, as you know, one of the tools of our trade. But none of them would carry that passion home, would mingle *this* world with the world of driving a taxi. Sometimes romances start in here, particularly after we do intense love scenes—" he smiled, and shook his head "—but they never last. Never. The passion in here never survives in the air outside."

Was that true? Moffitt, it seemed to me, was suggesting some sort of romantic Shangri-La specialness about this building, his class, himself; but wasn't what he was describing actually the kind of office politics that exists everywhere that people work closely together with some element of competition in it?

On the other hand, what he was claiming for his class was certainly true of office politics. No matter how mad somebody makes you at work, you don't spend your time being mad at that person on your day off. So I nodded, and got to my feet, and said, "Okay, Mr. Moffitt, point taken. Unless I find something else, while I'm rooting around, I'll think of all this as a dead end."

"That's what it is," he assured me.

We walked toward the head of the stairs together, and I said, "Thank you for not just simply exposing me to Pierce. He probably wouldn't have been amused."

"Not very," Moffitt agreed, with a smile. Then he said, "Shall I take that resumé of Matty's off your hands? You don't actually have a purpose for it, do you?"

"No, I don't." Giving it to him, I said, "You're the first person who's seen through me. What did it?"

"This is what I *teach,* Mr. Holt," he said, as though the answer were obvious. "I spend half my life evaluating performances. You did the *part* well enough, the stooped head to distract from your height, the insecure smile, the vague hand gestures, but the dialogue was off."

"That's been a problem all along," I agreed.

"You just weren't asking the right questions," he

said. "You weren't interested in the right subjects. When I began to sense there was something wrong, I suggested a topic that you'd *have* to be interested in, if you were actually who you claimed, and you refused to be detoured away from what you really wanted to know."

"I noticed you do that," I said.

"Then I looked you over more carefully," he told me, "and I saw the hair was wrong. And that moustache is pasted on, isn't it?"

"It is."

"It's excellent," Moffitt said, "but the hair somehow doesn't match your head, not well enough. I don't know how to explain it better than that, it's very subtle."

"It's passed till now."

"I'm sure it has," Moffitt agreed, "but I think I'm the first person who began to doubt you and *then* began to study you. And then, when I realized you were in disguise, I knew that had to mean it was because we would recognize you in your own self, and of course *that* meant you had to be the celebrity connected with poor Dale's death. Then I could see it was you."

"You gave me a bad moment," I said, "I have to admit that."

"If you don't mind," he said, "I'd like to make up for it with some good advice. May I?"

"Acting advice?"

"Of course," he said. "And the advice is, don't be in too much of a hurry to ask your real questions. Match the dialogue to the part. Be patient, take an interest in things you're not really interested in. Everything you want to know will come out eventually."

"Will it?"

"If you're very good," he said.

# 39

That evening, I was more discouraged than I realized. I knew I didn't feel like discussing my day, but I hadn't been aware just how silent and withdrawn I'd become until, after dinner with the Young family, Terry turned to me in the living room and abruptly said, "Well, Sam? Gonna quit?"

I blinked at him. The remark uncomfortably paralleled my own thoughts, except that instead of thinking of myself as on the verge of quitting I'd seen it the other way; the leads and trails had petered out, had quit me. What was I going to do tomorrow, what string should I follow? There was none that I could see. But I answered Terry's question by saying, "I can't quit. Not if there's anything left to do."

"And if there's nothing left to do?"

I put my hand up to rub my brow—still itchy from the wig I'd been wearing all day—as Gretchen came into the living room, having dealt with bedtime for the kids. Frowning from Terry to me, she said, "How can there be nothing left to do? Someone killed that man, didn't they?"

"And the girl," I said.

"Then they can't just disappear," Gretchen insisted, sitting on the sofa beside Terry and looking at me with concern. "There has to be a reason, after all. And you have to be able to find that reason."

"You'd think so," I said.

Terry said, "All right, now, wait a minute. Are you telling us *nothing* happened today? I thought you had people to see, an apartment to toss. You got nothing out of all that at all?"

"Not enough," I said.

"It's time for the actor," Terry decided, "to turn this over to a pro, somebody who knows what he's doing."

"The police," I said, "are as stymied as I am. I talked to them today."

"I don't mean the police," he said. "I mean me. A reporter. Somebody who knows evidence when he falls over it."

"Well, I wish you'd fall over some on my account," I said.

"Let's try." He settled more comfortably on the couch and said, "When we parted this morning, you were on your way to Wormley's apartment. Tell me about it."

So I told them about it, and about Mrs. Wormley, and about my meeting with Mort, and my meeting with Sergeant Shanley, and the oddball encounter with Pierce and Moffitt, and at the end Terry said, "I don't see anything in that acting class. I think Moffitt was right about that."

"So do I."

"So you don't exactly forget that scene," he said, "but you set it to one side. You also think about Mrs. Wormley."

I frowned at him. *"What* do I think about Mrs. Wormley?"

"Whether or not she had a motive."

"To kill her *son?"*

"It has happened, in this old world, once or twice," Terry assured me. "In fact, more people are killed by family and friends than by strangers."

"But— What reason would she have?"

"I asked you first," he said.

Gretchen said, "Would it be so she could sue you?"

Terry answered her, shaking his head, saying, "Too long range. Too many factors would have to fall out just right. I was thinking maybe she felt neglected, or maybe money was tight and she took out an insurance policy on him, something like that."

I said, "The chief characteristic of Mrs. Wormley that I've been able to learn is that she lived her life through her son, that his career was the most important thing in her life."

"That could change," Terry said, unruffled, "but okay. We'll set her aside, too, along with the acting class. Actually, what I most like is that missing audiotape."

"You mean, my blackmail theory?"

"Yes. It gives us a motive for murder beyond this general one that Wormley was a pain in the ass."

I said, "But that's a trail that just leads out into the blue. I don't know who was being blackmailed, or what the subject was. Or, you know, remembering what Sergeant Shanley said, I can't be really absolutely sure anybody was being blackmailed at all."

"I tell you what we'll do," Terry said. "Tomorrow morning, come on in to the office with me. We'll put the computer to work on it."

"How do we go about doing that?"

"If Wormley was blackmailing somebody," he said, "it had to be somebody he knew, right?"

"Right."

"And you have a pretty good list of the people he knew, including those cast lists from the acting class."

"That's right."

"So tomorrow," Terry said, "we'll run names through the computer, see if anybody has done anything newsworthy. Maybe the subject of the blackmail has already had some sort of public airing."

I frowned. "Like what? I don't see where you're going."

"Well," he said, "like, what if the place wherever Matty Pierce works was robbed six months ago and it might have been an inside job?"

I was dubious, and saw no reason to hide it. "Do you really think we're going to get anywhere that way? Isn't that just spinning our wheels?"

Gretchen said, "Terry's a bulldog, Sam, that's why he's so good at his job."

Grinning, patting Gretchen's thigh, Terry said, "That's how I finally wore *you* down."

"Yes, you did," she agreed, and said to me, "Terry knows how to just keep worrying at things. When you think there's nothing more you can possibly do, he thinks of six things."

"One will do," I said.

# 40

**T**erry doesn't have his own office at the *News,* but his space in the large main editorial room has a wall on his right, the back of a tall broad bookcase separating him from the aisle ahead of him, and a large two-sided cork bulletin board on wheels between his area and the desk of the guy behind him. To his left is editorial, loud and busy and seething with motion; but he likes that atmosphere, he enjoys the idea that it's getting into his prose.

Terry's space, besides his desk, contains a square metal wastebasket and two chairs. The wall and bulletin board and bookcase are covered with taped-up headlines, photos, cartoons, election buttons, correspondence, and all sorts of miscellaneous junk, in some places two and three levels deep. On the desk are his manual portable typewriter, on which he still writes first drafts, as well as the screen and keyboard to his computer terminal. If he feels like printing something out, the printer—shared by several other people—is on a table about thirty feet away.

We arrived a little before ten in the morning, carrying coffee from a deli downstairs. Terry exchanged words with a few other people, I did my gawky Ed Dante number (being back in the wig and moustache), and then he settled himself down at his desk and I produced my list of names. Terry switched on the computer, and began to ask questions.

We'd decided to be completists, and to go through everybody we knew Wormley knew, no matter how remote the connection. The writer and director and agency producer of the Kwality FoodMarts commercials, for instance, and Miss Colinville the receptionist from Kay Henry's office, and all of Wormley's fellow students at Howard Moffitt's class. Even so, I knew our net might not be cast widely enough. What if the killer were someone who'd been mad at Wormley since high school, and had finally caught up? Only my conviction that Kim Peyser had to have known the killer—or she wouldn't have let herself be killed so easily—kept me from fretting those possibilities too much.

Running the names through the computer took forever, and the first time through we didn't come up with anything at all that seemed useful. But then Terry said, "Let's try it the other way around. Let's see if Wormley himself was ever newsworthy, before his obit." And he tapped in the green letters DALE WORMLEY, and up came the morgue on that name: every mention in a review, every story about his murder, and then the notation: "Hanford Montgomery, with wife at time of suicide."

"Ho ho," Terry said. "What have we here?"

"We've seen that name before," I said. "Going through here, connected with somebody else. Hanford Montgomery."

So Terry brought up that name, and it turned out Hanford Montgomery was a wealthy architect from a rich New England banking family. He'd gotten ink several times for important governmental commissions his firm had received, and a couple of times for industry awards, and then once, nearly three months ago, on September 16th, when he'd shot himself dead at his weekend house near Short Hills, New Jersey; a very wealthy and socially significant neighborhood. Friends were quoted as saying Montgomery had been depressed about his health for some time. But the kicker was Hanford Montgomery's wife.

Rita Colby.

It was the third marriage for her, second for him. They'd been married four years. At the time of her husband's suicide, theater and film star Rita Colby had been attending the annual Theater Project scholarship fund banquet at the Waldorf-Astoria. Her escort had been the rising New York actor Dale Wormley.

"There it is," Terry said. "This is the thing you've been looking for."

I looked over his shoulder at the green letters on the black background. "It is, isn't it? September 16th; just after that is when Wormley told Julie Kaplan that good things were going to start happening for him."

"And Rita Colby," Terry added, "insisted on hiring the guy for her next play."

"You know," I said, "I've been to that Theater Project dinner, and it's just a mob scene, one of those places where everybody goes just to stay in touch with everybody else. A *long* cocktail party first, and then when you go on into the banquet room everybody tablehops all the way through dinner. Nobody can ever know for sure who's where when."

"Let's get all of this," Terry said, and hit the button to print out Hanford Montgomery's obit and the brief news item on his suicide and the somewhat longer entertainment page piece on the Theater Project banquet. He went away to the printer, came back with the sheets of paper, and handed them to me. "You're on your way," he said.

# 41

**B**ut was I? And if so, where to? I was as convinced as Terry that this was the thread I was looking for, but I wasn't one hundred per cent sure where that thread was supposed to lead me.

Was Rita Colby the killer? Did she have the strength to beat Dale Wormley to death with a piece of wood and then drag his body down the block and up a stoop and into a vestibule? I just had trouble imagining it.

On the other hand, I could see her having the coolness to dispatch Kim Peyser, and of course it was possible she'd murdered her husband and arranged it to look like suicide and then quickly called on a fellow Kay Henry client to accompany her to the banquet; no one there would know at exactly what time anybody had arrived.

Then, knowing just what crime he'd been the beard for, Wormley would have demanded the kind of payment in return that Rita Colby could provide; a boost for his career. But he'd gone too far, he'd pushed too hard, as of course he would have done, being who he was.

Had he wanted Rita Colby to sleep with the help? She would have refused, I could tell that much from our one meeting. And this would explain why she'd appeared to be so close with Wormley but had stayed so coldly distant from Ed Dante.

Terry and I talked this over, he wanting me to take these newspaper clippings to Sergeant Shanley, but me convinced it wasn't going to be enough to get the investigation active again. "I feel as though I should talk with Rita Colby," I said, "because something in here doesn't quite fit, which is what Shanley warned me about. But I don't know how to get in touch with her. I doubt Kay Henry would give me her phone number."

"Then why not look it up in the book?" Terry asked me, reaching for the stack of phone books on the corner of his desk, over against the wall.

"Are you kidding?" I asked him. "Rita Colby isn't going to be listed in the phone book."

Pulling the Manhattan directory out of the pile, opening it on top of his terminal keyboard, Terry said, "You'd be surprised who's in the phone book. If you know how to look." And, as he said that last, he was reaching for his pencil and small square pad of notepaper. "No reason for Hanford Montgomery not to list himself," he said.

"He's there?" I was astonished.

"Montgomery, H. Architect. East 58th Street, over by the river. Sound about right?"

A wealthy neighborhood. "Sounds perfect," I said.

He scribbled the address and number, tore off that sheet of the notepad, and handed it to me, saying, "Let Ed Dante give her a call. The worst thing she can do is tell him to go fuck himself."

"I can't think of anything else she might do, but I'll give it a try," I said, and reached for the phone on Terry's desk, but it rang just as I was about to touch it. So I pulled my hand back, and Terry answered, with a brisk, "Young." Then he smiled and said, "Hi, baby," so it was Gretchen. And then he nodded and said, "Yeah, he's here. Hold on." Extending the phone toward me, he said, "A message."

"For Dante?" I took the phone: "Hi, Gretchen."

"Your new agent called," Gretchen's voice said. "Kay Henry. He wants you to call him, some time today."

"Will do," I said. "Thanks, Gretchen." I hung up, and took from my wallet the slip of paper with Henry's number on it while explaining the message to Terry, saying, "I'll call him first, then try Colby."

Grinning, Terry said, "Maybe he's got you a job."

"More than my regular agent's doing," I said, punched out the number, and recognized the British accent of Miss Colinville when she answered. With my toothiest grin, I said, "Hi, honey, this is Ed Dante." (Terry gave me a repelled look.)

"Oh, is it," said that icy voice.

"Kay called me," I told her, knowing Ed Dante would presume to be on a first-name basis with her boss, and knowing also that Miss Colinville would hate that. "I'm calling him back," I explained, "but I could sit and talk with *you* all day."

"*One* moment," she said, and made a very loud

clicking sound in my ear, and then left me on Hold for a good long time as a punishment. I gave one of Ed Dante's goofiest grins to Terry, who tried to look disgusted but then just gave up and laughed.

Another click, less ear-jarring, and Kay Henry's voice said, "Ed?"

"*Hi,* Mr. Henry," I said, because only with the receptionist would Dante dare to call Henry by his first name.

"Morning, Ed," said his cheerful confiding voice. "Did they find your luggage yet?"

"Not yet," I told him. "I called Eastern this morning, they said maybe tomorrow. You know the way they are."

"Well, we'll struggle along. I don't suppose you've heard of the O. Henry Theater."

"No, I haven't."

"It's still under construction, down in the Village," he said. "They're opening with a limited run over the holidays, and I've talked to them about you for one of the parts. It's only three weeks, and scale, but it gets you back to work and still leaves you free for *Four Square,* if that should happen."

And makes it possible to be certain Ed Dante's really off the sauce, I thought. I said, "Thanks a lot, Mr. Henry, that sounds just perfect."

"I thought so, too," he agreed, "but it's up to you to make them want you."

"Oh, I know that."

"You're scheduled at six-thirty," he told me, "at the theater, the O. Henry Theater on Charles Street. You'll recognize it, it's a construction site, an old storage building going condo. You'll see Mr. Cardiff, he's the house manager."

I scribbled the information on another sheet of Terry's notepad, thanked Henry some more, with great effusiveness, and at last hung up, to face Terry's sardonic smile. "The first step to stardom," he said.

"Well, I've been looking for a job."

"Will you go?"

"I guess I'll have to," I said. "I mean, if this charade is still going on then; which I hope it isn't. But if it is, I'll want to keep my access to Kay Henry alive."

"And to Rita Colby through him," Terry suggested.

"Let's see if she's home," I said, and reached for the phone, which did not ring, so I picked it up and tapped in Rita Colby's number, and it was answered on the third ring by someone who sounded so like Miss Colinville I thought for one confused instant I'd called the wrong number. "Good morning," she said, and when my bewilderment kept me silent for an extra second she said, more emphatically, *"Good* morning."

"Oh, good morning," I said, realizing this had to be another secretary; Rita Colby's, if I'd dialed right. "Rita Colby, please."

"May I tell Miss Colby who's calling?"

"Ed Dante," I said.

*"One* moment," she said, exactly like Miss Colinville, and put me on Hold, exactly like Miss Colinville, but without the extra-loud click. Terry watched me, and I waited, and the *ur*-Miss Colinville came back to say, "Miss Colby would like to know the subject of the call."

"Tell her," I said, "the Theater Project banquet last September."

*"One* moment."

Terry said, "Playing hardball, aren't you?"

"Well, what am I going to say I want to talk to her

about? Acting methods? We aren't buddies, Terry, I can't just be making a social call. So let's shake the tree, and see what happens."

"Don't stand under it," he advised.

I nodded, and heard a click, and the secretary's voice came back, saying, "Miss Colby thanks you for your interest, but has nothing to say on that subject. Thank you."

I opened my mouth, but the click came first, and then dead air. So I hung up, saying, "And so much for that."

"So," Terry said, "now she knows you know."

I frowned at him. "That's the problem," I said. "She knows I know *what?*"

He laughed; more heartily than I thought necessary. "Too bad you can't ask her," he said.

# 42

**T**erry volunteered to look further into the Montgomery/Colby marriage, see if anybody on the gossip side of the news business had anything juicy to add substance to our story. I phoned Sergeant Shanley, but she wouldn't be available till mid-afternoon, so I called Anita and arranged to spend some time with her. Then I finally left Terry to get on with the work he was paid for, and I walked across town and downtown into the West Village, thinking that what I'd found—if in fact I'd found anything at all—wasn't the simple solution I'd been looking for but a brand new complication; not the end of something, but more like the beginning.

I got to Vitto Impero a little too early for lunch, so Anita and I spent some time upstairs in her apartment over the restaurant, and I gave her a recap of my adventures in the last two days, since we'd been together down in Brooklyn at the Youngs' house. When I finished, she said, "I don't see why you made that phone call to Rita Colby."

"Well," I said, "the idea that the death of her husband has something to do with the death of Dale Wormley makes a kind of sense, but there's great gaps in it. It's a brand new idea and I wanted to be able to talk about it, think about it. I just wanted the chance to have a conversation with Rita Colby and see what happened. But then, when the secretary asked me what my subject was, I drew a blank. All I could think was, okay, let's drop a depth charge and see what happens."

"What happens is," Anita told me, "Rita Colby now knows you aren't just the simple ignorant actor you said you were. If she's guilty, she knows you're on the trail. You gave *her* information, and didn't get anything back."

"Well, I did get something back," I said. "If there was nothing at all in the idea that there was something wrong with the story, if Rita Colby and Dale Wormley were just innocently at that banquet together when just coincidentally her husband was killing himself an hour's drive away in New Jersey, why wouldn't she have come to the phone, even if just to ask me what I'm talking about? The immediate refusal to talk is the smoke that tells me there has to be a fire around there somewhere."

"But haven't you used up Ed Dante now?"

"Well, I guess I have with Rita Colby," I admitted. "But will she tell Kay Henry? I don't see why she would, at least not right away."

"To get rid of you," Anita suggested. "She calls

Henry and tells him you're being a pest and she doesn't want you around his office any more."

"Possible," I said. "So what I'll do is, this afternoon I'll call the Henry office and see if my audition at the O. Henry Theater is still on."

"Would you go, if it was?"

"Sure." I grinned at her, saying, "That's a real acting challenge there. I have to go and be good enough to be considered, good enough so they don't call Henry and say, 'Don't send us any more amateur clowns like that one, okay?' But at the same time, I have to be not quite good enough to get hired."

"You plan to enjoy yourself," Anita accused me.

"In my secret heart," I admitted, "I'm enjoying this. Anita, for the last couple of days in New York, I've been *acting.* Win, lose or draw, learn something or learn nothing, this is the first time in *years* I've been able to actually use my muscles, do what I know how to do."

Anita gave me a sympathetic look and shook her head: "Poor boy. What are you going to do with yourself when you have to stop playing Ed Dante?"

"Which will be very soon, in any case," I told her. "I figure, by tomorrow night I'll have used it up. I'll move back into 10th Street and let whatever happens happen."

"Why tomorrow night?"

"Okay," I said. "Later today, Ed has his audition. He fails, but not by much."

"Lots of fun," Anita said.

"But also necessary," I reminded her. "Because *then,* I'm justified tomorrow morning in going back to see Kay Henry. I start by talking about the audition, and if I'm any good at all I get the conversation moved around to Rita Colby and her dead husband, and does she happen to have any guy in her life right now, and with any luck I get to find out what Henry thinks of it all." Grinning, I said, "Wouldn't it be nice, for instance, if she phoned him the evening of the banquet and asked him to arrange an escort for her to the dinner?"

"He'd have to know the truth, then," Anita said.

"He'd have to suspect, sure," I agreed, "which I'd look very hard for. But remember, Rita Colby's almost the entire support of that agency. It would take a lot for him to permit a negative thought about her to cross his brain."

"He has every reason to protect her, then," Anita said. She pointed at me, and added, "From you."

"I'll try to be subtle," I promised.

"As subtle as you were with Rita Colby?"

I laughed. "Even subtler than that," I said.

# 43

**A**nita and I had lunch together at the table in the back near the kitchen, surrounded by lawyers from downtown and executives from midtown and local people from the Village. This is the table where we'd had dinner with Julie Kaplan nearly six weeks ago, when I thought my troubles with the Dale Wormley killing were coming to an end. Now, six weeks later, it seemed to me they were just barely beginning.

Downstairs, we didn't talk about any of that, but about less troubling subjects. Anita picked at her food, as usual, but I had a good appetite for some reason, and Angela the waitress smiled in approval as I cleared every plate she gave me. I would have liked some white wine to go with the tortellini and the sole, but there was too much to be done this afternoon, so I contented myself with a bottle of San Pellegrino water, and several cups of espresso.

After lunch, there was still plenty of time before my meeting with Sergeant Shanley, so I went back upstairs and used Anita's phone to call Kay Henry's office, telling the chilly Miss Colinville, "Hi, hon, it's Ed Dante again. Just wanted to be sure my audition was still on for this afternoon."

"And what audition would that be?" she demanded, but then, before I could answer, she said, "Oh, never mind, just hold on *one* moment." And I got the phone away from my ear just in time to avoid the full impact of her punitive click.

Kay Henry himself came on the line half a minute later, saying, "Ed? Any problem?"

"No, sir, Mr. Henry," I assured him. "I just wanted to be sure everything was set for the audition."

"Absolutely," he said. "They're looking forward to you, Ed. I explained the problem with your lost photo and resumé, so they know if they're interested I'll send them the material in a day or two."

"Good," I said. "Fine. Thanks a lot, Mr. Henry."

"Just go in there and knock 'em dead," he told me.

"I will," I promised, and hung up, and told Anita, "She hasn't complained about me to Henry. What do you suppose that means?"

"It might mean she's worried," Anita said, "or it might mean she really doesn't give a damn about Ed Dante and his dumb ideas."

"An impregnable woman, eh? Let's hope not," I said, and kissed Anita goodbye. We'd agreed I would come back here this evening, after my audition. My last night in exile from my own house would be spent with Anita rather than with the Youngs; something pleasant to look forward to.

I walked up the west side to Midtown Precinct South, and had to wait about fifteen minutes before Sergeant Shanley came out to get me. "Sorry about the delay," she said. "There's always thirty things going on here."

"No problem," I assured her.

We went back to the same interview room as last time, took the same chairs, and she said, "So what do you have for me today? Been under any more beds?"

"Not exactly," I told her, and took the printed-out newspaper information from my inside jacket pocket and handed it to her.

She raised an eyebrow at me, but asked no questions, and settled down to read. I watched her, but her face remained expressionless as she went methodically through every sheet, turning each one face down on the battered metal desk when she was finished. At the end, she nodded and looked at me and said, "Filling in that theory of yours, huh?"

"Pretty much," I agreed.

"Let me see if I can come up with your story for you," she said. "You already had the idea Dale Wormley was blackmailing somebody, probably with some sort of evidence on a sound tape. Now your idea is, the somebody he was blackmailing is Rita Colby, because there was something funny about her husband's suicide and Wormley knew about it."

"Knew about it," I said, "because Rita Colby used him as her alibi for the time of her husband's death."

"So you say."

"Right after that event," I told her, pointing at the papers on the desk, "Wormley told his girlfriend Julie

Kaplan that things were definitely going to start getting better for him, that he *knew* he was headed for the big time. And that's when Rita Colby suddenly insisted he be given a part in her next Broadway play. Sergeant, a minor role in a play is not cast five months in advance, and unless there's some personal reason involved, it isn't cast without auditions, and it isn't cast without consultation with director and playwright."

"Personal reason involved," Sergeant Shanley repeated. "Doesn't that usually mean somebody's sleeping with somebody?"

"Not this time," I said.

She grinned a little. "Because Rita Colby wouldn't roll over for *you?* That doesn't prove anything, Mr. Holt, it really doesn't. Not to insult you or anything, but you know what they say: No accounting for tastes."

"Her reaction to me doesn't prove anything," I agreed, "but it does suggest something. But more important than that, if Wormley had been sleeping with Rita Colby, his regular girlfriend would have known it. *That* kind of secret you can't keep. Julie Kaplan is absolutely certain there was nothing going on there, and I believe her."

"You believe her because it fits the theory," the Sergeant suggested.

I spread my hands in frustration. "Are you just going to throw the whole theory out the window simply because I'm the one who came up with it?"

"Not at all." Tapping the sheets of paper on the desk, she said, "I'll follow through on this, of course I will, but I'll tell you right now what will happen. Shall I?"

"Sure."

"I'll call the police over in Jersey," she said, "and ask them if there was anything suspicious about Montgomery's suicide. They'll say no, of course, because if there'd been anything suspicious they would have acted on their suspicions at the time. But I'll tell them I have information that suggests the wife might at least have been in the house when her husband died, and not in New York at a banquet the way she claimed, and I'll ask them to check around and see if they come up with any corroboration of that. They'll say fine, and they'll talk to the first people on the scene, and they'll call me back and say there's no indication the wife was around. And that will be that."

"So you're telling me right now," I said, "that the whole thing is pointless."

She leaned toward me, looking concerned. "Mr. Holt," she said, "I'm not saying you're wrong about this. What I'm saying is, you're talking about an event that took place three months ago, and up to this point there hasn't been the slightest suggestion of anything funny there. You may be right about all this. At this point, my own guess is that it's even money you *are* right. But there's nothing here—" again she patted the papers on the desk "—to give me a handle, to give me something to work with. How could I go to Rita Colby and question her about the night her husband died? That isn't my case. It isn't even my jurisdiction. If I catch the interest of somebody on the case over in Jersey, then maybe something might happen. Maybe. But it's damn unlikely from that end, and impossible from my end."

"You need a smoking gun, you mean," I said.

"I need more than smoke," she told me.

# 44

**T**here was nothing to do after that but walk back downtown to Anita's place. I had two and a half hours before my audition at the O. Henry Theater, about six blocks from Vitto Impero, and I had plenty to brood about.

I knew Sergeant Shanley was right, of course. A theory wasn't reason enough to start the cops intruding on people's lives; particularly prominent people like Rita Colby. I could hope some policeman over in New Jersey *did* have mental reservations about the death of Hanford Montgomery, and that Sergeant Shanley's call would goose him into following up on his doubts, but, as Shanley had said, that was very unlikely. And there was no real evidential link between the supposed suicide of Hanford Montgomery and the murder a month later of Dale Wormley.

I passed this news—or lack of news—to Anita, and then used her phone to call Terry at his office to find out what he'd learned, if anything, about the marriage between Hanford Montgomery and Rita Colby. "Not much useful, I think," he said.

"Tell me anyway."

"Okay. It was a prominent-people wedding, up in Martha's Vineyard, lots of the well-connected and well-bred and well-heeled in attendance. His former wife, who'd been rich as hell, died of cancer two years before he married Colby. As for Colby, she was divorced twice, once from an actor, once from an Oklahoma oilman."

"Anything in those?" I asked.

"Whadaya mean, scandal? Cocaine, orgies, all of that?"

"It would be nice."

"But no," he told me. "They were just divorces. You know, regular let's-stop-meeting-like-this divorces."

"Okay. What about the Montgomery/Colby marriage?"

"Distant," he said. "Their life-styles were very different, their friends were different. They tended to lead separate lives. That famous banquet wasn't the first time Colby went out with an escort other than her husband."

"Then why'd they get married, for God's sake?"

"There isn't a couple I can think of," Terry said thoughtfully, "about whom that question couldn't be asked. They got married, that's why. If there was trouble between them in the marriage, they kept it quiet."

"Hmmmm," I said, because that wasn't what I'd wanted to hear.

"Also," he said, "while we're on the subject of bad news, Montgomery *was* depressed about his health. His first wife's cancer death apparently got to him in a big way, brought a tendency toward hypochondria into full flower."

"Hmmmm," I said again. "What did his note say?"

"Well, now," Terry said, "there we have a little something for your team. There was no note."

"That's unusual, Terry," I said.

"I know that," he agreed. "Most suicides leave a note. Particularly well-off literate intelligent suicides who want to make it clear it's depression or health reasons and they're not blaming their loved ones. I know that."

"So what have we here?" I asked.

"Probably, just a member of the minority," Terry told me. "It is not entirely unheard of for suicides to go out with no final message, it's just less common than the other way."

"Okay, okay," I said. "How did Montgomery do the deed?"

"Gun," Terry said. "His own, registered to him, a little revolver such as is found in a drawer in most master bedrooms in that county. Fired twice, the first time at a mirror in the bedroom. Second time, he shot himself in the ear."

"The ear? Isn't that unusual?"

"Not really," he said. "Suicides do understand that the concept is to get the bullet in touch with the brain. Some of them put the gun in their mouth, some put it in their ear. Not many shoot themselves in the eye."

"Goddamit, Terry," I said, "this is sounding more and more like suicide."

He laughed, but sympathetically. "I was thinking the same thing myself," he said.

"There's nothing else for my team? Just the lack of a note?"

"Sorry, pal."

I thanked him for his efforts, and told him I'd be staying here with Anita tonight, and then we hung up, and I had even more than before to brood about.

Was I on the wrong trail entirely? Was I haring off after Rita Colby and her deceased husband, when in fact none of that had anything at all to do with Dale Wormley's death? Had Wormley been given the part in *Four Square,* and had he been so sure things would be going well for him from then on, simply because Rita Colby *liked* him, because he'd been sympathetic at the time of her loss or something like that?

And did that mean Dale Wormley's murderer had come out of some other quadrant of his life? Howard Moffitt and his acting class, for instance? Or the Kwality FoodMart commercials? Or some corner of his experience I hadn't even come across yet?

How much longer could Ed Dante keep stumbling around New York with his dumb grin and his dumb moustache and his dumb hair, without getting exposed as a phony and without making trouble for Sam Holt? And what was Ed Dante accomplishing anyway? Nothing that I could see.

Well, I was discouraged, and I had good reason to be, but how could I stop? I had to keep trying because there was no alternative. Ed Dante had to keep shambling forward because he hadn't finished his job yet; even though it was looking very much as though he never would finish it.

But Ed Dante wasn't done yet. There was still hope, I hoped. And so, for now, Ed Dante had to get himself back in gear and get out there and fail an audition.

# 45

In recent years, the West Village has been undergoing a great deal of gentrification, the old warehouses and factory lofts and garages in the blocks near the Hudson River converting to condominiums, their ground floors filling with new delis and dry cleaners, and here and there, because this is Greenwich Village, new small theaters. The O. Henry Theater was one of these, in a building that had until just a few years ago been the home base of a moving and storage company; now gone to New Jersey, probably. Now the building, also renamed O. Henry, its old bricks freshly cleaned and pointed, its new name on the new canopy in front of its new glass-doored entrance, was nearing the end of its conversion: *Occupancy February* said the sign by the entrance, which also indicated, with an arrow, the direction to the sales office.

All of that was closed now, at six-thirty in the evening, after dark, and in fact at first it seemed to me that everything was shut down for the night here. But then I saw the worklight down at the far corner of the building closest to the river—visible at the end of the street, white pinpoints of light skipping nervously atop the black water—and I walked down there to find another entrance, closed with a temporary door in a sheet of plywood nailed to the frame, but with the theater sign already fixed in place above: *O. Henry Theater,* it said, in black letters on a white glass background, and with a black silhouette of head-and-shoulders that I suppose was meant to be William Sydney Porter himself.

I tried the temporary door, but it was locked, with a prominent padlock; nor did I see any light within. Had Kay Henry gotten his audition times confused? I was starting to turn away when a maroon Mercedes pulled to a stop at the curb and Henry himself got out, grinning at me and saying, "Ed! Right on time. Good man." Then he frowned past me at the entrance and said, "Where's Cardiff?"

"I have no idea," I told him. "I just got here myself."

Looking irritated behind his smooth exterior, Henry went over to the padlocked door, rattled the lock, and knocked briskly on the door. When nothing happened, he said, "Well, we'll wait for them inside," and withdrew a bunch of keys from his pocket.

Surprised, I said, "You have a key to this place?"

"The truth is," he said, grinning in satisfaction as he looked through the keys for the right one, "I'm one of the owners of the building. Rita, and I, and a dozen other people." Turning his broad happy grin toward me, he said, "I was the one who named the place. Did you think it was a coincidence?"

"Well, that's pretty good," I said, with Ed Dante's gawkishness. "Your own theater, and named after you."

"Not quite," he said, though still grinning. "A different first letter. Ah, here it is." And he bent over the padlock with the right key.

The temporary door opened to an unfinished lobby, its pseudo-marble floor covered with heavy sheets of mover's paper, its walls Sheetrocked but not yet painted. "Go on in," Henry told me, holding the door open with his foot as he fiddled the key back out of the padlock.

So I went past him and on inside, looking around. Light-spill from outside gave some illumination to the interior, or at least to this lobby.

From behind me, Henry said, "See the lightswitches over there? By the doorway to the auditorium."

"I see them," I said, moving carefully through the semi-darkness toward a row of half a dozen lightswitches without their switchplates.

"Turn on the two on the left."

"Okay." I did so, and brought up recessed lighting in bas relief pots on both sides of the lobby. I stood looking around at the place, the simple modern two-window box office to one side, as Henry closed the temporary door, which had another hasp lock on the inside, matching the one without. Moving smoothly, unhurriedly, Henry fixed that hasp into place and closed the padlock over it, saying, "There. Now we'll have privacy." Then, turning to me, his smile glinting as he took a small pistol from his pocket, he said, "We'll want privacy for this discussion, Ed. Should I go on calling you Ed, by the way?" And the pistol pointed unwaveringly at my face.

# 46

**H**ow stupid of me. That was all I could think at first, how stupid I'd been. Evening auditions are fairly common in off-Broadway theater, but in a theater as incomplete as this? And if the building isn't going to be ready for occupancy until February, how is the theater going to do a production, however limited, over the holidays? And how could I still have believed in the audition when there was no one present at all except the smiling Kay Henry, who just happened to be an owner of the building?

I'd walked right into this spider's parlor, as big and dumb as life, concentrating on my own performance and paying no attention at all to Henry's.

"I take it," he was saying, moving toward me from the relocked door, "Ed Dante isn't your real name."

So he didn't actually know who I was; could that be a help at all? "Sure it is, Mr. Henry," I said, playing the goofy Ed to the bitter end. "What's going on?"

"My very question to you," he said, and the barrel of the pistol angled downward, away from my face. "We're alone in this building," he pointed out. "You're going to tell me who you are and what you're up to. No question, you will tell me. If you take too long to answer my questions, I'll start shooting you. Not to kill, not to begin with. Just to hurt and to maim. For instance, my first shot will go into your left knee."

He extended his arm, sighting along it and along the pistol barrel, and I slapped off the lights I'd just switched on, spun away to the side as the pistol made a nasty *crack* sound, like a whip being snapped rather than a gun going off, and I leaped through the entrance into the dark auditorium, with no idea whether I'd been hit or not.

I stumbled over seating in the dark—plush, fortunately—and fell between rows as the lights behind me came back on. I scrambled away along the curving row, out of sight from the doorway just in time, because Henry's voice sounded back there, still calm, amused, saying, "Don't be stupid, Ed, or whoever you are. I can guarantee you there's no way out except the door we came in. And I won't let you near that door, Ed. I'm armed, and you aren't. All we need is to have a discussion, Ed. Nobody needs to be hurt. You'll answer questions, I'll be satisfied, we'll both go home."

I crawled like a snake under seats, hoping not to disturb the upraised seats or make any noise that would tell him where I was. Fortunately, he covered any sounds I might make by going on talking: "Ed, your story about the lost luggage never did play, you know that? It was just a way to explain why you didn't have photos and resumé, isn't that right? And when I checked into the career you described to me, the whole thing was just a fairy-tale, a pack of fibs from beginning to end. I called Equity, and they don't have an Ed Dante. Ed, Ed, how did you expect to get away with it?"

I no longer knew. At the extreme right side of the theater, I risked raising my head slightly, looking up across the rows of seats, and saw him there, just inside the lobby doorway, perched casually on a seatback, one foot up on the armrest, hand with the gun dangling over his knee. He continued to smile, calm and confident, as he chatted amiably at the theater and his quick eyes kept scanning, scanning.

I ducked back down. What to do? His voice moved over me, without apparent direction, showing how well-designed the acoustics were in here. A nice theater to work in, probably.

But not to die in.

"You're a good actor, Ed, you really are, that Nazi soldier you did was very impressive. No fooling. When this nonsense is all over, maybe we could talk about a career. A career *change* for you, Ed. What do you say?"

Flight was impossible. Someway or other, I had to counterattack.

"After we talked this morning, Ed, after I told you about the audition here, you called Rita, didn't you? Said you wanted to talk about the Theater Project dinner. You upset Rita a great deal, Ed, and I just can't permit that. If you want to talk about the Theater Project dinner, you can talk about it with *me*. Let's do that, Ed. What do you want to ask?"

He wasn't moving. His knowledge of this theater, this building, was such that he didn't have to move, he could just stay there by the only working exit—there'd be others, beyond the stage, mandated by the fire laws, but they'd be solidly locked now—and he could talk calmly and keep watching, and sooner or later the stalemate would end.

"My guess, Ed, is that you're a private detective. Did Mrs. Wormley hire you? What do you think you're investigating, Ed? Can't you even tell me that much?"

If I moved across the row two down from where he waited, I could get very close to him without being seen. If I could then distract him, stall him, *delay* him somehow for just a couple of seconds, until I got within arm's reach, there was a chance.

"Ed, I'm losing my patience here. Quit hiding like a child. Come out and let's talk this over. How much do you get paid, in your business? Is it worth all this, Ed?"

Ed Dante was finished now. I pulled off the wig and moustache, stripped out of the raincoat, left them behind on the floor, started crawling.

"You were spying on me, Ed. Think about it. You don't have that much goodwill to spend with me. But I *want* to make things all right. Just stand up like a man, Ed, and tell me what you want to know."

The lighting was soft; dim enough for my purposes? I could only hope so. And hope I remembered the voice, the mannerisms. I fixed my face in an expression of aggressive grievance and rose to my feet, two yards from Henry, glaring at him. "It's Dale, Kay," I said. "Why did you kill me?"

# 47

"**Y**ou should be dead, you know," Sergeant
Shanley said.

The hospital bed was not at all comfortable, the
sheets constantly bunching and creasing beneath me.
Shifting yet again to a slightly different position, feeling
the twinges in my side and my shoulder and my arm, I
said, "I know, Sergeant, I know. But I figured I was
dead anyway. I had to take the chance."

"Lucky," she said, and shook her head.

Well, that was true enough. When I'd risen up
directly in front of Kay Henry, doing my Dale Wormley
imitation—full circle: this had begun with Wormley
imitating me—the look of horror in his eyes had lasted
only a second, he was recovering even as I lunged at
him, and he managed to shoot me three times before I

knocked him down and pounded his head onto the pseudo-marble floor. The shock and the speed had thrown him off balance just enough to keep me alive, though, the three shots all off-target to the left, one cracking and ricocheting off a rib on my left side, one punching into my left shoulder and doing some carti-lage and muscle damage there, and one slicing through the flesh of my left arm, just below the elbow. I was bleeding like a fountain and only semi-conscious when I searched Henry for his keys, struggled to find the right one, unlocked that goddam padlock and went reeling out into the night on Charles Street looking for help. A cab that didn't want to stop for me changed its mind when I draped myself on its hood, and now, three days later, here I was in the hospital, my food being sent in by Anita from Vitto Impero and Sergeant Shanley here to tell me the story.

"Your theory turned out to be pretty good up to a point," she said. "The key to the thing was blackmail and a tape recording. But Rita Colby wasn't a murder-er, and she wasn't the one being blackmailed, and Hanford Montgomery really did commit suicide."

Laughing, even though it hurt my rib, I said, "But the rest I got okay, huh?"

"Colby's made a statement," the Sergeant said. "She and her husband were supposed to go to that banquet together. There'd been trouble in the marriage, he was jealous, thought she was playing around. They'd kept it pretty quiet, but it mixed in with Montgomery's de-pression and his health problems, and that's when he did himself in."

"Without leaving a note."

"Well, yes, he did," she said. "The tape. He made a cassette tape of why he was killing himself, blaming his wife, listing people he thought she'd been sleeping with, all of that."

"Ow. That's nasty."

"Colby insists none of it was true, it was just her husband's depression and paranoia. Anyway, when she told him it was time to get ready for the banquet, he pulled the gun and made her listen to the tape. When she tried to leave the bedroom, he shot the mirror to let her know he was serious. They listened to the tape, and she started to deny it all, and he blew his brains out."

"In front of her?"

"Yeah. She was rattled—"

"Well, she would be," I said.

"Anybody would be," Shanley agreed. "She phoned Kay Henry. He was always the one she turned to. He said come to town, bring the tape, you don't know anything, he'd get somebody to go to the banquet with her and claim they'd been there for an hour already. Then Henry called Dale Wormley, told him what was going on, and sent him to the Waldorf to meet Colby. They did their public act together, with her going to the ladies' room to break down every once in a while, and he stole the tape out of her purse. She didn't realize until the next day. She called Henry again, he said he'd take care of it, and then he said he'd taken care of it, the tape was destroyed. In fact, Wormley was keeping it, and telling Henry the price was stardom."

"Rita Colby was Kay Henry's entire career and livelihood," I said.

"So Henry went along with Wormley as best he could," Shanley said, "but Wormley just kept pushing and pressing."

"That's what he'd do, all right."

"Wormley wanted more and more, he got to be

impossible, and finally Henry felt he didn't have any choice. He followed Wormley, looking for his chance, and killed him. And he moved the body to that vestibule to give himself time to get home before it was discovered and he was notified."

"Then," I said, "he went looking for the tape."

"And found it, too. But unfortunately Kim Peyser walked in while he was there."

My rib gave me a bad twinge, and I lay back, grimacing. Sounding worried, Sergeant Shanley said, "Are you all right?"

"Well, no," I said.

"Let me leave you alone now," she said, getting to her feet. "We can talk some more tomorrow."

"One thing," I said, holding my left side with my right hand. "What about Mrs. Wormley?"

"Gone," the Sergeant said. "Home to Iowa, I guess. The Kaplan girl came back from Florida yesterday and threw her out."

That made me laugh again, and that made me hurt again. There was a fuzzy grayness at the periphery of my vision, trying to flow in. "I'm sorry," I said. "This thing is getting to me."

"I'm off," she said, and moved toward the door. "You want me to call the nurse?"

"No," I said. "I think I'll just pass out for a while."

And I did.